S.H.R.E.D.

GORGON RISING

Other books by Stu Jones

The Action of Purpose Trilogy

Through the Fury to the Dawn

Into the Dark of the Day

Against the Fading of the Light

The Zone (coming soon)

Other books by Stu Jones and Gareth Worthington

The It Takes Death to Reach a Star Duology

It Takes Death to Reach a Star

In the Shadow of a Valiant Moon

Condition Black

GORGON RISING

Stu Jones

Edited by Gareth Worthington

Based on the original story concept by Michael David Ward

This is a work of fiction. Names, places, or incidents are either the product of the author's imagination or used fictitiously. Any resemblance to actual persons living or dead, events or locales, is entirely coincidental.

Cover design by Stu Jones and Gareth Worthington
Cover Art by Michael David Ward
Interior design by Dorothy Dreyer

Paperback ISBN: 978-1-954386-03-7
Ebook ISBN: 978-1-954386-04-4

Published by Dropship Publishing
www.dropshippublishing.com
Printed in the United States of America
10 9 8 7 6 5 4 3 2 1

For Archer, who believed in this story from the very beginning.

-Stu Jones

For all of the precious life forms that call the sea home, and for Tania and her father Gordon for inspiring S.H.R.E.D. and imbuing it with the true spirit of Hawaii.

-Michael David Ward

A Note from the Author

It takes a village to raise a book. This one started in 2017 when I was approached about novelizing the original story and artwork of Michael David Ward's Super Humanoids for Reconnaissance, Espionage, and Defense. After years of trying to get it just right—this work is the end result. Michael, thank you for all your support, advice, suggestions, and guidance. And thank you for giving me the creative freedom to make this story my own. I hope I've done it justice.

A big thank you to my agent, Italia Gandolfo who initiated this process and who works tirelessly (and often thanklessly) behind the scenes. To my partner in crime and often co-author, Gareth Worthington for being there to consult with and for his help with the final content edit—*and* his brilliant work on the cover. Thanks, Mate!

A shout out to legendary author Jonas Saul for his proofreading and line edits and Dorothy Dreyer for her help in getting it ready for print. Those fine-tuning elements make the story. To all my friends and beta readers who encouraged and supported this project in its early days and my incredible family who put up with my manic writing habits without complaint. You guys really are the best.

And lastly, for all of us who dream of heroes and hope to see a glimmer of such heroism in ourselves. "So shall we go".

Stu Jones
March 2022

CHAPTER 1

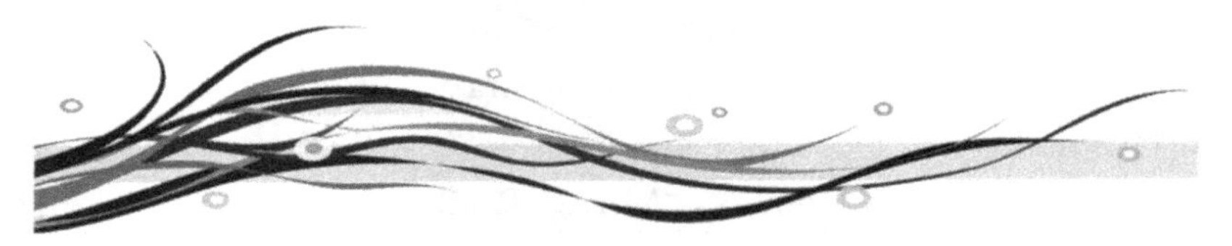

Sasha had a terrible idea, one that would get her thrown in prison—or worse. And just like every noble but ill-conceived scheme, it came from a place of greatness.

"Get out of the way, Bodhi," she said, stomping across the deck of *The Lorien*.

She shoved between the wiry dark-haired surfer and the steering wheel, prying away his white-knuckled grip.

"Okay, yeah ..." Bodhi stepped back wide eyed.

Out to sea sat a massive whaling vessel with red Cyrillic letters painted onto its bow. The enormous ship dropped into the trough of another large swell. A loud *thud* resounded as the craft struck the back of a humpback whale. Smaller metallic minions—catcher vessels brandishing big-bore cannons loaded with harpoons—kept pace alongside.

Pink bubbles frothed across the surface of the ocean. Another explosive harpoon forced air into the dying leviathan's hide with a distinct pop. The crew of the catcher vessels shouted to each other, their guided motor-assisted ropes whining with effort as they hauled the beast closer. One crew member leaned over the side. His rifle cracked again and again. The defeated creature rolled belly to the sky, bobbing on the surface of the crimson sea.

"Bastards!" Sasha screamed.

A third harpoon gun swiveled and aimed at the back of a second, smaller, baby whale gliding below the surface. Sasha's heart banged in her ears, the anticipation of another senseless death sending needles prickling across her scalp.

"Sasha, please don't do anything crazy," Bodhi said, holding up his hands in a feeble prayer. "Please—"

Sasha's face hardened. "Move, Bodhi. I can't watch this anymore."

The Lorien yawned, and Bodhi stumbled back. He grabbed for the stairwell railing and fell against the muscled bulk of their third crew member.

"Easy there, bro," Max said as he propped Bodhi back upright.

Sasha took the wheel and shoved down on the throttle. The bow of *The Lorien* plunged into the trough, flooding the deck and drenching the three friends with sun-tinged sea spray. Knees bent, the toned muscles of her legs flexed, Sasha gripped the wheel and twisted the balls of her feet against the deck.

"Sasha, don't do this," Max said as his strong fingers snaked around the steering wheel.

Bodhi clung to the railing as *The Lorien* bucked over another wave.

"Get your hand off the wheel, Max," Sasha said. "This is *my* boat. I'll do what I want."

Max released the wheel but stood close. "This is your *father's* boat, Sasha. He'll kill you if you mess it up."

"Well, I guess we'll chalk it up with all the other senseless killing going on," Sasha said.

"Hey, guys?" Bodhi shouted. He pulled out his phone and nearly fumbled it overboard as the yacht drove into another briny wall. "Should I get these evil pricks on live video? Cause, I kinda feel like I should film this ..."

Ignoring Bodhi, Max held his gaze steady on Sasha. "Hey," he said, his voice lowering.

Sasha kept her hateful stare fixed on the whaling vessel.

Max touched her arm. "Look, I understand where you are with this, I do, but this has stupid written all over it. Russian whalers are rough dudes. They've got guns. Don't do it. We can turn the boat around and forget all about this."

"Maybe *you* can, Max," Sasha said, her concentration unbroken. "I've turned a blind eye long enough."

"Check this out, guys." Bodhi hung on the railing, his phone held high selfie-style. "These Russian a-holes are out here killing everything that moves, but they didn't count on us being here."

The Lorien closed on the whaler with astonishing speed.

"Hit the air horn, Max. See if you can distract them," Sasha said.

Max sighed. "I'm not going to talk you out of this, am I?"

Sasha shook her head and feigned a smirk that she hoped might disguise her knotted stomach. "You might want to put your floaties on."

"Bodhi, stop screwing around and hold on to something," Max shouted and gave three blasts of the air horn.

A megaphone boomed from the deck of the big whaler. "*American vessel, we will not tolerate any interference in our operations.*"

Sasha aimed the bow of *The Lorien* straight at the hull of one of the catcher vessels. Sweat beaded on her brow, the afternoon sun hot on her back as she cranked the throttle to full. "Here we go. Hold on." She called out.

The Lorien rode a crest then slammed into the port side of the catcher. The squealing of wood, fiberglass, and steel filled their ears as *The Lorien* cracked and rolled. The third harpoon fired but, thrown off by the impact, missed its target. The majestic baby whale escaped into the safety of deeper water.

The catcher slowed, the ragged puncture in its bow gurgling and sucking as it took on water.

Sasha gave a whoop of triumph and backed the throttle down.

"I can't believe that worked," Bodhi shouted, still filming, his knuckles white as he clung to the rear rail of the boat. "Let's get the hell outta here!"

"No," Sasha said, eyes wild and her whole body on fire. "I'm not done with these jerks yet. Bodhi, grab the gaff. Max, get the hatchet from the toolbox."

Sasha backed off the catcher—with its crew of curse slinging, gesticulating men—and pressed then guided *The Lorien* alongside the hull of the giant factory ship. She glanced back at the partially hoisted dead humpback mother, streaming blood into the water, while Max and Bodhi scrambled to get the tools.

"Bodhi, quick," Sasha gasped out the words. "Hook one of the lines and draw it over. Max, when he pulls it against *The Lorien,* you hit it with the ax. This poor creature is going to feed the ocean, not their greed."

Sasha reversed the throttle allowing their broken yacht to move back toward the whale corpse. Bodhi hooked one of the ropes and tugged hard to draw it close. Max stood ready, the hatchet raised. With two powerful blows, Max severed the rope.

"Get the second one." She called out.

"*Criminal eco-terrorists will be fired upon,*" a voice from above barked through a megaphone.

Men with rifles leaned over the side of the great ship.

"Hurry," Sasha shouted, readying the throttle for their escape. She jabbed the coast guard emergency distress beacon on the console.

Bodhi secured the second rope, and again Max swung hard, this time severing the rope with one blow. Sasha slammed on the throttle and cut the wheel hard to the left. The water churned pink with whale blood as the freed creature drifted away from the ship.

Shots rang out. Bullets stabbed the water around them and slammed into *The Lorien*'s engine. Sasha, Max, and Bodhi threw themselves against the deck. The deafening gunfire ceased, replaced by the sound of a tireless wind and powerful waves as they lapped and sucked at *The Lorien*'s fractured hull. Sasha lifted her head but could only see smoke rising from the bullet-ridden engine block.

"*Stand,*" the voice behind the megaphone said.

Hands in the air, Sasha and the others climbed to their feet and turned to face the firing squad above.

"*There is no way out for you, now.*"

The edge of the summer sun kissed the horizon, throwing a hazy golden light across the north pacific as far as the eye could see. Yet off to the south, a plumed thunderhead rumbled low, heralding dark skies and rough seas.

An omen if ever Sasha saw one.

"Nothing to say?" the heavyset man with strong scarred arms and a beach ball-sized belly said. He paced back and forth in front of them, waving a small black TT-30 Tokarev pistol which he occasionally leveled at their heads to keep their attention.

Bodhi watched as one of the men monkeyed with *his* phone. Frustrated, the hairy fisherman clenched the device in his fist and pulled his arm back as if ready to pitch for the Yankees.

"Hey, hey, come on, comrade, not the phone," Bodhi pleaded.

The man grinned and hurled the phone overboard.

Bodhi pinched his eyes shut. "Ugh, you guys hate everything good in the world, don't you?"

Sasha licked her desiccated lips and tried to swallow. Her salt-caked, sunburned face and arms stung as she leaned to one side and tried to restore some feeling in her hands. Though Sasha should take comfort in knowing she and her friends were lucky to be alive, they'd been held against their will for hours now.

"Is my little Oriental princess uncomfortable?" Beach Ball said with a grin, showing a few gold-capped teeth.

"Rugs and food are Oriental. I'm an American, fatso. Hawaii is part of the United States." Sasha spoke in her bravest voice, though a slight tremor betrayed her.

"I don't think geography is their strong suit, Sasha," Bodhi said, twisting against the hemp ropes that gnawed into the flesh of his thin wrists.

Max stayed silent, his gaze steeled on Beach Ball.

"We're in U.S. territorial waters, and you're criminals," Sasha said. "They'll be looking for us."

Beach Ball leaned in closer. "But they won't find you," he whispered. "Look and see." He motioned to *The Lorien*, bobbing on the ocean some twenty feet off the port bow. Another man strolled past, brandishing a stick of dynamite, the fuse burning low. Sasha, Max, and Bodhi winced as the man tossed the dynamite into the fractured Lorien. The blast, powerful enough to rock even the whaling vessel, rolled over them. A boiling plume of smoke wafted up into the dusk orange sky. The men cheered.

Sasha bit her lip and swallowed back her anguish, imagining the fragments of her father's boat as they floated away and slipped beneath the surface. Max was right. Her father would kill her—if these men didn't do it first.

"Why bother holding us now?" Max said. "You've made your point, okay?"

"No, not *okay,*" Beach Ball said, pointing the handgun at Max.

"You are not children. You should know better than this. We must be compensated ... in some way." The man's gaze wandered over every inch of Sasha's toned frame.

"Hey, bro," Bodhi said. "Don't be a pig, okay. Nobody likes a fat pi—"

The butt of an old bolt-action rifle smacked across Bodhi's face.

"Hey!" Sasha shouted.

"Whoa, take it easy!" Max said.

The Russian with the rifle grinned and took a step back.

Bodhi's head lolled. Blood streamed from his busted nose. "Okay, it's cool. Point taken. Pigs are fine. I like pigs."

Sasha squirmed, her lips curled up in a snarl. "You're a bunch of cowards! You murder and rape our oceans. You're willing to beat a guy who has his hands tied behind his back. What's next?"

Beach Ball dipped his brow, which prompted the guy with the rifle to approach Sasha.

"What? Are you going to hit *me*, too?" Sasha said, her lower lip trembling. "Do it. I'm not afraid of any of you."

Beach Ball stepped over and leaned close to her face. "You should be." He turned and motioned to his men. "Poluchite ikh protiv rel'sov."

Beach Ball grabbed Sasha by the throat, lifted her high, and shoved her against the ship's railing. Sasha gasped and writhed. The dark ocean beneath her seemed to wash away the last remnants of the fading sun.

"Stop," Sasha wheezed. From the corner of her eye, she could see Max and Bodhi forced into similar positions, guns in their faces.

"Oh no, I'm just getting started," Beach Ball said, his vodka-soaked breath filling her nostrils and throat as he pressed his body against hers.

The men behind him leered.

Tears welled in Sasha's eyes, and a wild fear grew in the pit of her stomach.

Thunder rumbled into the distance.

Sasha struggled to speak through the grip on her throat. "Please stop."

"Here's what you don't understand, girl," Beach Ball said. "Your American laws don't protect you out here. The three of you died in a tragic accident at sea when your boat succumbed to the storm." He cast his stare toward the looming thunderhead. "No one will ever know."

"What are you going to do?" Max asked a Tokarev pistol pushed against his eye socket.

Beach Ball grinned. "We will shoot your brains into the water and dump you overboard, you and your wise-guy friend there." He flicked his head toward Bodhi before returning his eye to Sasha. "After you're dead, we'll keep this one around for a while to lift the men's spirits."

"Get your hands off her, you son of a—" Max struggled as a second man grabbed him and forced him back farther.

"Max!" Sasha strained against the men's groping hands.

A brilliant white light bathed them all, the sounds of engines and rotors filling the air.

The whalers stood frozen, their mouths hanging open.

"*This is the United States Coast Guard. Drop your weapons and put your hands in the air. Do it now.*"

The Russians dropped their weapons clattering against the deck and stood frozen, hands above their heads.

Sasha pushed off the rail and turned to see three USCG long-range interceptors in formation just off the bow. Above them, the rotors of an MH-60S stealth Jayhawk whipped the sea into a froth. The helicopter's side door stood shunted open, revealing a stone-faced gunner anchored behind an imposing M240 machine gun.

Max and Bodhi squinted beneath the blaze of the searchlights.

"'Murica," Bodhi said.

"Thank God," Max whispered.

Sasha said nothing. Standing straight, she took a step forward and delivered the hardest kick she could muster to Beach Ball's groin. With a piggish squeal, the top-heavy man pitched over onto the deck and curled into the fetal position, where he lay whimpering until the first of the USCG advance team cleared and secured the deck of the ship.

"Thank you," Sasha murmured as one of their rescuers cut her free from her bonds.

She'd live to be killed by her father, after all.

CHAPTER 2

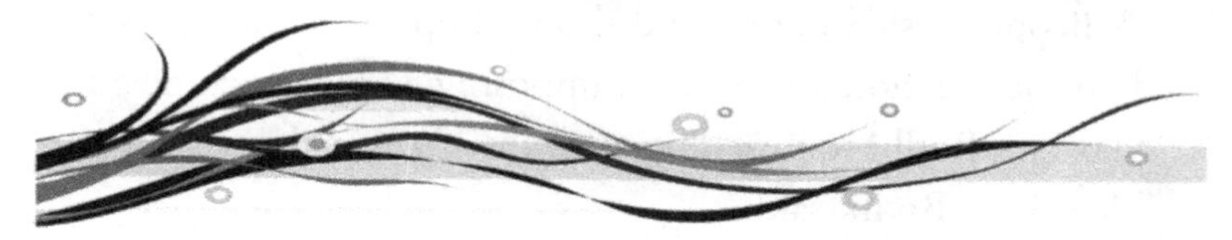

A flashing red light on the systems monitor marked *Heat Exchange Overload* strobed again in a series of blips blinding Orsen Rence. The station's master technician raised a hand to shield his eyes while using his other hand to probe for the override command key on the console.

"There it is again." He tabbed the key and blinked a few times in succession. Stars flared across his vision. He reached for the microphone control, rubbing at his eyes. "Hey, Marcus?"

"What is it?" Marcus Avery said, voice muffled through the static.

Orsen rolled his eyes, blinking a few more times in a failed attempt to clear them. "The heat exchange overload warning went off again. You sure that's not a problem?"

"Do *you* think it's a problem?" Marcus said, that condescending tone creeping into his voice.

"You're the project lead. You tell me," Orsen said.

"No, I don't."

"That's it?" Orsen said. "That's all you've got?"

He looked to the bank of monitors above, each one covering one of the many recorded sectors of the United States Department of Defense's Low Orbit Facility. With every sector monitored, from docking to engineering, command, and containment, nothing was private here. Thus, Orsen had long ago come to terms with the fact that his shower pod liaisons with the chief station engineer, Corana, weren't a secret to anyone.

Playing out on the small monitor labeled "containment," Marcus—covered from head to toe in a crinkled silver radiation suit—turned to look at the camera.

"What do you want me to say, Orsen? I'm a little busy here."

"I want you to give me something." Orsen leaned back in his seat, the cross-body harness holding him in place in zero gravity. "Technically speaking, the only reason I should see a heat exchange overload warning is if the LOF is in the path of a solar flare. I haven't seen any flares."

"Then no problem, right?" Marcus said. "Put it in the log and have AI diagnostics debug the program when we run station maintenance tonight."

Orsen pursed his lips. He had a lot of respect for Marcus. The guy was a legitimate genius in the realm of quantum field theory. But the man's ego had a penchant for getting in the way of reason, and Orsen couldn't shake the feeling they had missed something.

"Marcus, see, they built this warning into the system for a reason." Orsen continued. "If it keeps going off, I want to know why. That's my job. It's how we stay alive out here. Continuing to simply make it go away with an override command isn't a solution. Do you agree?"

"What are you boys arguing about?" Corana Luksova's voice rang out from the intercom, her Slavic accent sharp and sultry all at once.

Orsen shook the steamy memory of yesterday's shower pod get-together from his mind. "Corana, you getting any strange readings from the facility's systems?"

"A small spike in atmospheric control. Should be fine."

"See." Marcus waved at the camera. "It's fine."

"Yeah, yeah." Orsen leaned back in his chair again. "Volunteer for a special assignment, they said. You'll get to experience space, they said."

Orsen, Marcus, Corana, and an energy consultant named Rupert Fielding, were selected as the initial four-person crew assigned to the DOD's state-of-the-art Low Orbit Facility, hovering some one hundred fifty miles above the surface of the Earth. The contract had said a year. It wouldn't surprise him if the funding for the entire Erebos project weren't cut before the six-month mark.

Orsen's numb stare moved to the monitor labeled "containment grid," where Marcus currently busied himself by tinkering with the output module connected with the Erebos device—a giant multi-sided hollow orb constructed of rare earth metals. The strange device sat anchored in the center of the room, a faint green hue emanating from the outer shell. Orsen had never seen the inside of it himself. Still, as best he understood, it comprised a series of Casimir plates sealed in a vacuum, designed to measure quantum electrodynamics.

The project was worth billions of taxpayer dollars. Limitless energy potential by tapping into the vacuum structure of space; a technology both NASA and the United States Department of Defense wanted to get their hands on. But for all his lofty promises, after four months, they still had nothing to show for it.

Orsen squinted and sucked his teeth as the red Heat Exchange Overload light strobed again on the monitor. "Dammit. Are you serious?" he said, reaching for the intercom.

"Marcus," Orsen said, straightening. "You're wrong on this one. It's going off again. I think you should exit the containment grid until we can debug the platform and get a full system readout on what's causing this overload."

"Would you relax, Orsen? You're more jittery than my damn

cat." Came Avery's voice over the speaker.

Avery stood in his protection suit on a containment grid monitor, hands pressed on his hips. The visor of his face shield obscured the scowl that surely lay beneath. "The LOF is fine, and the Erebos is dormant," he continued. "A fact you love to rub in my face every chance you get. If it's okay with you, I'd like to finish my examination and get on with—"

A sudden pulse. The Low Orbit Facility shuddered, the walls shifting and creaking. Orsen sat forward, scanning the monitors. "What the hell was that?" he said into the open intercom.

Orsen watched as the Erebos thrummed, pulsing with an otherworldly emerald light.

On the monitor for the containment grid, Avery turned to face the giant orb anchored in place behind him. "My God. Orsen, are you seeing this?"

"Uh, I see it," Orsen said. "How did you …? What did you do?"

"Nothing," Marcus replied, his voice tinged with excitement. "I didn't do anything. It activated on its own. You didn't change anything?"

"I didn't touch a thing," Orsen said, opening the digital command system and confirming that the solar power inputs connected to the Erebos indicated it was disengaged.

The orb's green light shifted in hue, accompanied by an alien hum. Another audible drone pulsed from the contraption, followed by a third and a fourth, faster now.

"Orsen? Did you feel that?" Corana asked from one of the intercom terminals. "What's going on?"

Orsen licked his lips. "Corana, is Fielding with you?"

"In his bunk last I checked," she said. "Still isn't feeling well."

"Get him and make your way to central," Orsen said. "Now."

"Orsen, what's this about? You're scaring me."

Orsen watched as the flashing of the orb increased in speed, the strange humming growing louder by the second. The buzzing red heat exchange overload light came on again and penetrated his psyche like a nail driven between his eyes.

"Just get Fielding and get up here." He terminated the commlink, then initiated the mic for the containment grid.

"Marcus? Marcus, if you can hear me, you need to get out," Orsen said. "Marcus?"

On screen, Marcus stood transfixed, staring into the vortex of emerald light pulsing in waves from the Erebos device.

"It's amazing," Marcus said, stepping forward.

Another shockwave rocked the facility, and a shower of sparks burst from one of the panels above Orsen's head. "Marcus. What are you doing?"

Marcus approached the vibrant green sphere, his hand reaching out.

"I can feel it," Marcus said. "I can feel the power inside."

The monitor to the containment room flashed white.

"Woah!" Orsen said, shielding his face. He pulled his hands away and watched in horror as Marcus's body came apart, disintegrating in streaming ribbons of light.

A piercing wail filled the station, and amber lights in the ceiling began to flash.

"*Caution, fire detected in the containment grid,*" the station's AI said.

The door to Orsen's command center clanged open. "Orsen, what the hell is happening?" Corana said, pulling a tired and sickly-looking Fielding in through the hatch.

The camera feed inside containment went dark.

"Strap in. I'm going to have to cut it loose," Orsen said.

"Wait," Corana said, snapping Fielding into his harness. She turned to look at Orsen. "Cut it loose? The Erebos? It lit up?"

"Yeah," Orsen replied, punching several commands into the system and initiating a lockdown of the command module. "Like a nuclear Christmas tree. Marcus is … he's gone. We'll be too if we don't cut it loose."

Corana grabbed his shoulder, her voice a hoarse whisper as the station shuddered again. "Orsen, you can't. It'll fall to Earth. There's no telling where it will land. What it might …"

"The majority of the planet's surface is water. We have to take our chances. Get in your seat." Orsen prepped the containment grid's airlock control and pulled back the plastic shield covering a red lever. "I don't want to die out here."

Corana managed a feeble nod and slipped into her seat.

Another crushing tremor took hold, thrashing the walls as though LOF were in the midst of a category five hurricane.

Orsen's body, strapped to his seat, shook with the violence of the cataclysm. He pinched his eyes, his fingers hovering over the containment release lever.

"God help us for this."

CHAPTER 3

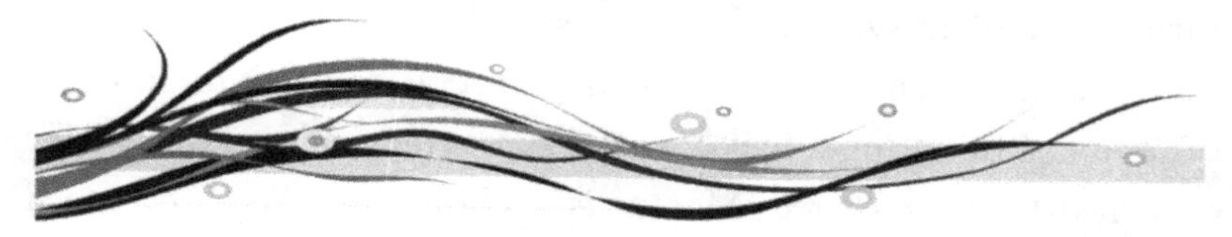

The primary administrative building of the United States Coast Guard base on Oahu was a square, multi-story structure of gray stone block with long dark windows, situated on the Eastern end of Sand Island in Honolulu Harbor.

Sasha watched the seconds tick away on a simple walk clock. 1:42 a.m. She drummed her fingers on the metal tabletop. A small plaque labeled *consultation* was stuck to the wall beside the door.

Consultation. What a joke. More like an interrogation, she thought.

Why were you out so far?

Who gave you permission to use the boat?

What happened to it?

Why did you attack that ship?

Sasha held one elbow, the fist of her other hand pressed against her mouth. There weren't any real answers to their questions. She released a breath and let it pass across her lips with a slight whistle. Some things were simply born of passion. They weren't supposed to make sense. Those gentle creatures needed her—the ocean needed her.

Her gaze drifted around the modest room. Stark metal desk, uncomfortable plastic chairs, monotonous blue walls, gray- and blue-checked carpet, and a thick plastic jug of purified water, thrust into the top of a water cooler—the motor of which rattled to annoying effect.

After hours of debriefing, Sasha just wanted it to be over. Hoped that soon they would let her go, give her back her phone, and let her call a friend to come get her. She'd have to figure out how to explain it all to her father. There was no good way to spin the situation. Her only comfort was the thought those whalers would think twice before terrorizing the oceans again. That, at least, felt good.

The door to the room pushed open, and a slim man in an astonishingly crisp USCG uniform stepped in. "Miss Kino, I'm Commander Roderick Hawkins. Mind if I sit?" He gestured to the chair opposite of her.

Sasha shrugged. "It's your place."

A brief dip of his head and he took a seat, his expression darkening. "Miss Kino—"

"Sasha," she said. "My mom is Mrs. Kino. Or was ... whatever."

"Sasha." Commander Hawkins cleared his throat. "This has been a long day for all involved. For you and your friends, a lot of danger."

"Are they here?" Sasha asked.

"They were released."

Sasha shifted in the stiff plastic chair. "So, when can I go?"

"Soon, but first, you and I need to come to a clear understanding about something." Commander Hawkins held her in place with his stare.

Sasha raised her eyebrows. "Okay?"

"I respect your conviction," Hawkins said. "What you did today was beyond brave—but it was also foolish, destructive, and inexcusable. You destroyed your father's yacht and almost caused an international incident in the process, an incident we are still trying to smooth over. You're lucky you're not dead."

Sasha balked. "They were whaling in U.S. territorial waters."

"Wrong," Commander Hawkins said, staring across the empty table. "They have a scientific research permit and were outside of the protected marine reserve. You attacked a foreign ship without cause."

"Without cause?" Sasha stood up.

"Yes, Miss Kino." The commander's formality returned. "Without legal cause. Now, sit down."

Sasha lowered herself into the chair, scowling.

The commander continued. "You don't have to like it, but under IWC law, that ship was allowed to capture and kill whales. Coming close to U.S. territorial waters was their mistake, but that didn't give you cause to attack them. We had to let them go."

Sasha's mouth gaped open. "You let them go? They held us hostage, put guns in our faces ..." she said, her voice cracking.

"*After* you attacked them," Hawkins said. We had no choice. Either that or spark an international incident involving Russia—a volatile situation we're not willing to risk."

Silence ballooned in the room, save the tireless rattling of the water cooler.

"I'm sorry," Commander Hawkins said, standing and sliding Sasha's cell phone across the table to her. "You should count yourself fortunate you're not the one going to prison."

Sasha lowered her gaze to the floor, face burning.

"Due to the situation and the loss of a vessel at sea, we've had to notify the owner, your father. He asked us to arrest you, let you stew on your bad life choices in a holding tank. When we declined, he volunteered to come get you himself." Commander Hawkins pulled the door open. "He's waiting for you in the lobby. You're free to go."

Her body felt as if it were a thousand pounds of sand, slipping through the gaps in her chair and piling on the floor beneath her.

Tears collected in the corners of her eyes, blurring the carpet squares into a watery mess.

"This won't happen again. Am I clear?" the commander said with a firm gaze.

Sasha pursed her lips, then stood and grabbed her cell phone which slid into the front pocket of her shorts. Her chest out and chin up, she wiped a strand of raven hair from her face and brushed past the commander. Without a second look, Sasha walked the length of the corridor and out into the silent lobby.

Only the groan of the old Ford Bronco seemed to permeate Sasha's senses as she and her father, Gordon, bumped along the coastal highway that would take them home. Her dad hadn't uttered a single word since the lobby. And even then, he'd only asked if she was hurt. To which she'd shaken her head. Her father was furious and for good reason. She'd destroyed their cherished family heirloom, a boat that had originally belonged to her grandfather.

The centerline slipped by beneath the truck's headlights, while above, the brilliant stars shone with majesty in the purple night sky. Sasha chanced a look at the sentinel form of her father, who had both hands on the wheel and his dark tired eyes focused on the road ahead. He wore an old pair of crumpled khaki shorts and a frayed T-shirt—both pulled out of the laundry, no doubt, in a moment of haste after receiving a call from the coast guard.

His silence was her agony.

"Papa, can we get this over with? Please say something to me."

The thick-framed man with long dark hair shifted in his seat, his face unreadable. "What is it you want me to say?"

"Anything Papa," Sasha replied. "Tell me you hate me. I can't take your silence."

"I don't hate you," he said with an even tone.

Sasha rolled her eyes and wiped a tear from her cheek. His graciousness was almost worse. "Papa, you didn't see what the whalers did to those poor creatures. I had to stop it. I didn't know how else to do it. I'm sorry, okay?"

Minutes passed. Time seemed to stand still. Her father shifted in his seat and exhaled, shaking his head. "You were made for the sea, Sasha. Your mother and I knew it on the night you were born in that silent cove north of Mākaha. The ocean calls to you—it always has."

Sasha bit her lip.

"I have great respect for the passion inside you, daughter, but this ..." He stopped, seeming to weigh his words. "This I cannot abide. You could have gone to prison, or your recklessness could've gotten you killed. With your mother in her present condition, what would happen to our family then? Did you stop to consider that?"

"No," Sasha whispered, her head low.

"No, I suppose you didn't," he said, his voice low. "Your grandfather's boat was our lifeline. It was going to help us pay for your college."

"I know."

"Do you, now?" Gordon looked at his daughter for the first time since the lobby. "Every action, good or bad, responsible or irresponsible, has an equal or opposite response from the natural world—a consequence. Sasha, our choices guide who we are and form the world around us. You can never choose a path without first weighing the cost."

Sasha remained silent.

"This time, your choice affected our family, bringing shame and loss upon us." Her father sighed and turned back to the road. "I hope it was worth it."

Sasha didn't reply. She turned to the window to watch the wind-blown palms flit past in the dark.

"We'll have to pull you from the competition next week, and you'll need to double your hours at the surf shop."

Sasha sat upright, her mouth open. "The United World Pro is the only surf competition that matters to me. You know that! I have to compete to defend my title."

"No, Sasha. You need to assess what's important in life. Insurance won't cover us on this. What will we do without the money I made running weekend island tours? Huh? You know we can't make ends meet. Besides, you still don't have a scholarship. If you ever want to go to college, we'll have to start saving more. I can pick up extra hours at the hangar, but that means you are working when you'd rather play. The surf competition is out of the question."

Her father turned into the driveway of their house, and before the wheels came to a stop, Sasha leaped out and slammed the door behind her. She knew she was wrong, but anger and pride won out.

She climbed the concrete front stairs two at a time. Grasping the railing, she hoisted herself onto the porch.

"You can't run away from this, girl." Her father's voice reached out to her from the ramshackle, single-space carport.

Sasha stood staring at the ramshackle residence dearly in need of a fresh coat of white paint. She grasped the front doorknob and jiggled it until the wonky latch disconnected and the door swung inward. The familiar smell of coconut and herbs wafted out. Sasha made a beeline for her room. With tears in her eyes, she slammed her bedroom door, then collapsed, exhausted, onto her narrow twin bed.

A few deep breaths slowed the cadence of her heart. Sasha could hear her father moving about in the kitchen. He would leave her alone for now. The text chime on her phone made the distinct sound of a dinner fork tapping a crystal goblet. She pulled it from her pocket and squinted at the bright screen that blinded her teary eyes in contrast to the dark of the room. It was Max.

U okay?

Sasha laid the phone on her chest, rubbed her eyes then looked at the screen again.

No.

The phone chimed again. She switched it to silent and read the text.

Ur not in trouble with the CG, are you?

Sasha sighed.

No, but I've really done it this time.
Can't compete next week ...

A double buzz sounded.

Sux.
Me and Bodhi r meeting down at Mākaha to carve a few night waves. Need to blow off some steam. U comin? I wanna see u.

Sasha needed sleep. Besides, her dad would be furious if she left. In the morning, she needed to visit her mom at the hospital. She'd tell her in person what happened. Sasha looked out the window and bit her lip. *To hell with it*, she thought. *Already in deep trouble, what else can I lose?*

Yeah. 10 min.

Exiting the window wasn't the problem. Retrieving her board from the carport without knocking anything over and creating a ruckus, that was another kettle of fish. She grabbed her board and gingerly weaved her way through the carport without incident.

Sasha breathed a sigh of relief as she stopped at the corner of Lahaina and Munuku, a physical and metaphorical crossroads. This little venture would only compound the problems she already had, but at this point, Sasha failed to see what difference any of it made. She'd tried to do what was right—what the ocean needed from her—and screwed up her life in the process. Fate had a funny way of showing its favor.

Sasha adjusted the longboard under her arm, the night breeze swishing her long dark hair about her shoulders. She closed her eyes, the fear and stress of the day melting away into the dark rustling of the island palms. She took a moment to look back at her dad's house. No lights on. She'd gone unnoticed, and if she played her cards right, it would stay that way. Her father wouldn't rise for work until six-thirty. She checked her watch. Four hours, with some time to get back home before anyone woke to notice she was gone.

After a brisk five-minute walk, Sasha stepped from the road out onto the sand of Mākaha beach. The sand sifted between her toes, and instantly, Sasha felt lighter. At two in the morning, the beach was silent like the town of Waianae around it. A small campfire down the beach suggested at least one other group of latecomers. Just some local boys, likely drunk by now. She could hear them laughing from way down the beach. For hard-core surfers, Mākaha beach was the birthplace of big-wave surfing. Steep lava-ridged valleys and mountains to the east made this cove one of Hawaii's most consistent and venerated breaks. In the summer, waves typically came in below four feet, but in the winter … well, that was the reason the International Surfing Championships started there in 1954. The same championship in which she couldn't compete next week.

Sasha sighed and made her way over to where her friends sat around a small fire, their boards knifed into the sand.

"Aloha," Max said, turning to Sasha as she approached.

"Aloha," Sasha said.

"Long day, right?" Bodhi said, his tone somber. He offered her a cold bottle of beer.

"Yeah, long day." Sasha declined the drink with a wave of her hand, then leaned down and gave Max a slow kiss.

Bodhi choked on his beer. "Jeez, bro, I'm right here. Third wheel much?"

"How did your dad take it?" Max asked.

Sasha stabbed her board into the sand and sat cross-legged next to him. "Like a knife in the back. How do you think he took it? Do your parents know?"

Max shook his head. "I got a ride home with Bodhi. I'm not saying a word."

Bodhi's eyes widened. "Dude, I still need a place to stay and want to keep my mom's insurance for a few more years. What we did today—not a conversation I want to have with her."

Sasha lowered her head, doodling a pattern in the pristine white sand with her finger. "I can't compete next week. We won't have the money for the entry fee, and I'll have to work more hours to make ends meet, now."

"But Sasha, you're the reigning champ. You have to …" Bodhi's voice trailed away.

Max gave a soft smile. "I'm sorry, Sash."

Sasha's gaze flitted from Max to Bodhi and back again. "Was it right? What we did today. Was it the right thing to do?"

The group of friends sat in silence for a few moments listening to the cadence of the surf and the laughter of the other group fading away as they trailed off the beach with their coolers.

"Sasha," Bodhi said. "It was right if you stayed true to your heart. What we saw today was murder. Somebody had to stop it, and that somebody was us."

"Yeah, but at what cost?" Sasha said, standing and pulling her board from the sand. "I've got a lot to figure out with my 'Aumakua, ya know? I'm going out for a bit."

"You want us to come out with you?" Max said.

Sasha stared at the stars and then the reflection of the moon, distorted in the lapping surf. "Nah, but thanks. I just need some time alone. Cool if I come in and get you guys after a while?"

"We're here for you, Sash," Max said with a wry smile. "Watch out for hammerheads."

"Thanks, guys." Sasha turned and headed for the water.

Bodhi looked at Max with a smirk. "It's the hammerheads that need to watch out, man."

Sasha slipped her board tether over her ankle and ran toward the water's edge, leaving behind moist footprints in the sand. The mellow water gave the incredible sensation of washing away her stress. She mounted her longboard and dipped her arms into the surf.

Paddling hard to catch the momentum of a passing swell, Sasha leaped to her feet and twisted her hips, the board carving into the wave. This was home. Here she felt free. On nights like this, she had her own private communion with Kai himself—the great ocean. Time ceased to exist, and the hustle and bustle, the cares of her world, fell away.

Heart pounding and lungs heaving, Sasha sat with her legs straddling the board and dangling into the water. She allowed herself a small smile. As long as she had this, as long as the ocean was there, she'd be okay. She could get through any trouble that came her way.

A dark shape glided past below the surface. Unlike most people, she didn't fear anything in the ocean. Each creature had its purpose, and the more predatory of those didn't attack people out of malice or ill will. They only did what the universe programmed them to do.

She also wasn't stupid and thought it might be nice to keep her legs for a while longer. Sasha watched as a dark fin pierced the water's surface ten feet away, then on the other side, another rose out of the dark waves. Just when she considered easing away to find another spot, a black and white snout pushed through the surface. A fine mist sprayed into the air from its blowhole.

Sasha broke into a beaming grin.

The orcas continued to circle, a majestic addition to the intoxicating mix of the starry sky and infinite oceanic serenity. As they moved, Sasha glided with them, out beyond the break. A sign. She wanted to call out to Max and Bodhi. She wanted them to see the pod, but they couldn't hear her, and she didn't want to scare off her new friends by shouting. Instead, she decided to savor the perfect tranquility of her unity with the universe, the sea, and these amazing creatures.

The clouds above reflected a momentary flickering in the sky, the slightest green-orange hue forming around their edges. A rumble rolled across the heavens. A brilliant flash, brighter than any bolt of lightning, set the sky on fire. Sasha flinched then slowly opened her eyes just enough to see the heavens alive with a luminous green glow.

An aurora? A plane crash? A meteor?

Another rumble, followed by a surge of sonic vibration, thrummed the air around her. The Orcas churned the water, stirred into a frenzy by the commotion. Sasha turned to see Max and Bodhi on their feet at the water's edge, waving their arms overhead. Their screams were drowned out by the rumble that grew to a roar.

Sasha shielded her eyes as the light enveloped her.

"It's coming at me—"

A massive spherical object struck the ocean with an ear-splitting crack. Sasha screamed and was ripped from her board and dragged under by the force of the impact. The sea seemed to boil, scorching her flesh and her eyes. She dug at the water, climbing for the surface, but the sinking orb dragged her farther into the deep, her flailing body anchored to it by some invisible tether.

In a moment of clarity, Sasha could make out a lone orca calf as it twisted downward with her. She reached out to it, her fingertips touching its dorsal fin briefly before they too were torn from each other in the vortex of emerald light.

Sasha's will left her, and, unable to hold her breath any longer, she gasped. Saltwater raked into her lungs—a gush of molten lava burning through her from the inside out. She clawed at her chest, her mind overcome with panic, her body wracked with pain. The glowing orb plummeted deeper still, dragging Sasha and the orca calf with it into the void—into the dark heart of the fathomless sea.

CHAPTER 4

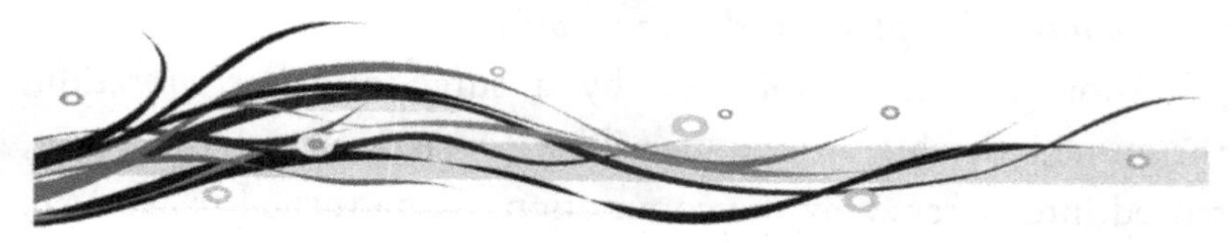

Max and Bodhi yanked their shirts off and dashed toward the surf.

Sasha hadn't resurfaced.

"The hell was that?" Bodhi shouted.

"Bodhi, I got this," Max said.

Bodhi slowed, his eyes questioning.

"I got her, man. Call for help. Use my phone. Go." Max splashed into the surf.

Bodhi bobbed his head. "Okay, yeah. Got it." He pivoted and ran back to the campfire.

Max dove into the dark waves and swam in the direction of the foreboding green light emanating from the depths. He took a deep lungful of air then dove below the surface, hoping to see something, anything. Starved of oxygen, Max rose and broke the surface. Panting and exhausted, he pushed on, paddling across the surface until he was above the green light strobing below.

Max dropped beneath the surface again. After a moment, his eyes adjusted to the sting of the salty water. Max could just make out a giant orb, waves of distorted green light pulsating from it across the seabed below. Was Sasha trapped beneath it? It was easily one hundred feet down, but he had to know. He returned to the surface for one last gulp of air before thrusting himself beneath the waves.

As he descended, the pressure gripped his head like a vice. Max pinched his nose and blew hard to equalize. His ears popped, relieving the pain. As he pushed deeper still, dead fish floated past, their eyes empty, their bellies pointed to the surface. His lungs burned a lake of fire in his chest. Max was no free diver, but he had to press on. Finding Sasha was all that mattered. Clawing at the water, Max pulled himself with increasing difficulty toward the glowing sphere.

As he drew closer, the object came into focus. It looked man-made, like some sort of huge metallic polygon. One shadow slid over the object, followed by another. Without the aid of a mask, his vision was blurry, but he knew the silhouette of a diver when he saw one. They were attaching some kind of rigging to the object. *Who could have made it down there so fast? Are they helping Sasha?* Max kept his distance, fighting the urge to return to the surface for air.

Suddenly, a heavy arm snaked around Max's neck and locked down on his throat. Max clawed at the muscled arm clad in some sort of hard reinforced neoprene. His attacker dragged him upward and away from the strange device, away from any chance of finding Sasha.

Max screamed, his ears ringing with agony. A curtain of bubbles poured from his open mouth. He kicked and struggled in vain against the inhuman strength that seemed to squeeze the life from him until a surge of electrical pain sent every muscle into spasm, and his body resigned. He broke the surface and immediately vomited seawater. With his muscles still convulsing and his consciousness leaving him, he was dragged away toward the hulking outline of a massive vessel looming dark against the distant horizon.

Bodhi waved his arms overhead at the approaching blue lights. "Might be the only time in my life I've ever been happy to see the cops."

The white patrol car, adorned with a single blue stripe and shield, pulled into the gravel lot off the side of the highway. A tired-looking, solidly built patrol officer exited the cruiser and made his way over to Bodhi. The man carried himself as if he'd been around the block more than a few times. He pulled a notepad from his shirt pocket with a sigh and clicked down on a ballpoint pen.

"What's going on here?"

"Hey, man … uh, sir. Where's the dive team? My friends are out there. We gotta get help—"

"Whoa, hang on a second, buddy. Slow down. Who are you?"

"I'm Bodhi."

"Right, I've run into you before. You got a last name Bodhi?"

"Yeah, Li."

"All right, Bodhi Li, tell me what's going on."

Bodhi eyed the brass name tag on the crisp navy-blue shirt. *Westfield.* He'd met this one a few times before, most notably when the officer had crashed Bodhi's house party a couple of weeks back. "Officer Westfield, we need the dive team, stat."

"What's your birthday, Bodhi?" Westfield said.

"Dude, I don't see how that matters. We need divers in the water, stat."

The officer raised his hand. "Relax with all the stat talk. I'm not an ER doc, kid."

"Whatever, bro, but I mean …" Bodhi pointed to the water.

"And you and your friends were out here doing what?"

Westfield looked at the sign to his right. It read: *NO Night Surfing*.

Bodhi pushed his hands out. "Totally not night surfing."

"You sure? Tell me what happened. The call notes said something about a meteor?"

"Yeah. I mean, no, dude, you just had to see it. There was like this green fire, and it fell out of the sky, and—"

"Hang on a second." Officer Westfield leaned closer and sniffed. "Have you been drinking?"

Bodhi swallowed. "No."

"You sure?" Westfield craned his neck to see the campfire and Bodhi's six-pack wedged in the sand.

Bodhi cast a guilty glance over his shoulder. "No way, man. I'm only nineteen. I don't do that juvenile delinquent stuff."

The officer gave him a suspicious look. "That's not what I remember from that little house party you and your friends threw."

Bodhi flushed. "You're just gonna stand here and not help. No dive team to help my friends? Is that right?"

"Look, kid," Westfield said. "I have to ask questions. They're not going to send a dive team because *you* think we need them."

"But we do need them."

"For your friends who were totally not night surfing?" Westfield's eyes narrowed.

"Okay, yeah, we were wrong, but dude. A meteor came out of the sky and fell on my friend Sasha. It might have even hit her, man. What if she's trapped under there? Max swam out to help her, and now he's gone, too!"

Westfield sighed, another marked unit pulling to the curb behind him. "Now you're saying there are two people out there? Sasha and Max. Gordon Kino's daughter, Sasha?"

Bodhi nodded.

"What about Max? He got a last name?"

Bodhi sighed. "Anderson."

"You three were out here alone?"

"Yeah, I'm not making it up. Sasha was out there—and I'm gonna be straight with you, dude—she was surfing. Max went into the water to help her after the meteor—"

"Hang on," Westfield said. "Look, I want to help, but I don't see any evidence of a meteor strike here. Your friend probably got out on another part of the beach."

"I saw it," a voice said from behind them. A young woman walked from the street out to where they stood. "You're talking about the meteor, or whatever that flaming green thing was? I saw it fall out of the sky, right there." She pointed toward the ocean where the object struck. "A girl was out there surfing."

"I saw it, too," another man said, keeping his distance under a nearby palm. "Thought I'd come to see if I could find where it hit."

"See," Bodhi said as he watched more curious people trickle in toward the beach. "I'm not crazy, man."

"You both saw it?" Westfield asked the newcomers.

"Yes," the man said.

Westfield raised his mic to his lips. "Two-forty to dispatch."

"*Two-forty, go ahead.*"

"Dispatch, send me the dive team and rescue to my location. Looks like I have a missing surfer over here on Mākaha."

"*Dispatch copy.*"

Westfield pulled his phone from a shirt pocket, dialed a number, and held it to his ear.

Bodhi squirmed, anxious to do something, anything.

"Hey, Sarge," Westfield said but stopped, staring at the shoreline as several landing craft came ashore, groups of men dressed in black tactical BDUs fanning out onto the beach. "Hang on, Sarge, let me call you back."

"Who's that?" Bodhi stared at the men clad in black.

"Stay here." Westfield pushed past Bodhi and called out to the strange men. "Hey, the beach is closed."

"That's correct, sir," a capable-looking man said and stepped away from the group as it spread out, creating a human barrier across the beach. "You and the other civilians need to clear out."

Westfield balked. "Now hang on a second, son. I don't know who you are, but this beach is the scene of a possible incident, and this area is within the jurisdiction of the Honolulu Police Department. I believe it's you and your friends who need to clear out."

"Negative, sir." The man remained calm. "This area is now under the jurisdiction of the United States Navy."

"I don't think so, buddy." Westfield raised his voice, his hand resting on his Taser. "You are now interfering in an official police investigation."

Engrossed, Bodhi looked on as others gathered around him to watch the confrontation. Just as he thought the seasoned cop might put his hands on the tough-looking sailor, the line of fatigue-clad men parted, and another man approached. Tall, with silver close-cropped hair and a gait that told everyone who was in command.

Bodhi took note of the subdued black eagle emblem in the center of the man's chest, down the centerline of his uniform.

"You're good to go, Chief," he said. "Resume the recovery operation."

"Roger that, sir." The sailor turned and marched back to the line of men, where he barked several orders about establishing a perimeter.

"Officer"—the Navy commander leaned closer to read the brass—"Westfield. Check with your department about your involvement in this situation."

"Excuse me, sir?" Westfield said.

"My name is Captain Jager, with the United States Navy. This area is temporarily under naval jurisdiction. Check with your superiors about your involvement here."

Westfield scowled but keyed his mic. "Two-forty to dispatch."

"*Two-forty, go ahead.*"

"I've got a Captain Jager here. Says he's with the United States Navy. He's telling me the beach is temporarily under naval jurisdiction. Can you confirm?"

"*Received. Stand by.*"

Jager took a step forward and raised his hand. "Ladies and gentlemen, may I have your attention?"

A hush fell over the small gathering. Bodhi wiped his hands on his shorts, unsure of what to expect.

"My name is Captain Jager with the United States Navy. This beach is temporarily off-limits. We will hold an official press conference concerning our business here, but what you need to know is everything is okay."

The crowd murmured, talking in hushed tones. Bodhi crossed his arms, squinting with suspicion.

Westfield's mic crackled. "*Dispatch to two-forty.*"

"Two-forty," he said.

"*Your traffic is confirmed. Per Lieutenant Mixon, immediately release the scene and get in service. Rescue and Dive have been canceled.*"

Westfield looked to his backup officer, who shrugged and headed for his car.

Jager's expression did not change. "Thank you for your help, Officer Westfield. We'll take it from here."

"*Two-forty, do you copy?*"

Westfield keyed his mic. "Dispatch, there might be a girl in distress."

"*Negative. Our information does not show any civilians involved. Release the scene and get in service per zero-zero-one.*"

Westfield shook his head. "I copy. Show me ten-eight. No report."

"You're gonna leave?" Bodhi piped up but immediately cringed when he felt Jager's gaze fall on him.

"Sorry, kid," Westfield said, turning for his car. "Looks like I'm in over my head on this one."

Jager cleared his throat. "I need everyone's attention. This is important." He paused for what seemed like dramatic effect. "Did anyone see anything strange this evening? If you did, my team may have a few questions for you." The small crowd murmured again, and a few people peeled off and headed for home.

Bodhi took a step back. He'd seen enough movies. Something wasn't right. As a group of bystanders broke away and headed toward the road, Bodhi slipped in with them, trying to look as inconspicuous as possible. He couldn't help Sasha or Max right now. He had to get out of there and figure out what to do next.

As he trudged in the loose white sand back to the street, he saw a dark sedan parked three spaces down from his Suzuki GXR 600. Inside, behind tinted windows, two shadowed figures sat, watching. The knot in Bodhi's stomach tightened. As he neared his bike, the doors opened. Two men dressed in black fatigues exited the vehicle and started toward him. His mind spun. *Do I talk to them? Do I run?* He fumbled with the key to the GXR's ignition.

"Hey, kid," the voice from behind startled him.

Bodhi turned to see Officer Westfield leaning against his cruiser. The patrolman straightened and made his way over. Bodhi cast a glance back to the dark sedan. The other men stopped, still looking in his direction.

"I'm going to need to see your driver's license and proof of insurance before you drive your motorcycle."

"Oh, um …" Bodhi checked his pockets, his fingers touching his wallet. He flicked his eyes back toward the men in black. "Officer, *I may be in a little trouble*. I don't seem to have my ID on me."

Westfield nodded, his gaze moving to the men in black and back to Bodhi. "You know, it's against state law to operate your vehicle without your driver's license and proof of insurance. If I follow you to your house, would you be able to show them to me?"

"Yeah, man … um, sir. That would be good."

"Get on your bike. I'll block traffic for you." Westfield winked.

"Thank you, sir."

Bodhi straddled his bike, rocked it upright, and slipped the key into the ignition. The GXR revved high as Westfield's cruiser backed onto the street, the light bar flashing. Bodhi pulled away from the gravel parking area and out onto Farrington Highway. One last look in his side mirror showed the men in black standing near their sedan. They weren't following him after all. He'd make the drive home, show this Westfield guy whatever, and thank him for covering for him. After he was clear, he could figure out what to do for Sasha and Max.

Shifting into third, Bodhi kept a moderate speed along the coastal highway watching as Westfield turned onto the road behind him and shut his light bar off. Bodhi glanced at his watch. 4:13 a.m. The roads, still clear and dark, he'd be fine with the officer following him home. Still, a knot twisted in his gut. Something crashed into Earth's atmosphere, and now the Navy wanted to act like it didn't happen. No one seemed to care Sasha and Max had gone missing.

As Bodhi rounded the bend toward Waikomos, an unmarked red dump truck swerved out onto the road from a darkened side street behind him. Bodhi looked back in time to see Westfield's patrol car crash into the side of the truck, bounce off, and drop into the drainage ditch where it rolled onto its side.

Four dark sedans emerged from shadows and surrounded him, matching his speed. Acting as one unit, the four cars pushed together until all four almost touched fenders with each other, leaving only the smallest room for Bodhi's motorcycle. The rolling trap came to a stop in the middle of the dark Hawaiian highway, the rounded canopy of the surrounding jungle rising high above them in the early morning darkness.

Bodhi removed his helmet and hung it on the handlebars of his bike. "Tell me you bastards didn't kill that cop, man. He was just doing his job."

The passenger side window of the sedan to his left rolled down, and a man in black fatigues leveled a Sig P226 handgun in Bodhi's direction.

"Don't make any sudden moves," the man said.

Bodhi raised his hands, his eyes wide. "You got it, dude. What's this about?"

The man in black raised his eyebrows as members of his team exited their vehicles. "I think you know."

A punch landed squarely on his chin, snapping Bodhi's head to the left. A firm hand clamped a pungent-smelling rag over his face. Disorientated, Bodhi panicked, clawing at thick fingers over his mouth. His world spun, and his struggling slowed under the influence of the powerful vapors. Jerked into the back seat of one of the vehicles, the last thing he heard was the slamming of the car door, and the bark of rubber against asphalt as the unmarked sedans sped off into the early morning darkness.

Suspended by his seatbelt in the upended, smoky confines of his issued Ford Taurus, Officer Westfield groaned and touched his face. His head pounded, and his lungs burned from the chalky remnants of a deployed airbag hanging in the air.

"Yeah, he's breathing. Looks unconscious," came a voice through his shattered driver's side window.

Westfield squinted. He tabbed the belt release and fell to the ceiling of his squad car with a grunt.

The voice outside rose in pitch. "Hey, I gotta go. I gotta go. I'll see you back at the rally point."

"Help me out," Westfield called out as the feet crunched their way back up the short embankment to the road. "Hey, can't you hear me?"

Above him, the rumble of a dump truck shook him to his senses. The kid, Bodhi. The way those men in black watched them leave. This wasn't an accident. Westfield scrambled for his radio mic, finding the spiraled cord which dangled from above.

"Two-forty to dispatch—priority traffic."

"*Two-forty, what's your status?*"

"I need additional units and for you to roll rescue to my location. I've been involved in a collision with a red dump truck. It may have been deliberate. The suspect may have fled the scene."

"*Is the suspect fleeing in the vehicle that struck you?*"

Westfield listened. The dump truck rumbled with a steady rhythm above. It hadn't moved. Westfield keyed his mic. "Standby."

Ducking low, he crawled through the low misshapen window frame now half-buried in soil and grass. Halfway out, his duty belt caught on a curve of mangled metal. Westfield unhooked his belt, let it flop free, and secured his weapon from its holster, a spare magazine, and his handheld radio. Crawling on his belly in a manner reminiscent of his days in the Army, Westfield got clear of the trashed cruiser and crouched with his Springfield Operator 1911 clasped to his chest. Scanning his surroundings, he worked his way up to the cab of the truck, the diesel engine still growling. Westfield flung open the passenger side door and raised his weapon in one swift movement.

Empty.

Westfield swore, reached into the cab, and turned off the ignition.

"Negative, dispatch. The suspect is gone."

In the stillness, distant sirens reached out from beyond the hills. Backup was on the way. The veteran patrol officer scanned the highway in each direction, looking for something to give him a clue where his assailant went. It was obvious now. The man on the phone hadn't wanted him dead. He'd wanted Westfield off his trail. The droning cadence of the big bore diesel engine was a necessary component in masking his escape.

Westfield groaned, touched a seam of blood running from his hairline, and looked north. The sky lightened to a pinkish hue beyond the mountains to the east, accompanied by the ever-shifting island breeze—no sign of Bodhi or his bike.

"Why'd they want you so bad, kid?" Westfield shook his head and dabbed at the lengthening trickle of blood dripping from his right eyebrow.

The question gnawed at his gut, even though he knew better than to bark up that tree. But after twenty years on the force, he also knew his cop instincts wouldn't let him leave it alone. Those kids needed his help, and he needed the truth.

CHAPTER 5

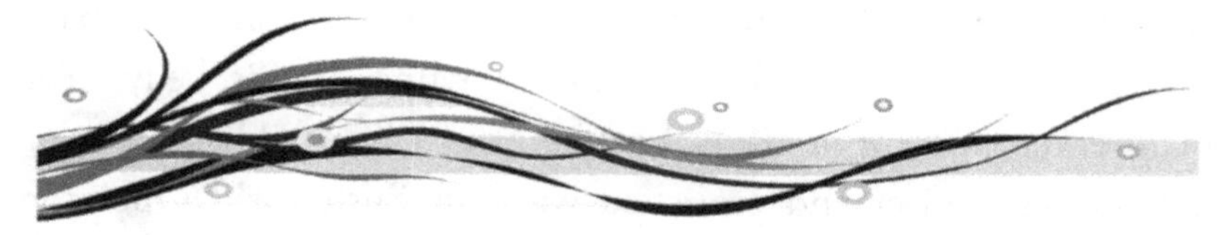

Captain Alric Jager stood on the beach with his arms crossed, an unlit cigar pinched between gnashed teeth. This operation couldn't have gone further off the rails. He shifted his weight and worked the cigar to the opposite side of his mouth. He'd done his best to keep a low profile for his unit, which was engaged in top-secret research and development for the Department of Defense's bioweapons division. But when the DOD's Low Orbit Facility had to jettison something called an Erebos device into Earth's atmosphere, his team, the closest secure asset, was called upon to retrieve it.

His group, reacting to a bad situation, was behind from the start. Worse still, the damn thing crashed in plain view of a bunch of civilians, and maybe even close to a girl who was out night surfing. To his benefit, the only witnesses close enough to debunk the story the public relations team had out there—about a malfunctioning satellite—were a couple of kids. He needed to contain the teenagers, get the device onboard his ship, *The Harbinger*, and everyone else would buy the satellite story.

In his last transmission, the master technician aboard the LOF said they had no choice. He cited rapidly destabilizing working conditions around Erebos. Something to do with disturbing the vector equilibrium in the vacuum structure of space. He claimed to have released the Erebos in an attempt to save the lives of his people on the station. Jager shook his head. *What the hell were they messing with?*

Jager cast his gaze toward the brightening sky and grunted. His division wouldn't be the only party interested in what happened here. Murong, the radical ideologue, would be watching with some high-altitude drone. Jager stamped out Murong's pathetic attempts to foil the DOD's operations every time he tried. But the bastard, like an STD making the rounds in a Vietnamese whore house, had a knack for popping back up over and over again. Murong had a particular distaste for Jager's super-soldiers and didn't seem to care that genetic experimentation was completely legal and sanctioned for certain military divisions. The president wanted elite warriors, and Jager delivered.

It was a good thing Murong hadn't found the Erebos first, or there'd be hell to pay.

The chief petty officer approached with a salute. "Captain."

Jager returned the salute. "At ease. What do you have for me?"

"Sir, we've secured two males in close proximity to the event. One entered the water after splashdown. One of our Strykers subdued and detained him. He's aboard *The Harbinger*.

"Good." Jager adjusted his cigar. "And the other?"

"There were a few complications." The young man shifted, uneasy. "The police—"

Jager raised his hand. "Was the mission accomplished without any civilian fatalities?"

"It was, sir," the young officer said. "The second male on the beach is detained as well."

"And the girl? The one who had direct exposure, what of her?"

"We've seen no signs of a girl in the water or around the device, sir. The only evidence we've found is a fractured surfboard with the name Sasha on it."

"Sasha," Jager repeated under his breath. He clamped his teeth around his cigar and squared his shoulders toward the chief. "Listen to me." Jager lowered his voice. "Priority number one is finding the girl. She was out there. Multiple eyewitnesses have confirmed it, and we have no idea what she's been exposed to. Find her. I don't care if she's a corpse."

"Aye aye, sir," the officer said. "Protocols for her retrieval?"

Jager leveled a withering gaze at the young man. "The national security of the United States of America is at risk, Chief. You do what you have to do to see this through. I don't need to know the details."

Cool ocean waves lapped at Sasha's back, kissed her lips, and sank into the thirsty sand. She groaned and pinched her eyes shut. Her fingers twitched, a leg stirred, and her toes dug into the fine pebbles. Pain washed over her from head to toe, setting each nerve bundle afire. She coughed, vomiting seawater from her lungs. The ocean surged again, and the foaming surf rinsed away the deposit.

A clawed hand, ugly and dark gray, reached forward and dug deep through shifting shingle. Sasha gasped and sat up. She clenched her fist and studied the beastly claw as it squeezed clumps of sand through webbed fingers. That wasn't her hand, but she could feel the sand in it as if it were. *What the hell?*

Sasha managed to drag herself another few inches along the sand, but almost immediately, her trembling body gave in to a blast of searing agony that seemed to scorch every fiber of muscle. She twisted onto her side, vision distorted by a broken sense of equilibrium. Sasha clenched her eyes shut, willing the sensation to stop, wanting nothing more than for the pain to end, to be safely back in her bed at home. Chin tucked to her chest, she swallowed back the rising bile as another lungful of warm island air filled her lungs.

Dancing rays of morning sunlight prickled her skin. Sasha opened her eyes, her stomach in knots, as she dared to look down at her legs and torso. No longer a beautiful golden brown, her body lay in bands of near black and bright white. Water beaded on her as if she repelled it. She gingerly touched the strange, taught skin of her abdomen. This couldn't be a dream.

Footsteps approached, and a shadow fell across her.

"Tito, set up a tight three-sixty on the girl and notify *The Argo* that we've found her," a voice said from over her.

"Roger. Sigma team to Argo command, do you copy?"

Men in wet suits surrounded her taking knees and facing outward. A dark-skinned man stepped past her and knelt, his eyes wide as he studied Sasha's naked body. She groaned again and clawed at another handful of sand, too racked with pain to care about the probing eyes of the men.

"You're incredible, Sasha," he said. "I don't know how to explain any of this, but we're going to get you some help. Everything's going to be—"

Something buzzed past her head—the flight path of an angry hornet hell-bent on death and destruction. There was a snap, like the sound of a nail gun, and the team leader coughed, his mouth chewing air as his hands flew to his upper chest. He toppled back onto the sand next to Sasha. The other men around her, once calm and methodical, now had a look of madness carved into their camo-painted faces. They threw themselves against the sand, the M4 rifles they carried barking flames as they fired at everything and nothing.

Sasha shuddered, her body stiffening. Through half-closed eyes, she watched one of the other men crawl to the team leader, the blood pumping through a useless barrier of cloth and fingers.

"We've gotta go. We've gotta move now. We're exposed here," one man screamed from her left as another shower of zipping rounds blew puffs of sand into the air.

"What about the girl? She's the mission."

"Dixon is down. The mission is scrubbed. Lay down suppressive fire and fall back in waves."

A soldier dove onto the sand between Sasha and the incoming gunfire. His weapon, a bulky belt-fed squad automatic weapon, exploded with the deafening sound of rapid-fire. On the other side of her, the team grabbed their man and ran in the opposite direction.

Sasha pinched her eyes shut, the SAW hammering away next to her only serving to spike her agony.

The gunfire stopped.

The machine gunner jumped to his feet and raced off as a fresh volley of suppressive gunfire erupted from their team farther down the beach, masking their escape.

Time seemed to stand still as Sasha faded in and out of consciousness, writhing alone on the disturbed sand of the now silent cove.

"This her?" A new voice said its face shadowed in the light of the rising sun.

"Of course, it's her. Look at her."

"A firefight is going to attract the police."

A new group of men surrounded her, their uniforms contrasting with those of the men who came before. Sasha struggled to open her eyes, the morning sun searing its way through her retinas and into her brain.

"Get her moving on the double. We're not going to wait for those terrorists to regroup. This girl is all that matters. Let's go."

The man engaged a throat mic. “Cricket, cover our extraction from your position.”

Sasha groaned, hoisted over the shoulder of one of the men as she mercifully faded out of consciousness. *Have I been rescued … or captured?* In her current state of all-encompassing misery, she had no way of knowing the difference.

CHAPTER 6

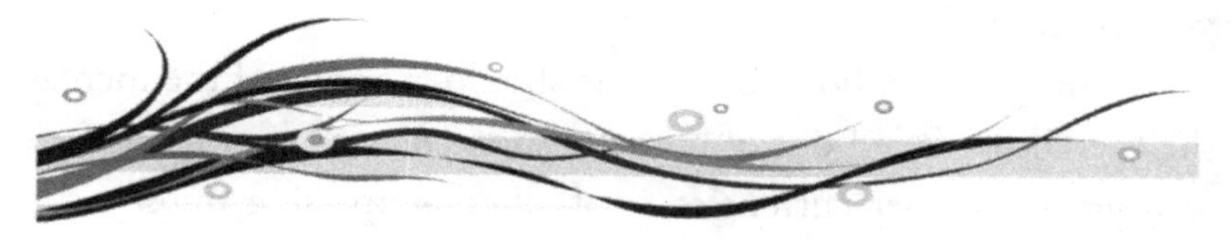

"I'm not getting another scan. I'm fine," Derrick Westfield said, sitting on the edge of the gurney.

"Officer Westfield, you were in a car crash, and you took a blow to the head. We need to make sure you're okay," the petite ER nurse said.

"I'm fine, Emily. Really." Westfield slid off the edge of the bed to his feet. "I appreciate you taking care of me, *again*, but I'm not going to sit on this cot with my feet dangling like a child anymore. I've got stuff to do."

"Stuff? Like what? You're going to work yourself to death." Emily offered a smile.

"Now you sound like my ex-wife," Westfield grumbled.

"No, your ex-wife nagged you. I'm worried about you."

Westfield ignored the comment. He looked at his torn, blood-stained uniform and over to the scuffed duty belt piled in a chair in the corner. He needed to change clothes. Sleep could wait.

Emily handed him his duty belt and rechecked the bandage on his forehead. "Three months ago, it was a hairline fracture to your orbital socket from that bar fight you broke up. Then came the badly twisted ankle from foot chasing some addict. Now, this? I'm starting to think you're finding reasons to land yourself in the ER so you can come and visit me."

"I'm committed to my job." Westfield grunted. "Next, it will be a gunshot wound."

Emily slapped his arm. "Why would you say that?"

"Cause it's the job. Can I go now?"

"You don't act a lot better than most of the people you escort in here, not waiting for us to finish your treatment before you walk out."

"Maybe, but the difference is, I'm ruggedly handsome." Westfield smirked.

Emily's eyes flared. "Oh right, of course, and charming as well. How fortunate for me to have you in my ER." She waited for him to fasten his belt. "Sign your release, and you can go, Officer Westfield. If you start feeling worse, get dizzy, nauseated, or overly drowsy throughout the day, come back in, all right?"

Westfield made his mark, handed back the clipboard, gathered his stuff, and made his way out past the nurses' station with Emily in tow.

"You heard me, right?" she said. "Come back in if you feel worse. Don't be stubborn about it."

Westfield glanced back at Emily. Dark curly hair pulled back in a ponytail, bright eyes and a genuine smile, with a curvy figure that—to his eyes—still managed to somehow be breathtaking even in scrubs.

"You sure I can't get you to meet me for a cup of coffee sometime?" he asked.

Emily scowled. "I don't date rogues."

"I don't either. See? We already have something in common," he said with a smirk, then exited through the double doors into the overcrowded emergency room lobby of The Queen's Medical Center.

An hour and a half later, Westfield emerged from his apartment a different man. Dressed in a rough navy polo with an embroidered badge alongside his name stitched into the chest and a pair of khaki BDUs, he pulled the door shut behind him. He ran his fingers around his waistline, grumbling at how it seemed to expand with each passing year. All things considered, besides the small bandage on his forehead and a dull headache he couldn't shake, Westfield didn't feel like a guy who'd worked all night, been in a car crash, and taken a trip to the hospital.

He pulled a cell phone from his pocket, wiped the screen with his thumb, and checked for messages. He'd missed a call from his daughter Janie while in the shower. Westfield frowned. He should call her back. She'd worry about him. *It'll have to wait,* he thought and stuffed the phone back into his pocket.

The veteran officer made his way to his dated Chevy 1500, unlocked it with the key, and slid in across the old cloth bench seat. The sour smell of baked sweat reached his nostrils. *Ugh, left my gym bag in here.*

His phone dinged.

Westfield grumbled and pulled the device from his pocket.

It was a text from Reggie in dispatch.

You wanted me to let you know if anything odd happened on 93 north ...

Yeah. What have you got? Westfield responded.

We've got cars responding to multiple gunshots at the end of 93, north of Keawaula beach. Could be related to your incident.

Thanks, Reggie.

Westfield turned on the truck's engine and, while pulling away, went ahead and touched the name Janie in his recent calls list.

"Dad?" Janie said a faint tinge of anxiety in her voice.

"Hey, honey. Sorry, I missed you," he said, piloting the old truck out onto the road and heading west. "Wanted to tell you I had a small accident this morning on duty, but I'm fine."

"A small accident? You had a collision with a dump truck, Dad. It's on the news."

Westfield grimaced. "Yeah, it sounds a lot worse than it was. The hospital checked me out and sent me home."

"And you're taking it easy today?" she asked.

"Janie, I'm fine. I'm not an old man yet," Westfield said.

"You're my old man. Someone's got to worry about you."

He couldn't much argue. "Will you meet me tonight for dinner after you get off? I'd like to see my girl."

"Sure, Daddy, that sounds good. Take it easy, okay?"

"Okay, honey." Westfield hung up the phone.

Janie was a good girl, grown into a great woman. Nothing like her mother.

The drive out past Mākaha was short, which was good because the longer Westfield drove, the more questions bubbled up from within. Passing the closed beach, he could see no evidence of the Navy or their activity from the early morning hours. He glanced at his watch. 10:47. *Need to find out from patrol about the gunfire and run down some other leads,* he thought. No guarantee this scene was connected to the strange business from last night, but gunfire at the end of 93? Only miles up the road from the meteor incident. Even closer to his crash where Bodhi disappeared. He didn't believe in coincidence like that.

Westfield eased his truck off the road at the end of the lane, ensuring not to block in the marked units and an unmarked but very familiar black Ford Taurus with tinted windows. An exasperated sigh escaped his lips. *Corley's dumb ass is already on scene.*

Alvin Corley was a golden boy and a first-rate jerk. Rising fast through the ranks and a stickler for policy and procedure, the young lieutenant wasted no time in making a name for himself—and pissing Westfield off every chance he got. They had history, and it wasn't good. If law enforcement was a coin, Westfield and Corley were two juxtaposed sides of it.

Westfield exited his truck and made strides toward the small cove from the shoulder. He ducked the tape and approached a patrol officer standing by several small yellow placards on the ground that marked a handful of large brass rifle casings.

"Hey, Derrick." The uniformed man nodded as he approached. "You okay? I heard about the accident this morning."

"Yeah, thanks, Mark," Westfield said.

"What's up?" Mark asked.

"Looking into a few things." Westfield examined the casings lying in a patch of matted-down grass. "What've you got?"

"I'm holding on to these rifle casings." The officer pointed to a pile of brass casings littering the grass. "Not sure what they've got on the beach, but with the large rifle caliber spread out like this, it looks like a sniper position if you ask me."

Westfield studied the placement of the casings and the distance to the other officers down by the water. "Corley is supervising on this one?"

Mark grinned. "Does that make you giddy?"

"As a schoolgirl." Westfield groaned. "Good to see you, Mark."

"You too, man."

Westfield watched his steps and stayed in the track already grooved into the sand by the onsite team as he walked down to the second scene. This kind of stuff didn't happen out here. What happened to him had to be related. As he approached the two detectives, Corley and Geruda, who stood talking and scribbling notes, he put on his most pleasant act.

"Gentlemen," Westfield said.

The two men turned, irritation smoldering in Corley's gaze, but it was Geruda who spoke first. "Hey Westfield, what's going on?"

"I was going to ask you guys the same," Westfield said.

Geruda shrugged. "We're still putting the pieces together, but it looks like a firefight. Not local boys either—like a literal engagement."

Westfield frowned. "Doesn't make any sense."

"But it does," Geruda continued. "There's the sniper position you came past on the way down, an apparent wound from a large caliber rifle round here." He pointed to specks of blood in a fan across the sand with a quantity of coagulated blood at the center. "And there are indentions in the sand here around this position indicating bullet strikes and, of course, all the brass. These men fired in all directions, almost like this group was trying to protect—"

"Hang on a second," Corley interrupted, his eyes burning a hole through Westfield. "Are you official here?"

A few other evidence technicians stopped working and looked up, eyeing the exchange.

"Corley," Westfield cleared his throat. "I'm only trying to—"

"That's a no, isn't it?" Corley snapped. "Don't tell him anything else, Geruda. This investigation is need to know—and he doesn't."

"Sorry, Derrick. Glad to see you're okay," Geruda said, turning back to examine the piles of brass glistening upon the sand.

"Corley—" Westfield started.

"That's *Lieutenant Corley*. And here's a news flash, Westfield—you're not a detective anymore."

Westfield bit his lip. He couldn't afford another write-up. "Lieutenant Corley, I had a guy try to kill me in a dump truck this morning. I'm trying to make sense of it."

"Make sense of it somewhere else." Corley dismissed him with a wave of his hand.

Westfield's skin prickled. "Look, I'm not sure you understand—"

Corley spun, fury in his red face. "Oh, I understand very well. You're a meddling has-been. Now get off my scene and go write some parking tickets. That's about all you're suited for these days."

Westfield had almost bitten his lip through, and he still couldn't stop the words from coming out. "So, I guess it's dark where you are, *that far* up the chief's ass?"

Geruda ducked his head to conceal a smirk.

Corley turned purple. "Get off my scene, or losing your job will be the least of your worries," he shouted, pointing away from the beach.

Westfield turned, ignoring the torrent of threats, and trudged his way through the loose sand back up to the road. *Screw Corley.* He had what he needed for now, and it left no question. Like Bodhi, the same people found the Kino girl, and they'd taken her, too.

CHAPTER 7

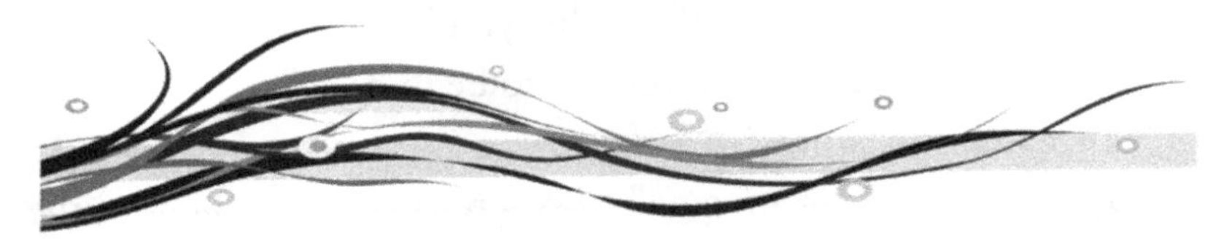

Max jerked awake. He tried to stand but stumbled back against the cold steel bulkhead and crumpled to the floor. The sound of his movement echoed in the dimly lit confined space. An oval hatch sat in one of the walls, complete with a simple dual bolt crossbar mechanism. Above the heavy steel door, inset high on the wall below the ceiling, was a single small fluorescent light, barely enough to illuminate the steel box in which he now found himself.

Max rubbed at his eyes, his whole body aching, the likes of which he hadn't remembered feeling since the days of track and field conditioning in high school.

"What happened?" The question mumbled from his lips, though he already knew the answer. A flaming thing crashed into the ocean. Sasha went under with it. He couldn't reach her before someone … who the hell grabbed him?

He stood again, slow this time, leg and back muscles protesting.

"Ugh," Max groaned, taking one step then stopping to stabilize himself on the cold steel of the wall. He arrived at the heavily sealed door with a few more clumsy movements. Grabbing the crossbar lever, he pulled, feeling it wiggle a fraction before stopping cold. Pushing the lever back into its resting position, he yanked up hard, straining, his back screaming. With a gasp, he let the lever go.

Without warning, the hatch in the door slid open at eye level.

A pair of cold blue eyes filled the hole. "Don't try to escape. Step back from the door, or we will subdue you."

"Subdue? Hey, I'm not supposed to be in here."

The hatch slid shut with a *clang.*

"You've got the wrong guy," Max screamed, pounding on the door. "I haven't done anything. Where are my friends? Where's Sasha!"

Max struck the metal until the bones of his fist ached. He stood there, bare muscled chest and shoulders heaving. His mind drifted.

Max was an athlete through and through. He was strong, confident, and capable of going the distance. There wasn't anything he couldn't do if he set his mind to it. But this was different. This wasn't sports. He'd been kidnapped, and now alone and isolated from everything he knew, Max felt his spirit sag beneath the weight of it.

And what about Sasha? Has she been captured too? Is she dead? Max couldn't bear the thought of it. They'd been together ten years. All the way back to junior high school. Sasha was his first love, and not that stupid stuff high school kids played at either. What they had was down to the bone. Real love. The sort of love a man dies for.

She's alive. I just have to find her.

Max sank to the floor, his back to the cold steel of the bulkhead. He pulled on his neck and scrunched his eyes shut. There was still time. *Think Max, where are they keeping you? Can you find a way out?* He slowed his breathing and tried to absorb all sensations. His stomach roiled in time with a rhythmic rolling of his body. *The ocean. I'm on a ship.* He pinched his eyes harder and concentrated. A faint metallic tapping, slow and deliberate. Somewhere below.

Max laid down and pressed his ear to the floor. There he

listened, straining to hear past the droning of some great engine. The tapping wasn't mechanical—the little inconsistencies, scrapes, and pauses between each strike against the steel told a different story. Max sat up and wiped the sweat from his face. *Concentrate, Max.* He lowered his head to listen once again. Over and over, the rhythmic tapping repeated the same pattern.

Morse code.

It was an SOS message.

Each breath came to Sasha as a shuddered gasp. Her lungs quivered with every pull of air. The specter of consciousness visited her now and again, tearing Sasha from the clutches of an endless nightmare. Each time she roused, a new wave of anguish pushed through her body.

The rattling of ill-fitting wheels grew into a deafening clatter in Sasha's aching head. She forced her eyes open, but through the blur, could see little—the haze gray world rushing by. Sasha groaned, her tongue lolling and useless.

"Please," she managed. Her fingers snaked around the smooth bars of a steel gurney as it bumped along what must have been a narrow corridor.

A slight woman in Navy blues walking alongside the rolling medical cot placed a cool gloved hand on Sasha's arm and squeezed it. "Don't worry, Sasha. We're here to help you."

Lifted over a barrier, the gurney pushed into a smaller, gray-walled room. Sasha clenched her fists, shaking with each new tremor of pain, and pulled against the restraints that held her in place. With a snap, the blades of a nearby fan moved slowly at first, then faster. A fine aqueous mist sprayed from the fan and enveloped her entire body. The tiny water droplets settled upon her skin, beaded, and rolled off, dripping onto the floor beneath.

"Easy now, this will sting but will help your pain," the slight woman said, installing an intravenous morphine drip.

Sasha groaned as the woman attempted, and failed, to force the needle into her arm. The woman gripped harder, pressing down.

"Hey, Beck, help me with this," she said.

Another woman, taller than the first, approached. "What's going on?"

"I'm not sure. I can't get it to—" The slight woman struggled with the needle. "I'm having a hard time getting this set."

Working together, their faces covered with masks, the two nurses braced Sasha and worked to insert the needle into her arm.

Sasha screamed again as the needle was driven with force into her flesh.

"Tape it," the tall nurse said.

"Yeah, but it won't stay in. It's like it wants to push back out. Can you feel it?"

The tall woman tore off strips of tape to secure the IV in place. "No, no, no, it's pulling free. I'm telling you. More tape. Cover it."

"Why would the IV pull free if she's not moving?" the slight woman asked.

"I've got it," the taller woman said. "It's secure. Hold it in place to make sure."

"Okay, administering an initial dose of morphine now."

Sasha's body relaxed, a warm calm snaking through her veins. A tear formed in the corner of her eye, then slipped down her cheek to mix with the building sheen of water covering her body. As her consciousness faded, she heard the door to the room open and footsteps approach.

The women snapped to attention and saluted. "Captain," they

said in unison.

"At ease, how's my girl?" the captain asked.

"Vitals stabilizing, we're sedating and medicating her for pain and working to re-moisturize her now," one of the women said, though Sasha could no longer discern which one. "We scanned her, and she's emitting some sort of energy field, but it appears non-harmful. We're ready to do the first round of bloods."

"I want hourly reports on her condition," the captain said.

"Of course, sir."

The man took another step forward and leaned over Sasha. Sasha could just make out his lingering smirk through tear-filled eyes and a half-chewed cigar dangling between his lips.

"Outstanding."

CHAPTER 8

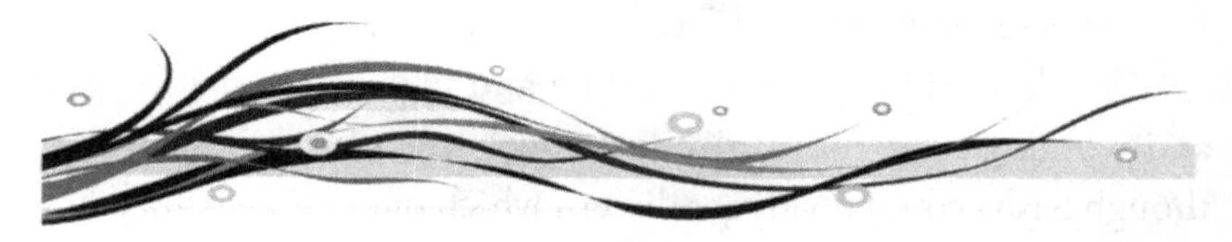

In the dark of the small, smoke-shrouded study, Zhou Murong leaned back in his chair, inhaling the musky scent of the tanxiang incense. With narrow eyes half-closed, he willed the screams, torturous memories of another life, to recede. The incense ember glowed faint, a small cone of gray ash perched on the top of the backflow cradle.

Allowing the calming vapors of the smoldering sandalwood to soothe the creeping feelings of madness, his gaze roved across the walls of his study. The wood paneling was clad with oceanic charts, news articles of his achievements, and rows upon rows of ancient tomes containing a wealth of scientific and progressive literature, as well as a gold leaf embossed copy of *20,000 Leagues Under the Sea*—the one copy of it he never opened.

The engine churned, droning with hypnotic effect, the minuscule shifting of his body the only reminder he was at sea aboard a submarine—*The Argo*, the most technologically advanced research and observation vessel ever designed. Equipped with state-of-the-art weapon systems and futuristic cloaking technology, it was a force to be reckoned with. He didn't relish the need for weapons, but he did need results. Sometimes those results came at a price.

Murong's stare followed the curling tendrils of incense smoke as they snaked from one ledge to the next. A knock, fast and efficient at the door, broke his trance. He took a breath.

"Enter," Murong said.

The door unbolted and swung in on greased hinges. A sturdy-framed man with close-cropped sand-colored hair and a weathered face entered and stood at ease. The merc, a former French COS soldier and kickboxing champion named René Lemeaux, gave a nod, not a salute, to Murong.

"Sir, I have the report from the beach."

"Dismiss with the formalities, René. We've known each other too long."

"The intel was good, Zhou. We found the girl. There's no question she was exposed to something … exotic."

"Where is she now?" Murong asked.

"Seconds after arriving on the beach and locating her, we were engaged by Jager's black ops team. Dixon was mortally wounded. He didn't make the extraction."

Murong lowered his head. Losing men was never easy, though for the greater good, often necessary.

"Sigma couldn't hold on to the girl," the merc continued. "If we'd tried, we would have all been lost."

"I see," Murong tented his fingers and leaned back in his chair.

The merc remained stoic.

"I need to understand something," Murong said, his words crisp and cool. "Why did you deviate from my plan?"

Lemeaux stood stock still.

"The drone identified her position," Murong continued. "We knew exactly where she was. Why make landfall the next cove over, almost a quarter of a mile, and move on foot to her position?"

"It was Dixon's call. Our team leader believed a stealth approach was tactically superior."

"But it wasn't. You were caught in the open when Jager's Strykers ambushed you, and now, as a result, your friend is dead."

Lemeaux averted his gaze.

Murong stood from behind the desk, calm and composed. The muscles of his lean, powerful figure, pressed through the silk button-down. He bore a questioning stare into the merc. "I am sorry for his death. But while it is not the military, I expect you to follow it to the letter when I give an order. That's what you're paid for." Murong's tone was hard as stone. "Believe me when I say, every possible outcome is considered before I ever put players on the board. I have viewed the problem from beyond the blind mind and sought out each and every answer to even the most mundane dilemmas. If you'd carried out my orders and taken the Hammerhead to her location, you could have extracted her in seconds while having a mobile armored cover and immediate heavy weapons support. Dixon would likely still be alive ..."

Lemeaux shuffled on the spot. "I understand. It won't happen again."

Murong gave a nearly imperceptible nod. "Good. You're now in charge of tactical operations." He traced his fingers slowly across the desk. "René, this girl could be the key to everything, and she's in incredible danger. No one knows what happened to her by coming in close contact with the Erebos. I have no doubt Jager will try to find a way to steal her out from under us."

"Zhou," Lemeaux said. "Now that she's in Jager's custody, what can we do?"

Murong paced behind his desk, his mind reaching for every potential outcome. "If we do nothing, Jager will exploit her condition to further his agenda. All my sources indicate he is currently developing super soldiers for the United States military. He'll use any data gained from studying the girl if he can. Can you imagine what would happen if such madness ran amuck?" Lemeaux cleared his throat. "And if we intervene?"

Murong stepped to a long mahogany bookshelf, his fingertips caressing the bindings of works by Krauss and Sun Tzu. "We'll lose more men, and we may not succeed at freeing her. But our intervention may yet alter the world's destiny in some unforeseeable way. Ripples in a pond can have an infinite impact. I don't see we have any other choice."

The merc captain waited, his hands clasped behind his back.

"Gather a fresh squad," Murong said. "We're going back after her."

"She's aboard *The Harbinger*. We don't have the ability to assault a microcarrier."

"Not head-on, no." Murong touched his chin. "This mission will employ a careful application of stealth. Silent insertion from a cloaked Hammerhead."

"I'll go," Lemeaux said.

"No, I need you to run the operation from here. Send Erikson, instead."

The Frenchman gave a reluctant nod.

"Only three men will board the ship," Murong said. "Utilize necessary force. Tell your men to find the girl. Free her if they can. If not, ensure she is warned of Jager's intent. Let the doubt germinate in her mind. It will drive her to us … eventually."

The merc captain saluted. "I'll take care of it."

Murong nodded, a look of quiet defiance spreading over his chiseled features. "As day fades to night, and the seasons dissolve away into the cycle, so shall we go."

"So shall we go," Lemeaux repeated.

CHAPTER 9

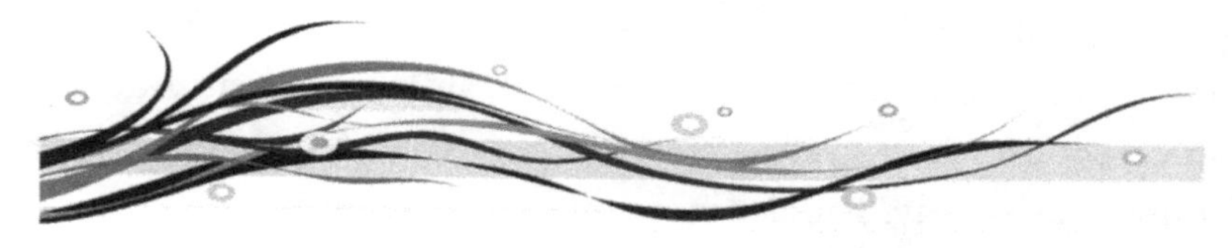

Westfield pulled his truck to the curb down the street from the simple, white, one-story residence. He was pretty sure this was Gordon's house. Placing the truck in park, Westfield took a moment to get his ducks in a row. Gordon was a sharp guy. He'd know Westfield wasn't straight with him if the delivery of this particular bit of unsavory news wasn't cohesive.

Back in the day, he and Gordon went through Army basic together. Following their initial training, they'd gone on to Fort Shafter on Oahu—Westfield with the 8th Military Police Brigade and Gordon with the 130th Engineer Brigade. Years passed, and they'd drifted in different directions, but that sort of bond wasn't easily broken by the passage of time.

Westfield put the truck in gear. *No good way to do this. Might as well get it over with.* He drove the battered 1500 a little farther and allowed it to crawl to a stop outside 435 Lahania Street. Westfield got out, pulling on his neck, fussing about the faint throb of a mild headache he couldn't seem to shake. The afternoon sun high above warmed his shoulders and face as he made the short trip up the driveway to the house. He rapped the flaky, cream-colored front door three times, then waited. No answer. He rapped again, then checked his watch. The day was growing long, and he really needed to get some sleep. A nap, at least, before seeing Janie for dinner.

The door clicked open, just a few inches. Gordon Kino

hovered in there, eyes red and puffy.

"Derrick?" Gordon said, pulling the door wide and stepping out onto the porch.

"Hey, brother." Westfield gave the barrel-chested Hawaiian a hug. "Been a while. I heard about Sasha and wanted to check on you. Knew you still lived out this way."

"Of course, it's great to see you." Gordon pulled away. "What can you tell me?"

"Well, I'm not official, and I'm not sure what you've been told, but I can start with what I know."

"Won't you come in? Damn, It's good to see you."

"Sure," Westfield said, following Gordon across the threshold.

A young teenage girl with waist-length black hair appeared in the doorway to a bedroom, her face streaked with tears. "Papa?"

"It's okay, darling," Gordon said. "This is Officer Westfield. He and I were in the Army together. Long time ago." He gave a weak smile. "He needs to talk to me about Sasha. It's okay. I promise to tell you anything new about your sister."

The girl simply nodded and disappeared back into the room.

"Do you remember my youngest, Mika? She's already had a hard time with anxiety over her mom's condition. Now, this. I kept her home from school today."

"Understandable," Westfield said.

"How's Janie?"

"She's doing great. Grown into a beautiful woman." Westfield instinctively swiped the screen of his phone open, revealing the background wallpaper, a recent picture of him and his daughter, their arms around one another. A tingle of awareness prickled his neck, and he turned the phone downward. "I'm sorry, Gordon. That was thoughtless of me."

Gordon forced a smile, swallowed, and cupped his hand

together. "No, I'd love to see her. Good to see that she's safe and well."

Westfield held the red-eyed gaze of his friend.

"Please," Gordon said, motioning to Westfield's phone.

Westfield clicked the screen on and handed it over.

"Oh, yes. She is a beauty. She looks so happy with you." His lip quivered. Gordon took a moment to master himself, then cleared his throat. "It's great to see you, Derrick." He handed the phone back. "Are we really this old?"

"I'm afraid we are, my friend."

"I feel stupid to admit I don't have a good reason for having not reached out to you over the last few years."

"Seven years," Westfield said. "Sasha was in middle school the last time we got together for a drink."

"Good grief."

"Forget about it, brother. Life happens, right? Sometimes it's easy to lose sight of people amid everything else."

"Yes, well, it's a point I intend to rectify. Can I get you anything, water? Something else?" Gordon moved to stand, but Westfield stayed him with a wave of his hand.

"If it's all the same, Gordon, I'd like to tell you what I know now. I appreciate your hospitality, and it's great to see you, but I worked all night and still haven't slept."

"Oh, of course," Gordon said, his expression darkening.

Westfield rubbed his hands together. "While on duty last night, I got dispatched to a citizen assist on Mākaha. It was Sasha's friend Bodhi who called it in."

Gordon shook his head. "This, right on the heels of the incident yesterday."

"What incident?"

Gordon sighed. "She and her friends tried to stop some

whalers, destroyed the family boat, and nearly got themselves killed." Gordon raised his red-rimmed eyes. "Kids, right?" He laughed, though the sound was devoid of amusement.

"You got me, pal," Westfield said.

"What happened last night?" Gordon asked, a muscle twitching under his eye. "All the officer said when he came out to the house was she went night surfing with friends. One moment she was there and the next, gone. They said she may have left without her friends or gotten out on another part of the beach, but that's not Sasha. I keep worrying that she drowned out there." Tears formed in the corners of his swollen eyes. "But she's an expert swimmer … I can't make sense of why she would disappear like that or why her friends wouldn't come tell me."

Westfield mulled the words over, contemplating his next move.

Gordon's gaze attempted to pry the whole truth from Westfield, but he couldn't do that to his old friend. Sasha and her friends had been kidnapped, and someone was willing to kill a police officer to do it. Gordon and his family didn't need any trouble. It was safer for him to simply believe she was missing, however cruel it seemed at the moment.

Westfield pursed his lips and rubbed the back of his hand across his chin.

"There's more to it, though I can't say how much."

Gordon nodded, hanging on to every word.

"Something crashed into the ocean this morning," Westfield said. "Dispatch blew up with meteor sightings. The Navy was on the beach in minutes. They said it was a malfunctioning satellite. That it might be emitting dangerous radiation. I spoke with Bodhi before he went home. He said Sasha was out there when it crashed into the water off the beach. After she disappeared, her friend Max went into the water to help her. I never saw either of them while I was out there."

Gordon licked his lips and wiped his eyes. "Do you think …? What do you think happened to her?"

Westfield shook his head. "The Navy claims they didn't find her while recovering the satellite. It's possible she and Max got out of the water somewhere else."

"Or she got injured or drowned." Gordon swallowed, staring off. "Is there anything else?"

Westfield fought back the need to blurt out the truth. "There are too many unknowns right now, Gordon. Time usually sorts these things out. It's best not to jump to conclusions."

Gordon shook his head dabbed at his puffy eyes with a handkerchief. "She's so strong, defiant, some might say, but her passion is unique. The only influencer in her life is the driving of her own heart. That business with the whalers yesterday? Her passion created that mess. Wild spirited, that girl." Gordon paused. "You'll tell me if you hear anything?"

"I will." Westfield rose and squeezed his friend on the shoulder. "I don't know yet what happened to Sasha, but I promise you this, Gordon." Westfield crossed the room and opened the front door. "I won't rest until I do."

CHAPTER 10

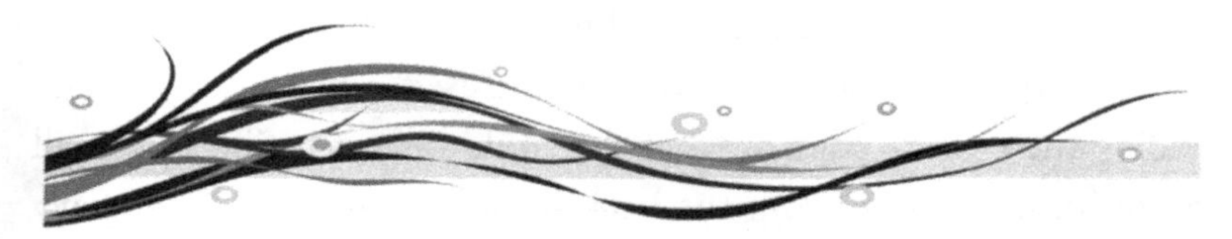

Alone in the damp, steel-walled room, Sasha lay in the fetal position, naked, on a hard metal gurney. The sticky flesh of her eyelids peeled apart, separating with great effort. She scanned the room through blurry tears.

"Where am I?" She mumbled, her head swimming in the fog of memories lost. Around her, the little creaks and moans of the ship echoed through the steel walls. Tiny fan-blown water droplets landed on her skin, pooled then trickled into the drain beneath her.

Sasha's whole body throbbed, though most intensely at the base of her skull. She tried to roll to her back but stopped short when a sharp pinch caught at the center of her spine. "Ow ... what the?" Sasha instead pushed herself up into a seated position, her legs dangling off the cot.

Her heart raced in her chest as she stared at unfamiliar limbs. The skin of her legs was jet black and glistened with a fine sheen of water. Her gaze continued to roam across her body. The pitch-black coloring extended from her webbed toes up over her legs and hips and flowed along both sides of her abdomen. Between the broad dark streaks from her lower abdomen up across her chest and neck, the skin was as white as a newly fallen snow. Sasha's hands flew to her bare breasts, but instead of prickled human flesh, she felt skin that was thick and rubbery.

"What's happened to me?" Sasha cried out, trying to slide from the table and stand—though her legs failed to support her, and she collapsed to the floor. "Somebody, help." Sasha crawled to the corner of the room and drew her knees to her chest.

She crouched there, scared and confused, the end of a finger tracing the outside edge of what she could only describe as a small white fin that jutted from the back of her calf muscle. The heavy steel door to the room clunked, the bolts slid back, and the door swung inward. A man in a crisp uniform with the markings of a naval officer entered and stared at her, a slight smirk on his square face. He moved to the large misting fan in the corner and switched it off. The droning cadence subsided.

Sasha watched the spinning chrome blades slow, the sounds of this place growing more distinct without the white noise. The groan of an engine, people talking, the clink clank of steel on steel.

"How are you feeling?" the man said.

Sasha shifted, unable to form any host of maddening questions filling her head.

"You've been through a lot. Is there anything you need?"

Sasha wet her lips with her tongue. "Why am I naked? What am I doing here? I can't remember." Her body shivered as she managed the words.

"My name is Alric Jager. I'm the captain of *The U.S.S. Harbinger*. We rescued you after your ordeal." Jagger moved to the nearby medical workstation. He selected a wool blanket and carried it over to the frightened girl. "Take the blanket. You can cover yourself for now, but the wool will dry your skin."

Sasha took the blanket, covering herself more out of shame than cold. "I don't understand any of this. Help me understand."

"Of course," Jager said. "I will answer any of your questions the best I can. The most important thing is that you are safe and, medically speaking, completely healthy. You're going to be just—"

"Bring me a mirror," she said, her voice quivering.

"Sasha, your body has experienced some incredible changes."

"I said, bring me a mirror!" she shouted, the sound echoing in the confined space.

Jager stretched out his hand. The question anticipated, an aide appeared in the doorway and placed a compact mirror in the captain's hand. He turned it over a few times and looked from the rectangular piece of reflective glass back to Sasha.

"Things have changed, Sasha. They can't ever go back to the way they were." He extended the mirror.

Sasha took the mirror, teeth clenched as she raised it to her face. She gasped, and the mirror slipped. The look of shock deepened as she raised it again, unable to pry her stare from the horror reflected back at her.

I'm a monster. No one will accept me like this. Max could never love me . . .

She threw the mirror at Captain Jager's feet. Tears slipped down her cheeks, crossing the band of black across her eyes and dripping from her snow-white chin. She moved a hand to touch a length of her hair, many strands fused into a host of thick locks like strands of braided rope.

"What will happen to me?" Sasha whimpered.

Jager dipped his head, "Well, I suppose it's up to you. Life is full of tough choices, Sasha."

"I want to know everything you know. Everything."

"Where would you like me to start?" Jager asked.

"At the beginning," she said, the sound of her words brittle.

"You're sure you don't want to recover a little more first?"

"I'm sure."

"As you wish," Jager said, motioning for the aide to bring him a foldout chair. "As I said, you are aboard *The U.S.S. Harbinger*, the most advanced stealth carrier ever developed. This ship is under my command as a part of the Navy's Special Projects Division."

Sasha raised a hand for him to stop. "What happened to *me*?"

Jager, unfazed by the interruption, unfolded the metal chair and took a seat. "Do you remember anything?"

Sasha swallowed. "I was night surfing, and I came across a pod of orcas."

Jager's eyebrows shot up. "Oh?"

"I was in perfect harmony with them, with the ocean. But there was this sudden light in the sky. Blinding and green and something crashed into the water beside me …"

"Go on," Jager said.

"I was drowning." Sasha brought her arms to her chest.

"The thing you saw was an experimental device called the Erebos—an attempt by government scientists to tap into the vacuum structure of space. Limitless energy potential, so I'm told."

"Why did it fall from the sky?"

Jager interlaced his fingers. "It was studied aboard a low orbit research station in Earth's atmosphere. When the conditions became too dangerous for the scientists on board, they jettisoned the device to save the crew. My team tracked it as it splashed down. You were in the wrong place at the wrong time."

Sasha lowered her eyes to study her black and white rubbery flesh once again.

"You were exposed to something, Sasha," Jager continued. "A zero-point energy field. Something we know little about. It seems to have changed the structure of your DNA, mixing it with the DNA of another creature. Noting the back and white color across your body, your proximity to orcas at the time of the incident makes a lot of sense. You're a miracle, Sasha. A great accidental miracle." Jager stood, folded the chair, and handed it to his aide.

"What will happen to me?" Sasha whispered.

"We'll take good care of you, Sasha. Whatever you need, you are welcome to request it. As soon as we are able, we will move you to more comfortable quarters."

"I'm not free to leave?"

Jager shook his head. "I'm afraid not. We can't let you go until we better understand what affected you. It could be a public safety risk." He turned for the door, standing on the threshold. "For now, rest and keep yourself moisturized. In the coming days, we will see what life has in store for you." He pulled the heavy steel door shut, and the bolt clanged into place.

The sound of the closing hatch echoed in the sterile metal room, which to Sasha sounded like the lid of some giant steel coffin dropping shut on the course of her life. Every part of the girl she was before stripped away in an instant. A life yet lived, fractured and broken, lost to the cruel machinations of fate.

Bodhi pinched a single copper-plated penny between his thumb and forefinger. He'd used it to tap out a distress signal on the steel walls—a stupid idea. The only thing he knew about morse code was the basic SOS message. He'd received no response, of course. *Probably a waste of time,* he thought.

Prowling the small empty cell, Bodhi tried to make sense of his current predicament. *Why would these guys kidnap me?* This was illegal, no matter who did it or their reason. They'd assaulted him and run a uniformed police officer off the road. Bodhi thought about the cop—Westfield—how he'd stuck his neck out for Bodhi and gotten hurt in return. *Hope the guy is okay.*

Bodhi took another lap around his cell, then stopped and touched his chin, which was still sore. *Jerk really belted me one,* he thought. He opened and closed his mouth a few times, supporting his cheek with the palm of his hand. He worked the situation over. It had to do with whatever fell out of the sky. His captors were military, maybe Navy, judging by the captain from the beach. *What was his name? Jogger?*

Bodhi shook his head and took a third lap. Whatever was going on, it was so secret, they couldn't allow any word of it to get out—even at the risk of kidnapping and holding American citizens captive.

"Freaking un-American, man," Bodhi murmured.

He could try to escape, but that was stupid. He wasn't Jason Bourne. Or he could hope Officer Westfield might try to help. Bodhi couldn't imagine the cop would be okay with someone crashing him off the road. Maybe he'd investigate.

Bodhi flipped the penny off his thumb and caught it, slapping it on the back of his hand.

"Okay," he said, "heads, I'm gonna go ninja assassin on these jerks next time they open the door and hope they don't shoot me on sight. Tails, I'll keep tapping my stupid message." Bodhi drew back his hand, cringing and squinting one eye.

Tails.

He released a sigh of relief. "Don't try to be a hero, dude. Keep doing your thing. They can't ignore you forever."

Bodhi leaned against the back wall and tapped out his SOS message with pained repetition. Rapid taps for the first three, slow taps for the second three, rapid taps for the third three, with five seconds between each cycle. He'd finished the fifth time through and was waiting to start again when he heard a muffled voice from above him.

Bodhi froze, pressing his ear to the cold gray steel. The rumble of the massive engines somewhere far below greeted his ears, the mechanical groans of a giant sea-faring beast. But mixed in with that drone, a voice reached out to him.

"Who's there?" Bodhi called out. He scrambled below the air vent in the ceiling, raising on his toes to get as close as possible to the metal grate. "Hey, can you hear me?"

"Bodhi?" came the muffled response.

"Yeah." Bodhi squirmed, unable to get any closer to the vent. "Who is it? I can't hear you."

"It's Max. Are you okay?"

"Max, oh my god, yeah, man. I'm fine. Where are you?"

"I don't know, man. Be cool. They can't hold us here forever." Max's voice sounded tinny in the air duct.

"Okay, okay, man," Bodhi said.

A guard banged on the door to his cell. "Shut up. No talking in there."

Bodhi faced the door. "Why don't you come in here and shut me up, you jack-booted fascist," he shouted, suddenly empowered after hearing the voice of his friend.

With a clank, the bolts in the door slid free.

"Bodhi, don't be stupid," Max's voice buzzed through the vent.

"Too late." Bodhi swallowed, wide-eyed, as two guards in midnight black BDUs entered his cell carrying black polycarbonate batons.

"You got something you want to say, kid?" The guard on the left slapped the end of the baton into his hand.

"Yeah," Bodhi said, bawling his fists and raising them, despite his fear. "This isn't right, and you know it, man."

"You are held in the interest of national security," the second guard said, his expression stoic.

"Not okay with me, man. I didn't do anything wrong. I'm an American. I've got rights, and you can't do this."

"We can and we will, and if you don't stop crying about it, I'm gonna give you a taste of this," the guard on the left pointed the baton at him.

Bodhi pressed his teeth together, the fury at being held against his will boiling to the surface. "Swing that baton at me, and I swear to god I'm going to shove it up your—"

"Bodhi. Stop," Max said.

But it was too late.

The guard on the left lunged in, swinging wide, a shot aimed for Bodhi's side. Bodhi ducked to the outside of his attacker's swing, then punched the man hard on the nose and shoved him face-first against the wall.

"I got more where that came from, you fascist pig," Bodhi shouted.

The second guard's baton laced into Bodhi's kidney from behind. Pain shot through him like a rod of lightning. Bodhi screamed, spun into the other guard, and drove him back against the opposite wall. The room filled with shouts as more soldiers clamored in.

A baton was shoved under Bodhi's chin. He was pried from the guard and twisted back against the wall. Bodhi gasped for air, grasping the baton, trying to keep it from crushing his airway. "Can't dew zhis," he wheezed, spittle hanging from his lips.

The first guard, whose name tape on his breast pocket read *Becket*, wiped a dribble of blood from his nose. "Where are the jokes now?"

"Gah," Bodhi sputtered, "Okay. You … got me."

"What?" Becket said. "I want to hear you say it."

The pressure released on Bodhi's neck enough for him to speak, the furious panting of the guards heaving in cadence around him as they pinned him against the wall.

Bodhi's lungs heaved. "You want me to … say it?"

"Yeah, I do," Becket said.

Bodhi licked his lips. "Okay, I'll say it." He paused and raised a flat palm. "Sieg heil."

The struggle commenced anew. Bodhi grit his teeth and kicked out at them as the men shoved him down the length of the wall and into the corner. Another blow whipped across Bodhi's face, followed by debilitating strikes to his thighs and stomach. He tasted copper, stars flashing in his eyes. A third blow landed against his head with a *crack*. Bodhi slumped, his hopes of escaping this hell, drifting away into an abyss of churning black.

CHAPTER 11

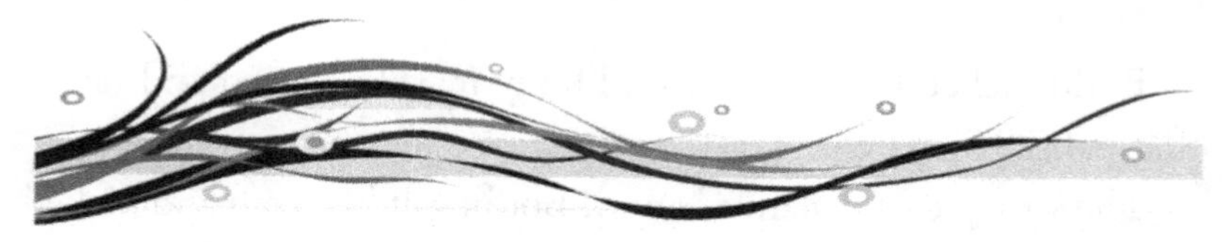

At the head of the mahogany hardwood table in the admiral's conference room, a fresh Dominican cigar between his teeth, Alric Jager rubbed his eyes. Behind him, a bank of monitors lay dark with the exception of a single panel playing a feed from the World News Network, though Jager's thoughts drowned out the reporter.

He pinched the bridge of his nose and clenched his eyes shut, willing the German nasal whine of his father's voice to fade. He'd stopped taking the little white Buspirone pills. Now he could feel it creeping on again, a lengthening shadow stretching its claws out across his mind. Jager wiped a bit of spittle from his lower lip. *Keep it together. Command will have a stroke if they find out.* He didn't need the damn pills. He could control the shadow by sheer will alone. Yet, his father's mantra still played over and over. *All that matters is success, boy.*

Success at any cost. That was the mission.

Jager's Special Projects Division had a reputation to uphold. In the short time since the unit formed, they'd easily achieved nearly every goal and smashed every standard set forth by the brass. Among the ranks of the Navy's enlisted men, people whispered about them like some sort of urban legend. The Grim Reapers of the United States Navy. It was said the men under Jager's command were capable of snuffing out the enemies of freedom with nothing but their combat knives. Each time he heard a story, it got longer and more elaborate. It was bullshit.

Mostly.

Ascribed a benign research and development title and given a dedicated crew of twelve hundred sailors, Jager's SPD was the most advanced military unit on the face of the Earth. Aboard *The U.S.S. Harbinger*, an XJ-437 Sea Blade class microcarrier, Jager possessed unlimited resources and absolute discretion at his fingertips.

The Harbinger, the first in its class, was part carrier, part destroyer, and the undisputed future of naval warfare. Designed by Axiom International, it was a third the size of a standard aircraft carrier, was large enough to carry substantial manpower, unrivaled firepower, three DF-16 Barracuda fast attack boats, and four modified F35-V Lightning III jump jets, while remaining fast and maneuverable enough to maintain fifty knots in a strong headwind still.

But tech had limitations.

Weapon systems could fail, run out of fuel and ammo, or need servicing. Biological weapons, on the other hand, were the future. Humanoid super soldiers capable of feats previously believed impossible. Fearless, tireless, obedient, and most importantly sentient—the ultimate fighting force. Jager grinned. Creating the pinnacle of human evolution would be his legacy, one to best even his father.

Jager checked his watch, then pulled the encrypted tablet across the table. He scanned the project names on screen: Project Erebos, Project Stryke, Project S.H.R.E.D., each file marked across its icon in red: *classified.*

Jager nodded to himself. It was time to make good on old promises.

Having called in a few favors, he now knew the whole truth. On the surface, the Erebos was an experimental multi-billion dollar government program designed to capture the clean, endless energy generated by tapping into the vacuum structure of space. But that was just the line they'd sold the press. The DOD wanted that limitless energy potential to power futuristic weapon tech. The sort of stuff that would make an arms dealer flush with excitement. As it turned out, the entire project was thought to be a dead-end waste of taxpayer dollars—until yesterday when it activated without warning and destroyed the Low Orbit Facility in which it was housed one hundred and fifty miles above the planet's surface.

Jager grunted in amusement.

The Navy's highly productive human bioengineering program, Stryke was on the other end of the spectrum. Funding for the program wasn't the problem; the problem was purely ethical. To do more than scratch the surface of expanding human potential, drastic things had to be done with the human genome—to which no military brass or self-serving bureaucrat wanted to put their name. At least officially. Only Jager had the stones for it.

The Strykers, Jager's special operations soldiers, had been spliced with the DNA of electric eels. Jager had often wondered why not a tiger or some other aggressive predator, but the eel had apparently been the creature of choice by the scientific team. Something to do with compatibility and the need to isolate desired traits. In this case, the desire to weaponize a human's innate electrical impulses. The first eel-based Strykers were a disaster—no control over their electrical convulsions, which discharged in response to even the slightest spike in adrenaline. And then there had been long-term effects—aneurysms, dehydration, heart palpitations, muscular spasms, and even a few strokes. It turned out electrifying a human messed with almost every biological system.

In the end, testosterone had been the key to the body's integration with the now heavily modified CV2 Black serum.

Large, slow-twitch muscle mass and more primal, violent tendencies were the trade-off for an ability to discharge a sizable electric current. That meant only men—most with previous special ops training—had been selected for the program. The end result was super soldiers with unprecedented natural strength and higher pain tolerances.

Jager smirked. His Strykers made the SEALs look like mama's boys.

Unfortunately, his team could not take the project any further without increasing the potential for test subjects to develop other negative traits. This point was made crystal clear to him by the higher-ups. They were not going to stand for him deliberately creating a bunch of super freaks that looked like fish.

Jager closed the Stryke and Erebos files, his teeth working the cigar.

Two programs, previously unrelated, now connected by sheer chance and an enormous leap forward in human evolution. His smile returned as he tapped open the folder marked S.H.R.E.D. - Super Humanoids for Reconnaissance Espionage and Defense.

He couldn't force the next unpalatable leap forward in evolution. But what if he didn't do it deliberately? What if during an unplanned incident, the pieces just fell into place, and he happened to ride the wave of progress surging from such an event? That was different.

The Department of Defense's Erebos probe was secure in a well-isolated section of the ship's cargo hold. No doubt it was still emitting the same cosmic radiation that altered Sasha during the initial moments of splashdown. Under the right conditions, he might be able to reproduce the same effects in other subjects. But little time remained. The radiation from the probe was already waning, now having lost thirty percent of its original strength since reentering the Earth's atmosphere. Then there was the matter of the Department of Defense wanting their device back. He could only stall them so long by claiming the recovery effort was more complicated than expected.

Jager's gaze rested on Sasha's picture—an athletic champion surfer with almond-shaped eyes, jet black hair, and a smile from ear to ear as she held high her first-place surfing trophy. No way for him to know yet how far she'd come or what she was capable of after such close contact with the Erebos. He scanned the initial report: highly oxygenated blood levels, thicker and more durable skin, fins. Webbed fingers and toes for faster maneuvering in the water. Indicators of enhanced strength due to redoubled muscle and tendon fibers and a localized short-range magnetic field she now emitted from her body. They'd only scratched the surface with the initial tests, but once they fully understood what happened to the girl, they might be able to reproduce it, *en masse*.

The door to the narrow conference room opened, and a handful of individuals entered in single file, the last of whom secured the door. Jager acknowledged them in turn as they filed in and took their seats.

Jager palmed the remote and pointed it at the TV, which winked to black.

Everyone waited in silence.

"Loose lips sink ships," Jager said with finality. He stubbed out his cigar, then wiped the saliva from it and placed it in his breast pocket. "It was a slogan used during the second world war on propaganda posters and among the troops to discourage the leaking of sensitive information which had the potential to damage the war effort."

His staff nodded, though their blank expressions conveyed they had no idea where he was going with this.

"Loose lips also sink careers," Jager paused, casting his gaze around the room. "What is said in this room stays in this room. Are we clear?"

Nods and murmurs of acknowledgment passed around the narrow room.

"The fate of the world hangs in the balance. North Korea, China, Russia, Iran ... politically, blasting them into the stone age is not an option," Jager said. "I was tasked by command with developing a suite of options outside the normal parameters of open war. This was how the Stryker Project started, and, as you know, it's been a resounding success. But, the time has come to take it to the next level." Jager leaned forward, resting on his elbows and tenting his fingers. "I'm initiating Project S.H.R.E.D."

The group tossed wide-eyed glances at one another.

"Captain, wasn't S.H.R.E.D. voted on and denied by the security council?" Commander Atcheson, the ship's XO, said.

"Yes, but that was before. The arrival of the Erebos device created circumstances we couldn't have predicted and put elements in play that will accelerate our ability to show the security council what S.H.R.E.D. is truly capable of. We have to seize this moment, and I need to know right now all of you are with me."

The men and women around the table nodded, solemn and resolute.

"Every one of you have wondered at some point why there's no brass above me in command of this ship—why not even a rear admiral was given command? I'll tell you why. There's a job needing to be done, and the people in Washington know it. They want to be able to say, *mission accomplished* without having to fumble over themselves trying to explain why we went so far tampering with the human genome." Jager pressed his fingertips against the hardwood table. "When project S.H.R.E.D. succeeds, and it will succeed, everyone sitting at this table will be a national hero."

Commander Atcheson cleared his throat and regarded the captain. "Sir." His eyes glanced to the others and then back to Jager. "I'm confident our loyalty to our country and to you has proven itself time and again."

Jager gave a curt nod. "It has."

"I also believe I speak for everyone when I say we are behind you," Atcheson continued. "But right now, we have three American citizens held against their will aboard this ship. They're barely legal adults. How are we justifying this?"

"This is a national security matter, and as of this moment, we are at war," Jager said, scanning the faces at the table. "That's how we justify it." He clicked open the S.H.R.E.D. file and pushed the image to an overhead projector. Sasha's image flashed on the forward wall. "This girl"—he jabbed his finger at the picture—"just became the next great arms race. The most powerful weaponized asset the world has ever seen. She just doesn't know it yet." Jager stood, palms pressed flat on the hardwood of the conference table. "Other countries will try to steal her from us. Terrorist groups like Sentry will try to repurpose her. Special interests inside our government who are opposed to what we are doing will attempt to stop us. We cannot, and we *will not* let any of them stand in our way. The safety and security of the United States and the good of freedom-loving people everywhere depend upon our courage to stay the course."

Jager stared at each member of his team before continuing. "Now, I'm going to ask one more time, and we're going to be done with this. I need your unwavering support. Do I have it?"

"Aye-aye, sir," the command staff chanted in unison.

"Good," Jager said, retaking his seat. "Let's get down to business."

CHAPTER 12

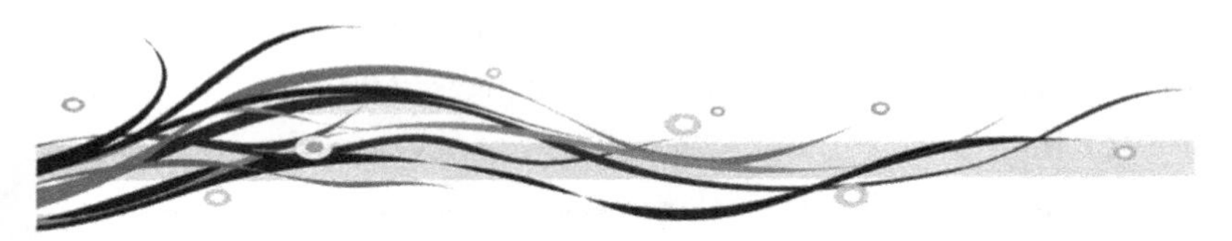

United States Navy Senior Chief Tal Alvarez sat naked on the gurney. A thick fog settled over his brain, muddling his thoughts and threatening to tangle his words when he spoke—an extreme irregularity in a man who had built his reputation on decisive thinking and straight talk. He balled up his fists, holding back the intense desire to thrash at the walls until either the bones of his hands or the steel gave way.

Today was a dose-day. A top-up to ensure he and his Stryker team remained mission ready. Though lately, something had felt off. A thick, foggy sensation in his brain muddled his thoughts and threatened to tangle his words when he spoke. The side effects were getting worse, and he couldn't afford to be off his game. Now more than ever, Jager counted on his team to do their job.

Focus, damn you.

He bore a stare into the back of Doctor Brenn Kingsfeld's head. The physician was specifically selected for monitoring the Stryker program due to his exhaustive experience with genetic modification, or so they'd been told. What experience the thin pasty man actually had for monitoring first-generation super soldiers was the subject of many a chow-hall discussion. The urge to throttle the wiry little doctor pulsed up from the pit of Alverez's stomach.

Get it under control. You're the damn chief, Alverez thought.

He averted his gaze and studied the narrow, white-walled room used exclusively for check-ups and serum updates for Project Stryke candidates. Stark, clinical and completely separate from the rest of the medical bay, the crew referred to it as *The Box*. Not exactly comforting. Once someone went in, they never came out the same.

The muscles of his jaw flexed.

"Is there a problem, Chief?" the doctor asked, a loaded hypodermic needle pinched between his spider-like fingers. Inside the syringe, a luminous amber liquid sloshed back and forth. CV2 Black, they called it.

Alvarez shook his head. "I didn't say there was a problem."

"Don't worry, Chief," the doctor said. "Everything we're seeing out of the Strykers is well within reasonable tolerances."

"And by tolerances, you mean the limits of standard deviation, the negative side effects you're willing to accept prior to screwing us all up and having to burn the entire formula to the ground." Alvarez locked the man down with an iron stare.

Dr. Kingsfeld returned Alvarez's stare, lowering the needle. "That's a bit of a dramatic way of stating it, but yes, you are in essence correct."

"I've told you what I've been feeling. Are you saying that's normal?"

"Normal isn't a word that belongs in this conversation, Chief," Kingsfeld said with a pompous chuckle, moving to insert the needle into Alvarez's hip.

Alvarez grabbed Kingsfeld by the wrist, the syringe hanging loose in the man's hand.

"Don't play games with me." Alvarez snarled. "You know what I mean. Answer the question."

The doctor screwed up his face into an indignant frown. "Do you mind, sir?"

"Yeah, I do mind." Alvarez pushed the needle toward the

doctor's face. "Talk straight, or I'll give you a taste of this stuff you've been pumping into us."

Dr. Kingsfeld stammered, his eyes wide as he was forced back against the wall.

Alvarez pushed closer, the tip of the needle touching the doctor's cheek. "If it's so safe, what are you afraid of?"

"This is highly irregular. I'll have to report—"

Alvarez gave the doctor's arm a jerk. "Are you going to tell me or not?"

"Yes, yes, of course. Please ..." Kingsfeld's voice took on the whine of a frightened schoolboy.

"I won't let you compromise the lives and wellbeing of my men. Neither will I let a pompous ass like you ruin our ability to accomplish the mission. You receiving me, Doc?" Alvarez held fast for a moment longer before releasing the man.

Dr. Kingsfeld stuck out his chin defiantly, hands trembling, and set the syringe on a sterile metal tray. "Ask your questions. I'm a busy man."

"What's happening to us?" Alvarez asked.

"You're going to need to be more specific."

"My men, they're reporting the same things I've been feeling. There is a clouded sensation in their heads, anxiety, memory loss, bouts of extreme anger, and the inexplicable desire to eat raw things—and I'm not talking about sushi, Doc. What is happening to us?"

"You are changing with each dose of the serum. This shouldn't come as a surprise. You all volunteered for the program. You knew there would be tradeoffs. It shouldn't be drastic if all the models are correct."

"And if they're not?"

"We'll all have to see what becomes of you and learn from the results," Kingsfeld said, his confidence growing. "That's science. Now, are you still willing to participate in the program? Or should I report this and watch you lose the command of your unit?"

Alvarez clenched his teeth and resisted the impulse to smash the doctor's brains in. He had gotten through SEAL training, survived for days behind enemy lines, days of hell with no sleep or food. At times it had been a close call, the desire to just get the hell out of there overwhelming. *Is this really what I want?* The question gnawed at him, though he already knew the answer, just as he had known back then—they'd have to kill him to make him quit.

Alverez caught a partial reflection of himself in a wall mirror. His skin had darkened, a mix of deep brown, pale yellow, and muted gray tones. His canine teeth looked longer and sharper, though that might be his imagination. What wasn't his imagination were the thirty pounds of solid muscle he'd packed on since starting the treatments. He looked like a completely different man, if he was still a man. Would his family recognize him when he finally made it back home to Texas? Would Maria and the children accept him? Or would they fear the monster that had taken the place of their father?

Too late to turn back now.

"Your answer?" Dr. Kingsfeld said, his tone condescending.

Alvarez turned around and leaned forward onto the gurney. There he waited for the sting of the needle, reciting the names of his cherished loved ones not to forget. He couldn't ever forget.

Maria, Tal Jr., Christopher, Kimmie, Vigo, Montressa …

CHAPTER 13

The chocolate milkshake wouldn't last forever, but that didn't stop Westfield from wishing it would. He tilted the wax paper cup, worked the straw into the bottom edge of the rapidly disappearing treat, and slurped. On the other side of the simple picnic-style table, a pacific island breeze tossed whisps of shoulder-length blond hair around the face of his dinner date. She tucked the strands behind an ear, smirking at his slurping.

"What's with the impish grin?" Westfield asked, lowering the cup and savoring the last sip.

"You, drinking your milkshake like a five-year-old, Dad," Janie said, popping a ketchup-laden fry into her mouth.

"What? I always drink my milkshake like a five-year-old," Westfield said, smiling. "How long have we been having this date?"

"Mmm, since I was about six."

Westfield nodded with fake seriousness. "Yeah, which means I probably learned the kid slurping technique from you."

"How often do you eat like this anyway?" Janie said with a scolding look. "It's good, and don't get me wrong, I've always loved our daddy-daughter dates, but ..." She pushed at a grease-soaked burger wrapper.

"What are you trying to say?" Westfield feigned offense as he ran his hands around his midsection. "This physique hits the gym hard but never turns down cheeseburgers." He grinned.

"Exactly what I'm afraid of." She took a sip of her diet soda.

"Have you had your heart health checked recently?"

"Janie, come on," Westfield grumbled. "I'm a career cop. I don't need a doctor to tell me my heart health is bad."

Janie pursed her lips the way she always did when she worried about him. "Work going okay? You seem a bit stressed."

Westfield shook his head, glancing in irritation at a guy in the plaza behind him laughing too loud. "I'm fine, honey. Work is work. Same ol', same ol'."

"What about the accident this morning? You sure you're okay?"

"Sweetie," Westfield said. "Stop fussing about me. I can take care of myself. I'd know if something was wrong. All right?"

Janie raised her hands and finished the last of her fries without further protest. He watched her chew, the perfect moving lines of her jaw, the button nose, and a smile capable of thawing out the Arctic. He shook his head. *How in the world did such a perfect creature come from me?*

He knew Janie couldn't help worrying about him. She'd felt responsible ever since her mother left ten years ago, both of them wondering what in the hell happened. Westfield wasn't a great fill-in mother, but he'd done his best to be a good father.

Janie's phone chimed a trio of notes, the screen illuminating. Her fingers crept for it. She bit the edge of her lip, glanced at him, and grabbed it.

"Ha. I win. Dinner is on you next time," Westfield said.

"Dad, it's work. Doesn't count."

"Yes, it does. No phones. That's the rule."

Janie rolled her eyes. "Okay. But it's work. You'd look too." She glanced at a second message as it popped up on the screen. "Great. So much for off days. Shandra needs me to work this weekend."

"Mmm, I know the feeling."

"It's fine." She flicked a strand of golden hair from her face with a smirk. "I've got bills."

Westfield chuckled and crumpled the brown paper bag around the rest of his fries. He didn't need them.

"So." He cleared his throat and wiped his hands and face with a napkin. "You seeing anybody?"

"Dad." Janie sighed. "No, and get out of my love life."

"Come on. A father has a right to know who's scamming on his daughter."

"Scamming? Dad, really, let's not have this conversation, please. I'm a grown woman." Janie placed her trash back in its grease-stained brown paper bag. "Oncology keeps me way too busy for a love life. I go in early, stay late, and work on my off days." She waved her phone at him. "No time for love." She cocked her head. "Except that which I hold for a certain stubborn old man." She nudged his knee playfully under the table.

Westfield smiled and nudged her back. "No one's too busy for a love life, sweetie."

"Yeah, I heard about you stalking the ER nurses at Queen's."

"Stalking?" Westfield adopted a wide-eyed wounded look.

"I'm just telling you what I heard." She laughed and tossed her bag in the trash.

"Innocent until proven guilty," Westfield said with a mischievous smile. "I'll walk you to your car."

Westfield had just passed through the front doors of Honolulu Police Department's West Precinct when his phone rang. He glanced at it. Unknown number. He didn't usually answer these, but the last couple of days had been unusual, to say the least, and he had the creeping suspicion he shouldn't let it go to voicemail.

"Westfield," he said, placing the phone to his ear.

"Officer Westfield. Be careful how deep you dig," the voice said in a strong Chinese accent.

"Who's this?" Westfield asked.

"My name is Doctor Zhou Murong. You may have heard of me. I'm sort of a big deal."

"Can't say I have, Mr. Big Deal. What do you want?"

"What I want is world peace, equality, and equity for all people," Murong said. "I want our oceans to be preserved, our animal brothers and sisters to be respected and cared for. What I'll settle for is a little street justice."

Westfield stifled a laugh. "What's that supposed to mean?"

"Let's say we have some mutual interests at this time."

Westfield balked and pulled the phone from his ear, looking at the unknown number on the screen as the seconds on the call ticked past. He considered hanging up but resisted the impulse and put the phone back to his ear. "Which is? Cut to the chase."

"Oh, I don't need to cut to the chase. You've already well involved yourself in something you do not yet fully understand. A matter that will, without question, have global implications."

"Global implications, huh?" Westfield said. "You mean this business with the missing kids? The jerks who ran me off the road? Or the thing that crashed in the ocean and the wise guy Naval Captain?"

"All of it." Murong seemed to weigh his next words. "The girl, Sasha, was exposed to something that may have fundamentally altered her DNA. I don't usually speculate, but there is no doubt this is why Jager wanted her."

"Exposed? To what?"

"Something ... not of this world."

Westfield let a stream of air whistle from his lips. He glanced around the mostly empty lobby of the west precinct. "Why the call? What do you want from me?"

"Be careful," Murong said, his voice lowering. "The more you dig into this, the more your life and the life of those you love may be at risk."

Westfield chuckled. "I'm a career cop, buddy. My life is always at risk. And veiled threats aren't going to stop me from doing my job."

"Good," Murong said. "As long as you know what lies ahead. We need an advocate on the ground. Someone who can blow this wide open, should the need arise."

"You've got the wrong guy, Doctor whatever-your-name-is," Westfield said. "I'm not an investigative reporter. I want to know what happened to those kids and why someone was willing to kill me to get to 'em. That's all."

"Officer Westfield, I don't make mistakes. I'm talking to exactly the man I mean to be talking to. Listen to me. Sasha and her friends are alive, for now. They are in the custody of Jager's black ops unit. How long they stay, that way is another matter I might have some sway over."

"Where are they?" Westfield said.

Silence.

"At least tell me more about this Jager guy. What's his story?" Westfield said.

"Tread carefully, Officer Westfield. These people have much to lose. And so do you."

The phone clicked in Westfield's ear. He frowned and looked at his phone. Call failed. He swore under his breath and slipped the phone back into his hip pocket. He pulled his ID, touched it to the nearby card reader, and listened for the snap of the locks disengaging. One heavy step at a time, deep in thought, Westfield made his way to the second floor and the bank of sleeping general access computers. He wiggled the mouse at the terminal on the left and watched the screen blinked to life.

The phone call tickled at the back of his mind. Westfield rubbed his eyes and checked his watch. The numbers were nearly indistinguishable. He squinted—9:00 p.m. He extracted a set of drug store reading glasses from his floral print shirt pocket with a sigh. Another reminder that he was getting too old for this nonsense.

Before he sat, Westfield took one more glance around the empty second floor. This time of night, the admin was all gone, and the shift guys were busy with domestic disputes. What he was about to do wasn't unethical, but it also wasn't official and could step on toes if he didn't go about it right—specifically, Corley's toes. A weathered smile formed on the veteran patrol officer's face.

Opening an internet search browser, Westfield started broad with search terms such as "Navy special operations" and "Dangerous satellite crash" and from there refined his search further. After a few minutes of scanning enormous amounts of information that was irrelevant for the most part, he searched Dr. Zhou Murong. In an instant, thousands of articles, social media posts, and photographs of a lean, intense-looking, Chinese billionaire and self-claimed eco-activist flooded the computer screen. Westfield shook his head and clicked on a highly polished photo of Murong, who sported a shock of styled black hair and chiseled features. The clearly egotistical asshat was standing on the deck of his private research submarine, *The Argo*. Article after article lauded him as an ecological hero and a champion of the world's oceans. Conversely, a plethora of other websites and postings referred to him as an eco-terrorist who stood in the way of governmental and scientific progress at every turn. Someone claimed his research group Sentry was a front for a mercenary faction he used to enforce his agenda.

And this guy personally placed a phone call to me. Why? The question gnawed at him. *What in the hell have I gotten myself into?*

Westfield stood, rubbed his hands through his salt and pepper hair, and walked a lap around the room. His knees and feet ached, and he needed a whiskey. He completed his circuit and again took a seat at the computer. Westfield blew out an exasperated breath and typed in the next search: *Alric Jager + Special Projects Division.*

Nothing. At least, nothing he didn't already know.

Most of what filled the screen indicated that Jager was a captain in the United States Navy and commanded a research and development unit.

"Okay, how about the state database," Westfield whispered.

He accessed the system and ran a search.

"Good grief," Westfield said, scanning the results. "Not even a parking ticket, this guy." He noted the P.O. box listed on the driver's license of an Alric F. Jager. *Might be worth checking out,* he thought.

After a few minutes, a broader search of relatives revealed the first actual lead. Jager's father, Friedrick Jager, came to the states in 1946 as a part of Operation Paperclip. A Nazi scientist whose greatest achievement for Nazi Germany during the second world war was advancements in eugenics as performed on labor camp prisoners at Mauthausen. Many conspiracy theorists seemed to believe his usefulness to the United States outweighed his status as a war criminal, thus the whole reason he was never tried and executed. In an old Nazi propaganda piece, Dr. Friedrick Jager was quoted as saying he was on the cusp of fulfilling his life's work—

creating the master race.

Westfield sat back in the creaky chair, the fabric worn thin from the repeated rubbing of duty belt leather. He put his hand over his face with an exasperated sigh. "Mary, Joseph, and baby Jesus. Make that two whiskeys."

CHAPTER 14

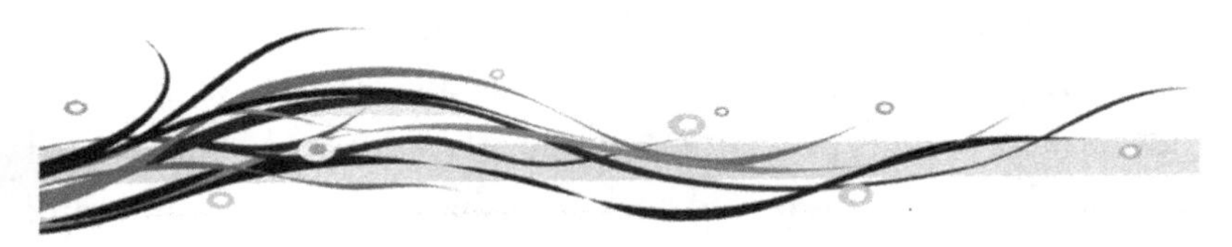

They'd given Sasha an actual room. On the surface, it was a nice gesture. It was actually akin to upgrading an inmate to a better prison cell. This one had a two-way mirror set into the far wall. Her every move was monitored and recorded. A lab rat, tested and studied. Sasha listened to the steady *beep blip* of the heart monitor and tried to suppress her irritation at the unending cadence. She closed her eyes and allowed the misting fan to cover her in yet another fine spray. The past few days had been a hellish tour through a wild gamut of emotion; sorrow, fear, loneliness, regret, shame, and now … rage. Boiling hot, it pooled deep inside her like a lava flow, raw and unbridled anger driven by the sheer injustice of it all.

Sasha stepped walked to the mirror and gazed at her strange reflection. It wasn't an ugly form. In a strange way, she was beautiful, a human-orca hybrid with smooth taught, muscular limbs and striking black and white coloring. Something straight out of a comic book foldout that Bodhi might have plastered on his bedroom wall. But she wasn't human anymore. Beyond some teenage fantasy, how could she ever live in the world again? What would her family say? Society wouldn't accept her, not looking like this. She couldn't even wear regular clothes. The fabric pulled too tight, dried her skin, and pinched the little fins that jutted from her legs, arms, and spine. She was an aberration—a beautiful monster.

Max would never look at her the same again.

Sasha leaned forward and grabbed the metal sink at the mirror's base. How had she gotten here? It all started with those godforsaken whalers no matter how she played it back. She wanted them dead. Sasha's lips pulled back over sharp white teeth and pink gums, and her clawed fingers squealed against the basin. She tore the sink away from the wall. A burst pipe gushed water across the floor. The heart rate monitor behind her accelerated, the sound driving her insane. She spun with a snarl and eviscerated the monitor with a swipe. Sasha grabbed the torn device and flung it against the opposite wall. Chest heaving, she stared at her formidable body in the mirror. With all this raw power, could she change her destiny? *What if I didn't have to be a victim?*

With eyes lowered, shoulders heaving with each breath, Sasha clenched and unclenched her webbed hands. The door to her cell unbolted and swung open to reveal Jager's composed form. He stood there for a moment, observing the carnage in her room. He gave a brief nod as if approving of the destruction she'd caused.

"What?" Sasha said, her chest heaving. "Come to marvel at the freak?"

"Sasha—"

"No, no, please. I insist. Step into that room there"—she pointed at the two-way mirror—"and you can observe me like some zoo animal. Watch me go to the bathroom and everything."

Jager placed his hands together. "I know it's not ideal."

"Not ideal? It's my life, and you're treating me like some experiment." She jabbed one clawed finger at Jager. "You can't keep me here. I want out."

Jager seemed to take a moment to digest her words, his gaze meeting hers without an ounce of uncertainty. "If you're done, and you're ready to let me talk, I have a proposition for you."

Sasha's lips peeled back into a snarl. "I don't want or need anything else from you. Let me go—"

"I discovered the location of the whalers," Jager interrupted.

Sasha grew still. "What are you talking about?"

"You know exactly what I'm talking about." Jager took a step across the threshold and into her cell. "You want out, and I want to see what you're capable of. The business with the Russian whaling vessel … I've read the coast guard's reports. I'm talking about a little old-fashioned revenge, pure and simple."

Sasha swallowed, the prospect of going after Beach Ball and those primitive jerks was so appealing it caused her skin to tingle.

"You can go, or you can stay here. It's up to you, Sasha." Jager shrugged and turned to leave.

"I'll go," Sasha blurted out. "But stop calling me that name like we're old friends. We're not friends."

"Very well. We'll brief in ops in twenty." Jager grinned. "I think I have just the call sign for you."

Sasha approached the open door with caution as a female sailor motioned her out.

"Captain Jager is waiting to brief you," the woman said.

Sasha took another tentative step toward the hatch, taking note of the powerful men in black assault gear lining the hallway. She swallowed, keenly aware of only the sweeping patterns of black and white covering her bare skin.

"Are you sure I can't have some clothes?" Sasha whispered to the sailor, motioning her out.

"They won't do anything but slow you down," the woman said with another wave of her hand. "Come on."

"Okay, fine," Sasha muttered, stepping into the hallway.

The men in black fatigues flanked her on either side but kept their eyes forward.

"And what's this about?" Sasha said, motioning to the men as the sailor led the way off to the right.

"These men are an escort for your protection."

The men shifted as one, falling in step with Sasha.

"From who?" Sasha said.

"Everyone." the sailor said as they ascended a set of stairs and entered what looked like a small movie theater, complete with dark wood paneling, a projector, and plush reclining chairs.

Jager turned from speaking with several men in suits and motioned to her. "And here she is."

Even in her twisted state, the men couldn't help but gawk at her nakedness.

"Callsign Gorgon," Jager continued. "The primary asset in the S.H.R.E.D. program."

Gorgon. Sasha felt herself flush with a new wave of anger. She knew the tale of Medusa, a vibrant young woman whose body was twisted by the cruelty of the gods. It hurt because it was true and caused Sasha to loathe her similarities to the mythical beast even more.

"As you know," Jager stepped to the front and continued addressing the packed room from behind a podium, "what's happened to Sasha is a result of her simultaneous exposure to a zero-point energy field while in close proximity to other complex life forms, specifically, a pod of Orcas. By every reasonable scientific standard, she should be a gelatinous blob right now. Instead, we have been gifted with a miracle—the next great step in human evolution. Our tests indicate she is imbued with enhanced strength, muscular resilience, and much greater oxygen absorbency in her lungs. In addition to this, her agility and speed, especially in the water, will far surpass that available even to our Strykers. Tonight, we are going to see what she's really capable of. Please take a seat."

Sasha stood near the back of the room, her arms folded. The small fin on the back of her forearm bent, causing a pinching sensation. She twisted her arm over, examining the foreign protrusion.

The lights dimmed. An image of the familiar whaling vessel popped up on the large screen behind Jager. He explained the operation was a highly covert use of the United States Navy's newest asset and how she would be operating alone, without official support. Her target was *The Vladimov*—a Russian whaling vessel known for its aggressive action as well as trespassing in U.S. territorial waters. Jager detailed the schematics of *The Vladimov*, flashing photographs of the ship and identifying points of weakness best suited for sabotage. He noted the number of crew onboard and the sorts of weapons they'd likely have access to. He stressed this last point to Sasha, urging her not to underestimate the unpredictable nature of these men.

"Are there any questions?" Jager said.

"Yeah. Can I go now?" Sasha said, already tired of the formality.

A ghost of a smirk pulled at the captain's mouth. "Dismissed." Murmurs filled the air as the room emptied, leaving Sasha and her escort detail.

Jager stepped down from the podium and approached Sasha.

"Yes, you can go, but there's one last thing." Jager motioned to a man carrying a black lockable case. The man set the substantial metal case on the table and opened the lid. Inside, several large chrome rings sat each in its own cradle. The man removed a ring and held it out toward Sasha.

"What's this about?" She looked at Jager and took two steps back.

"It's a GPS tracking device coupled with a highly sophisticated digital radio communication system. It will let you communicate with us, and we can keep track of your movements for when you need assistance or evac."

"It's a collar—like something a dog would wear." Sasha's eyes narrowed. "Not me."

"It's important. You are operating as a military asset. We have to monitor you if you plan to leave this ship."

"Can I take it off?" Sasha placed her hands on her hips.

"I'm afraid not. We have a certain liability here. We will be able to remove it later." Jager pressed his lips together into a thin smile. "I'm sure you understand."

Sasha looked around at the room, her options dwindling.

"If you're not ready, you can always return to your room, but our window of opportunity to execute this mission is dwindling," Jager said.

"How about I just leave instead?" Sasha said, turning toward the door, her jaw clenched.

"I don't think so," Jager said with a shark-like grin.

The squad of Strykers dropped their hands to their weapons. The closest soldier, a Hispanic man with bulging muscular shoulders, held her in his stare, a stoic rigidity set in the signature brown and gray flesh of his face. Sasha glanced at his name tape: *Alvarez.*

"You may be a lot of things now, but bulletproof isn't one of them. Best to go along and play nice," Alvarez said.

"Not only am I a prisoner, but I'm also forced to play your game?" She glared at the stoic captain.

"I told you, you couldn't leave—national security risk and all. You want out, and you want a crack at those Russian oxygen thieves aboard *The Vladimov*. I'm giving you an opportunity at both. This is your chance. Take it or leave it. It makes no difference to me."

After a long, tense moment, Sasha huffed and nodded. The strikers lowered their weapons, and the briefcase man stepped forward. He adjusted a sliding bar on the collar to fit her neck. Looping it around, the end pieces snapped together with a small chime.

"What's that?" Sasha asked.

"An indicator the device is operational, and your comms are up," the briefcase man said. "Simply speak, and it will register your vocal vibrations, initiating a commlink."

Sasha pushed her tongue against the inside of her cheek. "Okay. What now?"

Jager regarded her with a cool gaze. "Now we release the Gorgon."

CHAPTER 15

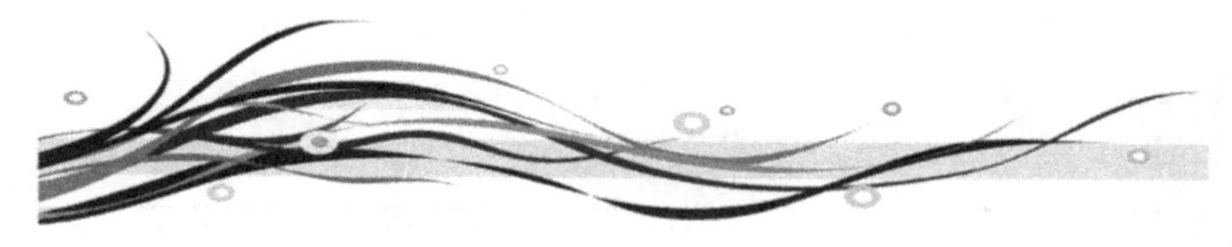

Under the cloak of a moonless night, the Hammerhead special research and assault vessel sidled up against the hull of *The U.S.S. Harbinger.* A state-of-the-art prototype developed by Murong International, the Hammerhead was fast and silent, as well as capable of full submersion for limited periods. With a suite of offensive capabilities, it represented the pinnacle of waterborne stealth assault technology.

Three men crouched low and secured the last of their equipment on the bow. Adorned with gray camouflage fatigues, painted faces, and ultra-compact MP-7 submachine guns loaded with tranquilizer rounds, the three Sentry operatives waited for the go signal.

"Argo command to Sigma team, stand by for jump-off," Lemeaux said over their headsets.

"Sigma, copy," the team leader said from the rearmost position in the stack.

Black waves slapped and sucked against the Hammerhead's sleek hull as its two thousand horsepower electric engine maneuvered it closer.

"Your orders are to find and secure the girl," Lemeaux said. "If you are unable to do so, it is imperative that you are not taken captive. Do what you can to minimize casualties and use any means necessary to escape if the mission is compromised."

"Sigma team, copy. We are good to go," the team leader

whispered.

The Hammerhead's rubber bumpers touched the side wall of the great ship.

"Mag gloves on. Let's move," the team leader said.

Stepping forward, the point man pushed a flat palm against the hull of the massive ship. With a soft clunk, his left magnetically charged glove stuck to the sidewall, followed by his right. Pulling himself upward in chin-up fashion, the frogman bent his back and brought his knees to his chest. *Thunk, thunk.* The next man followed suit. Then the third.

One at a time, like babies shuffling on all fours, the frogmen ascended the slick vertical surface. Reaching the top, they paused and peered out onto the quiet jump deck of the ship—the primary launch point for a series of vertical takeoff or "jump" jets. The coast was clear—for now. The team leader disengaged his mag gloves and climbed onto the deck, scanning for threats. The rest of his team followed.

Readying their MP-7 submachine guns, they approached the island, a lone structure on the starboard side. The island contained the primary flight control and the bridge, but it was only their guide, not their destination. Bounding across the shadows, the frogmen slunk past a series of F35-V Lightning III jump jets, staged and ready to deploy.

As they approached the stairs to the lower levels, a young sailor rounded the corner. The team leader's MP-7 rose, the safety flicking free as he squeezed off a rapid three-round burst from the integrally suppressed weapon. All three sticky projectiles smacked against the exposed skin of the man's neck and face. The young man's eyes grew wide, his mouth forming unspoken words, as his skin absorbed the powerful tranquilizer. The team leader descended the steps in one lunging stride and grabbed the shocked sailor by the shirt before he hit the ground.

"This is it." The team leader said to his men as he peered down the second stairwell. "We split up from here and scour the ship for the girl. You have your orders. So shall we go."

"So shall we go," the others replied in unison.

Sasha walked the narrow corridor, led by Jager and flanked by Strykers. Her stomach roiled. How could this have happened to her? How was this existence her life? She would never go to college or pursue her passions or get to find out if things would work out between her and Max. Sasha hung her head. *What about my family?* she thought. *Father and Mika will be worried to death by now. Mother, sick as she is, needs me to help care for her.*

A wave of anxiety passed over her as she placed one webbed foot in front of the other, the gray, lifeless steel walls of the corridor sliding past in a monochromatic blur. In a matter of days, everything she'd known had been uprooted, replaced by a life of ugliness, imprisonment, and forced compliance to government entities she didn't understand.

Am I actually capable of the things Jager said? What am I supposed to do with that sort of power? As much as she wanted a crack at those whalers, she hadn't wanted to wear the collar. Though padded and lightweight, it gave her the constant sensation of choking. She tugged at the device around her neck to see if it would give.

"Warning." A small electronic voice said from a speaker built into the collar. *"Attempts to remove this device will result in the deploying of countermeasures."* Sasha jerked her hand away.

Jager chuckled without turning around. "I was wondering how long it would take you to pull on it."

Sasha's eyes darted up, embarrassed. "I was only—"

"I wouldn't tug on that if I were you," the man with the briefcase said from behind her.

"Why?" She glared at him. "It's tight."

"Countermeasures." The man smirked. "It's titanium anyway. You'll never get it off. Not until we say."

Sasha turned away from the briefcase man with a scowl and continued to walk the cramped hallway.

They ascended a flight of stairs and passed a row of secured doors, each with a military police guard standing in front of it. Black polycarbonate batons slung, the men stood stock-still at attention, holding their salute as Captain Jager passed. Sasha looked at the black block lettering stenciled over the doorway to each room. Containment 1, Containment 2, Containment 3. Sasha's brow furrowed. *Containment for what?*

Her gaze met with that of the MP standing in front of Containment 2. As she passed, he dropped his salute and nursed a swollen busted nose.

Salty ocean air filled Sasha's nostrils as they approached the exit onto deck three. Her limbs tingled with the desire to bolt, to explode through the door and dive into the sea. Her breathing became rapid, and her heart thumped against her ribcage.

Shoving past the guard, Sasha crossed the threshold out onto the exterior platform. Gasping, she grabbed the railing. The wind whipped across her body, the open expanse of the dark sea churning below. She took a breath in and held on to it, savored it. Raising her chin to the brilliant night sky, its beauty forced her to exhale. All at once, she felt free.

Behind her, Jager stood flanked by his Strykers in all black. "Whenever you're ready ..." he said.

Without a word, Sasha pushed from the railing and turned

down an external set of stairs to a short landing where a go-fast boat sat waiting.

"Here we are," Jager said, pulling a half-chewed cigar from his pocket and admiring it. "Your chariot awaits. We'll give you further directives once you're closer to *The Vladimov*." He appraised Sasha once again. "Unless you've gotten cold feet?"

She took stock of the hard men around her. "I haven't gotten cold—"

A shrill cry echoed from the top of the stairs behind them. Everyone turned. A sailor stood wide-eyed at the top of the stairs with a knife to his throat. Behind him, a shadowed figure in black and gray camouflage stood ready.

"Help," the petrified man squawked.

The Strykers all seemed to coil in unison, their weapons rising.

"Take the collar off and release the girl, or this man dies," the dark operative called out. "The girl is not a creature you can cage and control."

"God-forsaken Sentry scum," Jager growled.

Sasha's mouth hung open as she looked to the Sentry frogman and back to Jager.

"He's not alone," Jager shouted to his men. "Lock down the ship, and take them alive. I want to know what they know."

Before Sasha could cry out for them to stop, the frogman raised a compact submachine gun around the side of his hostage and opened fire. Projectiles flew past. Jager pushed Sasha to the ground, and the Strykers launched themselves forward. Tracking them with expert precision, the Sentry operative landed good hits on half of the Stryker squad.

A few of Jager's men stumbled, struggling forward under the influence of the powerful tranquilizer. The rest made for the stairs, vaulting them in two strides.

After removing the knife from the sailor's neck, the frogman shoved the man down the stairs and into the rising Strykers, which knocked them back. The frogman locked eyes with Sasha as she stood transfixed by the display.

"Don't let them control you, Sasha. This is your life. Don't be their pawn!" The operative called out to her as the strikers rushed him again.

"Get in the boat," Jager yelled, pulling Sasha to her feet and pushing her forward. "Go."

Sasha dropped into the boat as it lowered from the platform and turned in time to see the Strykers close in on the frogman with supernatural speed.

The frogman pulled a Sig P223 from the tactical holster at his waist and pressed the barrel flush under his chin, leaning back over the rail. "So shall we go," he called out to the sky. The muzzle flashed, and the report echoed out into the night.

Sasha screamed as the Sentry operative's body toppled backward over the rail and disappeared into the boiling black sea below.

CHAPTER 16

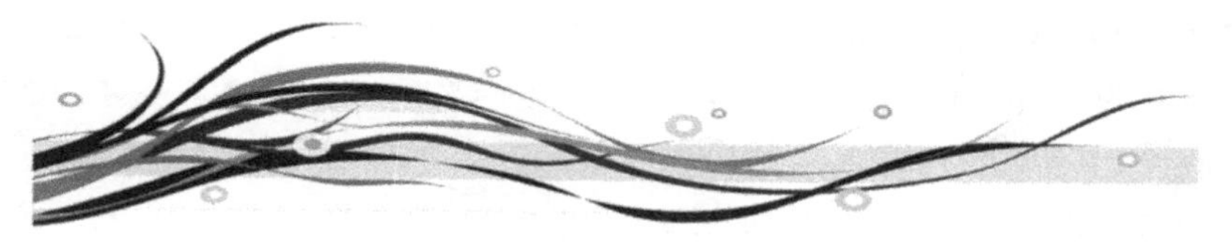

Max listened to Bodhi's screams from below with hands squeezed a bloodless white.

"I've had enough of this," Max said through clenched teeth.

He'd done his best to remain calm and tried to be the voice of reason. But that anger streak, the one who got him kicked out of two different high schools, now rose to the surface. "Your anger can't make things right," his father once scolded him. That was before Max was told that if he got kicked out of another school for fighting, he was on his own. No more financial assistance and no more place to stay. Not a man to mince words, his father would've made good on it, too. Max bottled it up, graduated high school, and swore not to let his anger dictate his actions in life.

A wave of prickly rage tingled its way up his spine. He was about to have a hard time holding to that promise. Max took a few steps toward the door, but it unbolted and swung open. A military police officer stood in the arch.

"Listen." Max licked his lips. "I don't understand what this is about since no one will talk to me, but you're not going to keep us here anymore. You can't, legally. I'm an American citizen. I want to speak with an attorney right now."

The MP sneered.

"This is funny to you?" Max clenched his fists tighter. "I hear my friend down there screaming. You won't get away with this."

The MP raised a small black device and pointed it at Max's

chest. "Don't fight it. It'll only hurt worse."

Max sobered and raised his hands. "Hang on, guys. Wait a second. Not like this. Okay? Let's talk about—"

A scream erupted from Max's throat as the Taser probes struck him in the chest and thigh, sending an agonizing jolt of electricity through him. He fell in an awkward half spin and flopped against the steel floor. The jolt stopped. Max scrambled to his feet, breathing labored and muscles on fire. He snagged the prong imbedded in his thigh and yanked it free. The MP's Taser initiated again, rapid electrical snaps echoing off the metal walled surroundings. But this time, without the second lead attached, Max felt nothing.

Max charged for the MP, but two broad-shouldered, dark-skinned men in black fatigues burst into the room and intercepted him. Max took a swing, but the soldiers overpowered him with little effort and secured both his arms.

"Hit him again. We'll complete the circuit," one of the soldiers said to the MP. "On three …"

The Taser snapped again.

"Get your hands ovvv—!" Max's stretched wide. Pain, hot and electrical, ripped through his body. The Taser stopped, and his scream tapered, replaced by a whimpered groan. Max hung limp in the soldiers' grip.

The MP laughed. "Good thing we had a couple of Strykers on hand."

"Secure him and get him to the lab ASAP. Captain Jager's orders," the lead Stryker said, turning his dark eyes on the MP.

"I was told to get him ready for blood work," the MP replied.

The Stryker shook his head. "We've got what we need already. The timeline has changed. Get him to the lab, now."

Cruising at its top speed of forty knots, the sleek, black-armored Navy DF-16 Barracuda knifed through each passing swell with ease. A fine spray of seawater drifted across the open stern of the boat where Sasha held to an exposed side rail.

"Two minutes out," one of the black fatigue-clad men said as the engines slowed to a growl.

Sasha stared, lost in thought, at the whitewash of foam pushing from the bow as the Barracuda sank into a moonlit trough. That man shot himself right in front of her. But why? To warn her? Was it worth his life? He'd called her by name. *Don't let them control you, Sasha.*

A sailor snapped his fingers in her face. "Hey, you still with us?"

"What?" she scowled.

"I said," he tapped on the tight collar around her neck with an index finger, "show us we can trust you, and you'll get a longer leash."

Her countenance darkened.

"Don't deviate, or we deploy countermeasures," the soldier motioned to the open briefcase with a small remote station for her collar nestled inside. "You do understand your mission, correct?"

"I understand you want me to do your dirty work," Sasha said.

"No, ma'am. It's your dirty work. This is not a sanctioned U.S. Naval operation. We were never here. So, tell me now, do you still want a crack at these guys or not? They're criminal scum. What's the problem?" He motioned off the bow to the glowing silhouette of a whaling vessel nestled on the dark horizon.

Sasha's stomach turned over. Should she go after the ugly men who'd held her and her friends prisoner only days ago? They should get what they deserved for their conduct and their endless raping of the ocean. *Who else will bring them to justice? The law? Clearly not. This is my chance.*

The squad leader cleared his throat. "Now or never."

"I've come this far." She raised her chin. "I'm going to do it."

"Good. Rally on this position when you're done." The squad leader marked his watch. "You have twenty minutes."

Sasha looked from the squad leader to the whaler. "I have to swim all the way over there?"

The squad leader chuckled. "Honey, have you seen yourself? You'll be fine. All you need to do is swim faster than the sharks out there."

The sailors laughed.

Sasha couldn't get off the cramped boat fast enough. "Get away from me," she snapped, lips pulled back over sharp teeth in a snarl.

The squad leader took a step back and raised his hands. "Twenty minutes. Not a moment longer."

In one graceful movement, Sasha swung her legs over the side rail and slipped into the dark waters of the pacific. Beneath the surface, an endless black enveloped her, the currents pushing and swelling around her newly formed body. Sasha allowed herself to drift, the silence beneath the waves blocking out even her own chaotic thoughts.

She clawed at the water, her webbed fingers finding purchase and driving her forward. Darting through the water like an arrow loosed from a bow, she glided for what felt like forever, the oxygen in her lungs not even half spent. She slowed amongst a ribbon of bubbles and rose to the surface to check her position. Far behind her, the Navy boat bobbed up and down. She'd made it almost three-quarters of the way in one breath.

Was this a curse? Or could it be a gift from Kai, the debt of the ocean repaid to her? A swell of resolve filled her chest in the hope of finding those whalers and giving them what they richly deserved. Another deep gulp of air and Sasha sank below the midnight black waves, powering forward through the dark, turbulent water.

Energy tickled across the length of Sasha's entire body. She belonged here, in the depths connected to all of Kai's creations—a nervous school of fish stirred up by a recent shark, the distant echoed call of a whale. Her mind cleared with each stroke of her arms, her mission, and the drive to see it through stronger and clearer. Right now, at this moment, she felt free.

Sasha broke the water's surface. The smell of diesel mixed with the heavy air of a coming storm. A bark of laughter echoed down from the deck of the whaler. With powerful strokes, she approached the stern of the ship. The rear turbines chugged as she passed through the current and grabbed the landing of the whale ramp. Cautiously, Sasha eased out of the water and pressed herself to the cool steel of the ramp wall. A man shuffled past the top of the ramp and dropped a mostly empty vodka bottle which clinked and rolled away across the deck. He grumbled something in Russian, groping around for where it may have gone.

Sasha took a moment to gain her composure. If the crew were already drunk, this might be easier than she thought. She crouched and slunk upward to the top of the ramp, a shadow in the dark of night. A flicker of lightning and a rumble of thunder followed. A drop of warm rain smacked against her shoulder. A wraith in the night, Sasha slipped onto the deck and stood behind the bumbling drunk man. The man turned, following her animalistic shadow to her webbed feet. His withered gaze followed her lithe body to her angular face. A moan escaped his lips as Sasha's hand closed over his face. She shoved him back and over the rail. His gargled cry cut short as he smacked against the dark waters below.

A voice hissed in Russian from the dark.

Sasha dodged to the left, the deafening crack of a rifle ringing in her ears and the hot flash of the muzzle blast far too close. Furious, she advanced on the terrified man as he stumbled back, his useless fingers trying to work the bolt action weapon. Then, she tore the weapon from his grasp and slammed the wooden stock across his lower back. The weapon shattered in a spray of wooden fragments, crumpling the man against the deck and sending him sliding into a corner.

Lights snapped on all across the ship, anxiety laced voices of the crew rising from below decks. The door to the stairwell burst open, and a flood of men stomped onto the deck. Sasha leaped for the roof of the stairwell housing, effortlessly bounced off it in a triple axel, and landed perched on the guard rail right in front of them. A finger of lightning streaked across the midnight sky, setting her otherworldly figure aglow.

The men staggered back, fumbling with their weapons. And there he was, standing with his fat mouth hanging open right in the middle of the stunned group of whalers: Beach Ball.

"You had this coming," Sasha said, then dropped from the rail to the deck and flexed her clawed fingers.

Beach Ball cried out, shoving another stupefied man forward.

The terrified men shuffled back and forth, clubs and crowbars in hand. Sasha tensed, her body a coiled spring. The lightning flashed again, strobing into the eyes of the men before her. Sasha hurled forward, crashed into the first man, and flung him headlong into another man with a rifle. The gun went off, and a spray of red erupted from the chest of the thrown man.

A crowbar cut the air to Sasha's right, arcing toward her head. Driving into her attacker, Sasha stole his energy. The force of her shoulder blow cracked the bones of his arms and launched him into the opposite wall. She hit another stumpy troll of a man with a swipe of her claws, leaving an ugly swath of open gashes from his forehead to the bottom of his chin. He fell screaming, his hands flying to his ruined face. Shouting in terror, two men ran the length of the ship while a third threw himself overboard.

A blast of pain rocketed through Sasha as a steel pipe smacked across her neck. She turned and glared into the piggish eyes of her former captor. Beach Ball took two staggering steps backward and dropped the length of steel against the rain-slicked deck. Another step, and he tripped over a coil of unkempt rope, landing on his seat in a puddle.

Rain streaked down, covering Sasha's nimble body in a glistening sheen that seemed to electrify with each repetitive stab of lightning across the night sky.

"No ..." Beach Ball's lips quivered, the pouring rain bathing his bulging jowls. "Get away from me, *sea witch*."

Sasha closed on the fat man, her eyes aflame. Her lips parted in a savage grin revealing stark white, fangs.

"Time to pay for your sins, asshole."

The Barracuda throbbed in idle, rocking in the turmoil of the growing storm. The young lieutenant strained his eyes against the dark and let a whispered curse hiss from his mouth. He wasn't in the mood to entertain this circus. He listened to the staccato of gunfire rippling across the open water, punctuated by the occasional scream. A fireball from a small explosion rolled upward from the deck of the Russian whaler.

"She's doing a number on them, LT," the petty officer said,

watching with the others from the starboard rail.

"Yeah, she is," the lieutenant said. "Like captain told us—she's a weapon, and this is what weapons do." He glanced at the briefcase and shook his head. Apparently, this Gorgon, as Captain Jager called her, needed to be kept on a leash.

The collar she wore could generate 100,000 volts and could be triggered at a distance of up to two miles. Enough to subdue an enraged elephant. The trouble was, if she went AWOL and he had to light her up, his team would have to extract her from whatever mess she'd created. That scenario wasn't something he wanted at all—the less exposure for him and his team, the better. On the flip side, they couldn't just ditch the most powerful biological weapon on the planet unattended.

He rubbed his eyes and checked his watch. Seven minutes left.

"Hey, Smokey," the lieutenant said.

"Aye aye, sir," the young radioman said from the helm of the Barracuda.

"Hit her up and tell her she has five minutes. Then get Zero Team on the horn and let them know they're up. We're not going to cut this too close."

"Roger that," the radioman said, raising the mic and adjusting the channel. "Barracuda to Gorgon. You copy?"

"I've got you," Sasha responded in a wash of static.

"You have five minutes. Repeat. You have five minutes until extraction."

"Yeah, I'll be there."

A heavy boom reverberated from the hulking whaler, the lights on the deck winking out. Darkness closed in across the water as far as the eye could see, the final screams and the pop of gunfire fading to silence amidst the rumble of thunder and splash of rain.

"The other transmission," the lieutenant said, looking to the radioman. "Send it."

"Roger." The radioman tabbed the channel down. "Control to Zero, encrypted channel, do you copy?"

"Zero copy. Confirming encryption. Go ahead with it," a voice said, dry like the crackle of dead leaves.

The lieutenant shuddered. The Strykers were only men. Hyper-advanced supermen, but still, men all the same. They were the good guys. Sure they were different, but were they different from the asset he'd just deployed moments ago? *She's still human, too, isn't she?*

The radioman looked to the young lieutenant. "They want to confirm their directives before proceeding."

The lieutenant tried to steady his nerves. A bad feeling gnawed at his guts. The men aboard *The Vladimov* were criminals. Outside of their questionable whaling activities, they smuggle everything from guns and Chechen terrorists to human slaves. Who cared if they all ended up dead? Besides, orders were orders. He chewed the inside of his cheek.

"Wait till she exfils from the whaler back to the Barracuda and then take the ship," the lieutenant said. "It's a clean sweep operation. Knives only. It needs to look like her."

He held a clenched fist to his mouth as the radioman repeated the order of operation to the Stryker team waiting somewhere out there amidst the undulating dark.

"Zero, copy direct," the voice replied. "Clean sweep. No survivors."

CHAPTER 17

Derrick Westfield sat in his truck in the parking lot of the Mega Donut. A large wax paper cup of steaming coffee beneath his nose sent soothing vapors about his closed eyes. The bold scents of the dark roast coaxed him back to life. Two whiskeys had turned into four and then eight. It wasn't a path he often tread, and at this moment, his throbbing head reminded him why. The veteran cop rolled the taught thick muscles of his neck, trying to relieve the budding tension at the base of his skull.

He took a tentative sip of the boiling black liquid, then flinched as it scalded the tip of his tongue. A few drops spattered the front of his shirt. "Sonofabitch," he mumbled, wiping at the little dark spots soaking into his short-sleeve, flower print, button-up.

Westfield closed his eyes again and tried to concentrate on the matter at hand: Jager.

The post office box angle was a dead end. Releasing an individual's personal information was a quick way to get fired, and the branch employees knew it. Regardless, the case gnawed at Westfield's gut. He'd served in the Army and been on the job as a cop in a military base hotbed long enough to know Jager's type: driven, calculating, not the sort to cross. *Ruthless* was the word that came to mind.

If Westfield wanted to find out more about Jager and the secret projects division, he would have to go about this from a different angle. Another tentative sip of blistering hot coffee prompted more curses. *Do they even intend for this stuff to be drinkable?*

Westfield watched as Len Mitchell's black Suburban with tinted windows finally pulled into the empty parking lot. This was a long shot. Len, a buddy of his from his academy days, had been recruited by the FBI. He'd bounced around for a while before returning to work a post in Hawaii. Westfield didn't have a whole lot of contact with the guy anymore, but he did know he frequented the Mega Donut on his way into work. LEOs were bad about having routines, and this guy was the proof.

Westfield set the coffee on the dash of his truck and stepped out into the crisp early morning. The island breeze ruffled his collar and his close-cropped thinning hair. He quickly stepped to the Suburban's rear to catch Len exiting the driver's compartment.

"Len," Westfield said.

The G man jumped, grabbing the top of the open door. "Damn, Derrick? Are you trying to give me a heart attack?"

"Sorry, man, I needed to speak with you. Must've changed your number."

Len adjusted his tie and swiped at his wavy brown hair. "Well, what so important you have to stalk me while I'm getting coffee?"

Westfield stepped forward and produced a file folder. "I've been digging into something, and it isn't adding up."

Len eyed Westfield. "What the hell is this? What's with the flower print shirt? Are you on the clock?"

"Always," Westfield said. "This is connected to a case I worked on a few nights ago." *Not a total lie,* he thought.

Len kept his hands close and scrutinized the extended file as though touching it might give him the plague. "What's this about? I just came to get some coffee."

"It's in the damn file, Len," Westfield said. "Would you look at it already?"

Len snatched the blue folder and flipped it open, his fingers hovering over the paperclipped documents and articles inside. The color drained from his face. "What are you doing with this? Where did you get this?"

"I'm a cop, Len. I did some investigating." Westfield frowned. "This is important, man. I know you have information about the thing that crashed off Mākaha. And don't tell me it was a damn meteor."

Len rifled through the pages until he landed on a picture of Jager. He snapped the file shut and shoved it against Westfield's chest. "Are you stupid?"

"Hey, relax—"

"No, shut up." Len cast a look over his shoulder as a large woman with jiggling arms and two full bags of donuts exited the store. He watched her lumbering form as she passed before snapping his terrified gaze back to Westfield. "You have no idea what you're messing with here," he said, his voice a strained whisper.

Westfield hardened his expression. "I'm doing my job, Len. A couple of kids are missing, and nobody cares. I want to know why."

"I can't talk to you about this. If our history ever meant anything to you, you'll leave this alone and forget we ever had this conversation," Len said as he practically fell back into the driver's seat.

"Len," Westfield protested.

The FBI agent slammed the door and threw it in reverse without fastening his seatbelt. The Suburban lurched backward, the bark of rubber on asphalt.

Westfield sidestepped the vehicle. "Hey! Look out, you crazy bastard."

The Suburban hit the street with a screech, then rocketed into the flow of traffic.

"You gotta be kidding me." Westfield expelled a loaded sigh. "What the hell is going on here?"

Sleep wasn't in the cards. She'd tried. Sasha trembled with a terrible restlessness, a relentless tingling ache that slowly drove her insane. She stopped pacing the small metal enclosure long enough to face the dark glass of the one-sided mirror and glared into its inky depths. In the dark reflection, the beast's bared teeth and white eyes looked back. She grabbed a handful of the collar still clamped around her neck. A small chime pinged.

"Warning. Release the restraint collar or countermeasures will deploy in five seconds. Four. Three."

She jerked her hand free.

"You people said I had to wear this when leaving the ship," Sasha shouted. "I left, and I came back like you wanted, and now I want it off!"

"*Sasha,*" Jager's intercom voice filtered into her room from small circular speakers set into the ceiling. "*It has to remain on for your safety.*"

"My safety?" She narrowed her eyes. "Or yours?"

"Sasha—"

New voices interrupted, and the microphone switched off.

Sasha strained to hear the murmurs on the other side of the glass.

With a click, the speakers came alive again.

"You did an outstanding job on your mission today, Sasha," Jager said. *"You should get some rest now."*

"Mission? I didn't want any of this." Sasha held her clawed hands in front of her face. "I didn't want to be a military asset. You did this to me."

"No, Sasha." Jager's voice was calm and cool. *"Fate did this to you, we only cultivated and harnessed your circumstances."* He let the words sink in. *"Think of all the ways we can help mankind. The medical advancements alone are incredible. Genetic modification to withstand or recover from a previously incurable disease—"*

"But you don't want me for medical advancements," Sasha said. "You want me to be a weapon." Sasha's skin felt hot and tight. She took a step back in front of the misting fan.

"We're the United States military, Sasha," Jager said. *"Developing and safeguarding weapons that protect our way of life is what we do. Surely you understand."*

"I understand. I just don't want to be a part of it," Sasha shouted, her voice wavering on a razor's edge, loud and furious in the confined space.

A bloated pause filled the room. The lack of response grated on her nerves, ratcheting her already swelling anger higher. "Well? Nothing to say?"

A click. Sasha turned as a small paper-thin flat screen in the top right corner of the room winked to life and projected a news report. Smoke billowed from a fire onboard *The Vladimov* while firefighters attempted to quench the flames and salvage anything they could. At the bottom of the soundless image, the ticker read: *Russian whaling ship attacked by a mysterious creature. No survivors.*

"No survivors?" Sasha said, her eyes wide. "Turn … put the sound on."

With a click, the voice of a broadcaster filled the room.

"This is a live shot of the deck of The Vladimov, *and as you can see, rescue efforts are underway to salvage the ship and put out the fire*

in the engine compartment. At this time, rescuers are still holding out hope they'll find survivors, but the outlook is grim."

Sasha turned to the dark glass of the mirror behind. She pressed her lips together and tried to suppress their quivering, her eyes filling with tears. "But I didn't …"

"*Watch the news, Sasha,*" Jager said through the wall-mounted speakers.

She turned back to the screen, her hands raised to cover her mouth.

"The United States quickly condemned this tragedy, followed by an earnest pledge by President Fulsom, via Social Link, to offer assistance. The attack happened in international waters, and little is known about what transpired. Russian authorities have released this single surveillance camera footage captured from the deck of The Vladimov at the time of the incident."

The shot switched to a grainy black and white video, captioned: "*Mysterious creature attacks* The Vladimov." Sasha squinted at the image, the black blobs of shuffling men on the ship's deck, suddenly illuminated in a flash of lightning. Her blood ran cold. There she was, perched on the rail. As the flash receded, the men stumbled and ran, some falling to the deck and others freezing in place. But the image of the Gorgon was gone.

"*Congratulations. You've joined the ranks of Bigfoot and Nessie,*" Jager said.

"But I didn't kill all …" her voice died in her throat. "Some of the men must have survived."

"*Are you saying you didn't kill anyone, Sasha?*"

Sasha lowered her head, guilt and shame a yoke upon her shoulders. *Beach Ball wouldn't have survived, a good number of the others, too. But all of them?* Tears streaked down her cheeks. She'd been so angry. Willing to do anything to get even. But was this what she'd wanted?

"I didn't mean to," she mumbled.

"Exactly, Sasha." Jager's voice had lost its edge. *"Which is why we have to keep you under observation for now. No one yet really knows what sort of greatness or destruction you are capable of."*

"Turn it off," Sasha whimpered.

The TV went black. Thoughts of her mother and father and little sister filled her head. Better days. Days when she still felt in control of her simple life. But now? *What am I now?* Sasha leaned back against the wall, careful not to pinch her fins as she slid to the floor. The blown mist mixed with tears of regret as the whirring sound of the blades melted into a cacophony of white noise.

"*Rest now. Some rest will do you good,*" Jager said, his voice almost fatherly.

CHAPTER 18

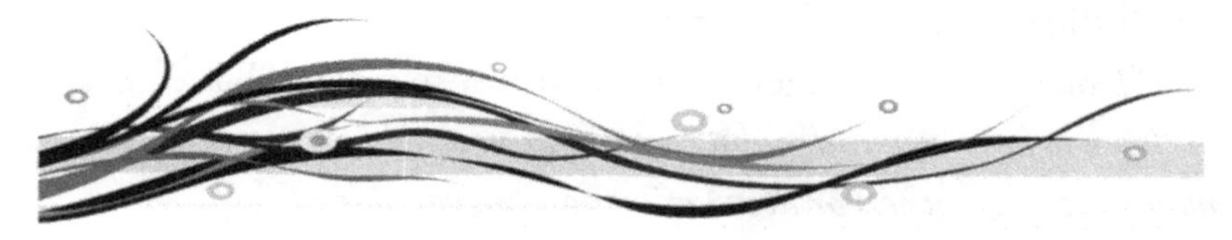

Commander Atcheson shut the door to the conference room. Jager grunted, and rotated the unlit stub of his Dominican. "You have something for me?"

"The ship is secure, Captain. We believe a total of three of Sentry's operatives boarded, but other than the one you encountered, they left no sign. There are no indications they had access to any sensitive areas."

Jager's eyes narrowed. "Double security patrols. This will not happen again." The silence ballooned. "Is there something else?"

"A small matter of importance." Atcheson seemed to weigh his words. "I felt you should know that a Honolulu police officer is probing into our operation."

Jager chewed on his cigar. "And?"

Atcheson rubbed his hands together, a nervous tick he'd developed years ago while serving in war zones around the globe. "It's the same one our people dealt with earlier. He won't let it go. He's asking questions."

"Let him spin his wheels. He doesn't have any other ability to injure our operation." Jager looked his XO over. "What's got you spooked about this?"

"Captain, we all have a lot riding on this. If information about this operation gets out before we can justify the means with appropriate ends ..."

"Go on."

"We have intel. He approached his contact, an old friend of his who now works with the FBI. A field agent by the name of Len Mitchell who may have some limited knowledge of our operation. Our sources indicate this Officer Westfield was asking questions he shouldn't. About our confidential level projects. About *you.*"

Jager sighed and pulled on his neck. Exactly what he didn't need right now. Some dumbass street cop playing detective and sticking his nose where it didn't belong. He switched the half-chewed cigar to the opposite side of his mouth. "What's this guy's name again?"

"Westfield. Officer Derrick Westfield."

Jager grunted and pulled the wet chewed end of a Dominican cigar from his mouth and glanced at it. "All right. Put together a file on him. I want everything. Family, friends, associates, where he might be getting his information, everything."

"Aye aye, sir," Atcheson said.

"I'll personally put a call into his command," Jager added. "I've got contacts over at HPD Headquarters who owe me a few favors. They've already helped sweep the Erebos' splash down under the rug."

"Very good, sir."

"Anything else, Atcheson?"

"No, sir. I'll take care of it." Atcheson turned for the hallway.

"How about a salute?" Jager said, his expression cold like chiseled granite.

Atcheson cleared his throat, his face flush. "Of course, sir," he said with a salute.

Jager waited a moment, forcing the XO to hold the position before dismissively returning the gesture. "That's more like it," he said.

Atcheson left, pulling the door shut behind him.

Jager stubbed out his cigar and glanced out the window. Too many storm clouds on the horizon. It was time to change the course of destiny. Exiting into the hallway, Jager took the stairs to the lower levels, his mind clear, his focus absolute. He stepped onto deck four and strode the length of the narrow hallway, passing row upon row of holding cells without a glance as he moved with purpose to the containment sector of the ship—to the Erebos device. The failed scientific project gave rise to something even more incredible, mutating Sasha's code and changing her into something remarkable. Who could say how advanced she'd become or how she might further evolve? The girl may be the next step in human evolution. Though, day by day, she became more volatile. Jager had to figure out how to gain her cooperation, and fast. *The restraint collar will control her, but for how long?*

Jager rounded the corner. Terrible moans emanated from behind a sealed chamber ahead. Behind a thick wall of glass, one of Jager's project leads, a quirky man named Gerald Hanson, jabbed notes on this tablet.

"Captain," Hanson said.

Jager looked the man in the lab coat over. "Well? What's the status?"

The scientist swallowed, apparently composing his thoughts. "It's remarkable, sir."

"I want specifics." Jager's gaze bored into Hanson.

"The subject known as Bodhi has been in direct contact with the Erebos' energy field as well as a male orca specimen for six hours," Hanson said. "He received the full battery of S.H.R.E.D. serum injections derived from the edited genetic material we obtained from Sasha.

Jager pulled a fresh cigar from his pocket, sniffed it, and placed it in the corner of his mouth. "Go on."

"Scans already show the subject experiencing a one-hundred thirty-seven percent increase in muscle mass, improved cellular rigidity, and high levels of genetic modulation. I mean, it's incredible."

A shriek echoed inside the chamber. The sound elongated, stretching into a moan.

"Why is he making that sound?" Jager said.

"Well, sir," Dr. Hanson forced a smile, rubbing his hands on his lab coat. "The process of genetic alteration appears to be ah … quite painful."

"I'd say so," Jager said, peering through the thick glass of the viewport. Emerald light danced in waves across his face. In the first of three large tanks, next to the thrumming Erebos probe, lay the first test subject. The one called Bodhi. Face obscured by an oxygen mask, his body hovering suspended. In the tank in the center, next to Bodhi's tank, sat the sedated floating form of a fully-grown orca with various tubes and hoses attached to it.

"But look," Hanson continued. "Notice his grayish coloring. He's changing skin tones. The same way she did. And there"—he pointed—"look at his back. Do you see it?"

Jager squinted against the strobing glare, able to identify a nubbed protrusion pushing from between the subject's shoulders. "It's a fin."

"Like Sasha," Hanson exclaimed.

The exotic energy from the Erebos is only a fraction as powerful now as it was when it first crashed and exposed Sasha, but the combination of the direct injections of the serum plus prolonged exposure is working as it did with her—only slower."

"Tell me something," Jager said, turning to the Hanson. "Why orcas? Why can't we use a mako shark or some other hyper-aggressive apex predator?"

The scientist's face seemed to light up at the opportunity to display his knowledge for the captain. "Good question." He held up a finger. "See, there is a distinct reason it worked the first time with Sasha. I believe the orca, an air-breathing mammal, made the genetic gap between the species easier to bridge. Biologically, a shark, for example, is so different from a human, it could prove difficult to assimilate the two."

"But you could use a dolphin? Or any other mammal for that matter?"

"Potentially." Hanson shrugged. "But if you're looking for the combination of an aggressive, water adept mammal, the orca is it, sir. They're called the wolves of the sea for a reason."

Jager seemed to consider this. "Side effects?"

His enthusiasm snuffed, Hanson secured a tablet from a nearby table. "It's hard to tell as of right now, but he's showing diminished neural activity. It should return to normal when we're finished."

"Should?" Jager clamped his teeth around the cigar, eyeing the nervous man.

"Yes, sir." Hanson jabbed at the tablet with a narrow finger and wiped the sweat from his forehead with his coat sleeve. "We simply don't know what will happen yet."

"The other subject. Is he ready?" Jager interjected.

"Yes, but—"

"Shoot him full of the S.H.R.E.D. serum and throw him in the other tank."

The light in Hanson's eyes died. "Sir, we have no idea what's going to happen with the first subject. Putting them both in such close proximity to each other within a powerful morphic energy field could wildly affect their genetic framework."

"Do it." Jager growled, grabbing hold of the man's white coat. "I didn't ask for your opinion."

The scientist swallowed, his Adam's apple bobbing with some difficulty. "Yes, sir."

Jager eyed the man's name tape. "And don't forget, I need them strong, smart, and compliant, *Hanson.*" He emphasized the man's name with a snarl. "That's your job. Don't screw it up."

CHAPTER 19

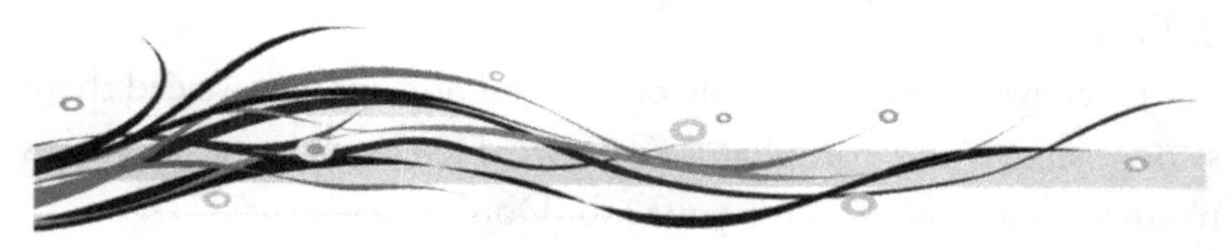

The inner workings of the busy naval vessel reached out to her, the droning cadence of mechanical things mixing with the clang of something dropped and the chatter of distant echoing voices. But also, something else. A cry from somewhere deep within the ship, sustained and agonizing. She could feel it more than hear it.

Sasha sat bolt upright. Beside her, the misting fan continued to hum. She turned her head strained her ears. *Is my mind playing tricks on me?* She swung her feet over the edge of the specially modified cot with cutouts for her fins, then scooted to the edge and placed her feet on the floor, listening. The sound was gone.

"*Sasha, is everything all right?*" a voice sounded over the speakers in her room.

"I thought I heard something ..." her voice trailed off.

"*What do you think you heard?*" the voice responded, clinical and condescending.

Sasha didn't reply. She focused on listening.

"*Sasha.*"

"Be quiet for a second," Sasha snapped.

There it was again. Sasha stood from her cot, the clawed fingers of her webbed hands flicking open. After the past few days, she'd given in to accepting the notion that this terrible existence was now her life. But what about Max and Bodhi? *Why won't Jager tell me what happened to my friends?* A knot the size of a fist grew in the pit of her stomach. *If I'm a prisoner here, could there be other people held against their will? My friends?* They were all there when the space object crashed into the ocean. Sasha crouched, searching again for the sound so faint one might dismiss it as the groaning of the ship.

"*Sasha. I need you to tell me what's going on.*"

She ignored the voice, dropped flat to her belly, and pressed her ear opening to the cool, wet metal floor. Her breath held in her chest, she could now hear the sound again, far away like the sorrowful call of a night bird in the distance. But this wasn't that. This was a scream of agony.

Suddenly a host of dark questions with no good answers flooded her mind. Her ear suctioned from the puddled floor as she stood then made her way toward the dark glass of the observation room. The words of the mysterious doomed frogman echoed in her mind. *Don't let them control you, Sasha. This is your life.*

"What is it you people are doing here?" Sasha said, facing the glass.

"*We are trying to help you.*"

"No. Don't sell me that line of crap." Sasha took a step toward the wall-length obsidian mirror. "What sort of work are you doing here, really? Who else are you holding against their will?"

"*Sasha, we're not keeping anyone against—*"

"No more lies," Sasha shouted, her brow knitting in fury at the faceless voice behind the glass.

In the upper right corner, a small white strobe flickered. Sasha glanced at it and back to the glass. "What is that?" She could feel the heat looming beneath the surface of her fragile composure, a red tidal wave of death and destruction. "Well?"

"You should calm yourself, Sasha. Getting excited won't be good for you."

"Won't be good for *me*? Is that some sort of threat?" She

turned, eyeing the smooth, riveted walls, the single door, and the strobing white light above. She gnashed her teeth.

"*Calm down, or we'll be forced to—*"

"Do what? You'll do what to me?" she shouted, her voice shaking. Moving to the aluminum chair to her left, she grabbed it and cocked it over her shoulder. "I want out. Let me out of here. Right now—"

The blast of white-hot electrical current struck her like a lightning bolt, crackling and snapping against the skin of her neck. Sasha's eyes flared wide with pain, the muscles of her body locked tight. She couldn't move, couldn't breathe. She toppled to the side, crashed through the nearby table, and sank to the water-soaked floor. Twitching and jerking, Sasha writhed. The collar around her throat continued to snap like a live wire.

A gasp escaped her as the brutal electrical jolt ceased—the skin at her neck, a charred black swath of smoking flesh.

"You … you can't …" Sasha moaned.

Voices conversed in excited whispers through the intercom on the other side of the glass.

"*Incredible. She's still conscious. One hundred thousand volts should kill a person outright.*"

"*Well, she's not a person anymore, is she.*"

"*Your mic is hot.*"

A squelch and a click followed by silence.

Sasha swallowed and pulled her trembling arms into her body, clutching them close, trying to stop the burning that tingled from her scalp to the tips of her webbed toes. Slowly, she rolled to her knees and hunched forward to try to stand again.

"Don't get up. A team is coming in to sedate you," the voice said.

"I don't want … to be sedated," Sasha said, her voice trembling.

"Stay down, monster," the cold electronic voice said, *"or you'll get it again."*

Monster. That was what she'd been reduced to. After all the pretty lies Jager spun, these people didn't care for her. They weren't trying to help. She was a monster—a weapon they needed to control.

Her heart banged in her chest. She swallowed a gathering of sticky saliva from the back of her throat and tried to ignore the smell of hot electricity and charred flesh—her flesh. In the darkest corners of her heart, something awakened. Raw. Primal. Furious.

"*Her heart rate is accelerating,*" the voice over the speaker said.

"You. You're the monsters." Sasha grunted, then stood on shaking legs, her teeth bared.

"Do it. Hit her again."

"But the captain said—"

"I don't care what the captain said, hit her again. That's an order."

"Don't—" Sasha managed, her hand outstretched as a second bolt of lightning lanced through her. She screamed again, the horrifying sound of innocence dying. Her body shook, her eyes full of pain and betrayal, spittle frothing from her lips. She dropped to her knees, her arms flexing, reaching for her neck as one hundred thousand undulating volts of directed electrical current knifed through her. Groaning with effort, she slipped her fingers inside the collar on either side and yanked with all her might. The snapping electrical current seared into the tips of her fingers as she pulled.

"*Stop her, you idiot. Do you want Jager down here?*"

"*I'm trying.*"

The metal collar squealed as Sasha stretched it.

"*Crank the voltage. Give her more.*"

"*There is no more!*"

With one last yank, Sasha tore the restraint collar, popping and fizzing in a shower of sparks from around her neck. In a single stride, she vaulted forward. Her body crashed through the dark glass of the observation room, slamming one of the two men inside against the far wall. In a bumbling fit of terror, the other fell to the floor, scrambled to all fours, then ran screaming for the hallway. As he did, he slapped a large red button on the wall labeled *containment breach*.

The screaming high-pitched wail of an emergency beacon filled the air, the walls around Sasha flickering with intermittent flashes of red. Instinct, strong and powerful, told her to run, but her higher brain held her fast: what they'd done here was illegal, and she needed evidence. She scanned the various consoles. *There, a flash drive. No time to waste. Jager's men must be on their way.* Any data she could grab was no good if she couldn't get it off the ship.

Snatching the data stick from the console and looping the lanyard around her neck, Sasha gave one last look to the unconscious man slumped against the floor and turned for the door. She stepped into the strobe-lit flash of the corridor and hovered there, her heart beating fierce in her breast.

On either side of the corridor, two pairs of Strykers squared up, the dark brown tones of their flesh offset by midnight black BDUs. They tensed, the banded muscles of their arms taut. No one moved.

"I don't want to fight," Sasha said over the wail of the alarm, her heart still thrumming. "But I'm not staying locked up here anymore."

"You don't have a choice." The one named Alvarez said through clenched teeth. "Get back in, or we'll put you back in."

Sasha knew she should be afraid of these men, but then she

remembered about how easily, accidentally even, she'd killed the whalers. How moments ago, she'd torn a titanium collar from her neck and crashed through a seemingly impenetrable two-inch-thick layered sheet of armored glass.

Sasha steeled herself as the four Strykers advanced on her from either side, their fists raised. "I don't want to hurt you," she said.

The Strykers stopped, exchanging amused glances. One of them closest to her, a man with a cropped mohawk, let out a chuckle.

"We're not the ones who are about to get hurt, *darlin'*."

Sasha's skin flushed hot. Her eyes narrowed to slits as she flexed her clawed fingers. "That's what you think."

Jager picked up the pace, storming his way toward the observation deck of the Island, curses muttered under his breath. The containment alarm assaulting his ears meant only one thing; Sasha had broken out.

"Ready for you, sir." A young ensign extended a scoped Krytak 7740 modified bolt action rifle.

Jager snagged the weapon, threw the door to the observation platform open, and stepped out against the rail. "What's the status?"

"She's loose," the sailor said. "Four Strykers, including Senior Chief Alvarez, are en route to control her."

"That won't be enough. Send everybody," Jager growled. "What else?"

"Sir, she …"

Jager cast a scathing glance at the young man. "Spit it out, son."

"She may have seized sensitive information on her way out of the lab." The sailor fidgeted, unable to hold the captain's hardened gaze.

Jager shook his head, a snarl of disgust on his lips. "That defiant little bitch."

He took a moment to insert a magazine into the mag well in the underside of the rifle, careful to avoid the needles of the two precision tranquilizer rounds. Fired at fourteen hundred feet per second, the barbed tips were designed to embed in the target's skin, and auto inject their payload. Each one was capable of incapacitating a rampaging rhino in a matter of seconds.

A muffled *whump* sounded from somewhere below him—the familiar sound of a body smacking steel. The door below burst from its hinges and careened across the deck, followed by the tumbling body of one of his Strykers.

"Good God," Jager murmured as Sasha emerged from the hole.

Behind her, a Stryker charged his with head down. Jager watched as the girl spun and grabbed the Stryker by his uniform. She twisted and flung him across the deck headlong into a pile of stacked metal transport crates.

Alvarez and the last Stryker limped onto the deck, followed by a fully armed security contingent.

"Get control of her, dammit," Jager shouted above the shriek of the containment alarm. He watched, morbid curiosity gnawing at his guts, as Senior Chief Alvarez and the other Stryker converged on Sasha.

With a scream, Sasha lunged into the closest Stryker, knocked his hand away, and punched him square in the face. The Stryker gave a garbled scream. His knees buckled, and his nose gushed blood as he stumbled back and fell against the deck. In a flash, she was on Alvarez, slashing at him with her claws. Even with the limp, the lead Stryker evaded her attack, side-stepping and landing a body shot on her that would've turned a heavyweight boxer's guts to paste. Sasha didn't even flinch. Instead, she evaded a second blow and hammered him with a double overhanded fist.

Alverez hit the deck and lay there unconscious.

Jager worked the action on the rifle, forcing the first tranq round into the breach. He locked the bolt in position and flicked off the safety. Shouldering the heavy weapon, Jager braced it on the railing and acquired his target through the glass of the scope. "I've got you now," he said, his finger jerking the trigger. The specialized round fired with a *whoomp*.

Sasha flinched as the loaded injector struck her in the shoulder, the multi-prongs ejecting and latching into her skin.

Jager grinned. "Bullseye." The beauty of the tranq darts is that they were designed to be too painful to pull or claw out, the victim left them in place to deliver the full dose.

With a snarl, Sasha grabbed the injector embedded in her shoulder blade and pulled. Her skin stretched and distorted until, with a wild cry, she tore it free. A wash of blood streamed from the wound. Sasha stumbled, then righted herself and made for the edge of the deck.

Jager stared, grinding his teeth until they felt they may crack. "How is that possible?" he muttered through stiff lips. "Even half of that concoction would have dropped a pissed-off silverback." He clenched his teeth and worked the rifle action, ejecting the spent cartridge, then racked the second tranq into the chamber. Obtaining proper eye relief on the scope, he found his target again and tracked her as she stumbled forward to maul another hapless sailor who ventured too close.

"Unbelievable," Jager said, his finger moving to the trigger. Under no circumstances could the girl be allowed to escape—with sensitive information no less. Jager steadied his breathing and aimed for her lower half, hoping to disperse the effects of the drug faster after already hitting her high. Another *whoomp* as the second round fired and struck her in the back of the leg.

This time she didn't stop, didn't even register the hit. Sasha just lumbered for the edge, only a few feet away now.

Jager dropped the rifle against the rail and stood stock straight. "Shoot her!"

The last men left standing fumbled with their weapons, raising them too slowly. Jager grabbed at the railing, his eyes wide. "Shoot her, damn you. That's an order!"

A ripple of gunfire tore across the deck. Bullets pinged and zinged in little showers of sparks as the Gorgon fell, tumbling from the jump deck of *The U.S.S. Harbinger.* A distant splash and she was gone, swallowed into the depths of the deep blue sea.

CHAPTER 20

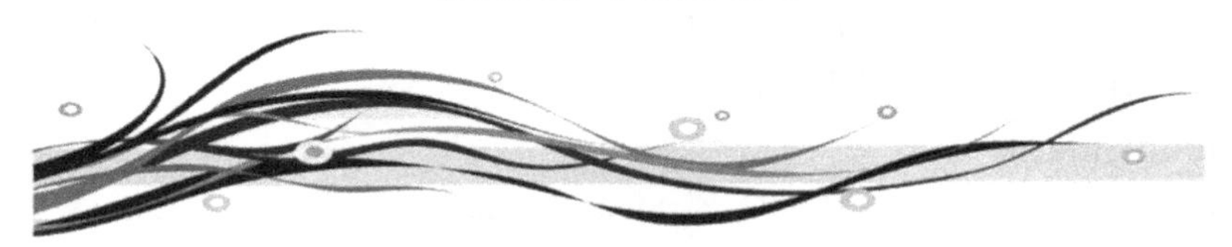

Murong sat cross-legged atop a silken pillow of crushed memory foam in his dimly lit room aboard *The Argo*. A haze of incense drifted about the room, obscuring the outlines of maps, nautical charts, and various sources of literary, scientific, and mystical literature. He closed his eyes and waited in the dark of his mind, absorbing and categorizing all the sounds and vibrations from within his submarine.

In this place, he could contest his demons, master them even, at least for a time. The past failures, memories that refused to release their hold on him, faded away. As Murong sank deeper into meditation, the tortured screams of his family began to fade, and for the first time in days, he felt a small measure of relief wash over him.

The trill of the intercom on his desk dinged like a dinner bell.

Murong's fragile calm shattered. He sucked in a long breath, hoping to quell the tide of anger already rising in his chest. The intercom trilled again. With the grace of a cat, the leader of Sentry crossed the short length of his personal space and tabbed the button on the small square pad. "You've interrupted my meditation," he said.

"*Apologies, Doctor Murong, but we have something you're going to want to see.*"

"It's about Sasha." Murong took in a deep lungful of the soothing jade incense blend. "Am I right?"

"*Yes, sir. Her genetic signature popped live on our bio scanner. She's separated from the Harbinger.*"

Murong pursed his lips. "Keep a lock on her. I'll join you momentarily."

"*Copy.*"

Moving to the closet, Murong took the time to slip from his day robe, the muscles of his lithe frame accented in the dim light of the small space. He pulled a pair of pressed black Italian cotton trousers from the closet, stepped into them then shrugged into a crimson silk shirt. A gleaming black leather belt and polished designer loafers completed the look. He checked his hair and touched at the crow's feet at the corners of his eyes that seemed to deepen with each passing year. Though he often entertained the mystic arts of his ancestors in an attempt to gain clarity, never would he enter into a public space wearing traditional garb of any sort. *Apparel oft proclaims the man*, he thought.

Exiting his room, he navigated the short, segmented corridors of the submarine and headed toward the control room. Men and women he encountered along the way, his crew—his followers, simply stepped from the center of the walkway and pressed their backs to the walls.

"So shall we go," one of the crew at the entrance to the control room said.

"So shall we go," Murong repeated, then stepped through the hatch. "What have we got?" he asked the room of sailors.

"Hard to say, sir." An idealistic-looking young man with plump features sat at one of the terminals. "But we've got her signature clear as day, fifty meters down almost directly below *The Harbinger*. She's emitting some form of radiation. It's showing loud on the spectrum."

Murong leaned over and studied the bank of monitors. "What

is her status?"

"Unverified," the plump man said. "She isn't in motion, though. Think she's waiting to see what action *The Harbinger* takes?"

"Or?" Murong said, anticipating the terminal operator's hesitation.

The man licked his lips and smoothed a few strands of wiry blond hair. "Or she's incapacitated, maybe even ..."

"She's not dead," Murong said. "Her signature wouldn't be so strong. What's the status on *The Harbinger*?"

The young man seemed to hang on his benefactor's words, the other occupants of the control room watching the exchange in silent anticipation.

"Sir, *The Harbinger* will send Strykers to retrieve her soon. Five minutes, tops, if I had to guess."

Murong nodded, angling to get a better look at the glowing green terminal. "Set a course to get us close and prepare to create a diversion. We have one chance to get this right. We must not allow her to fall back into Jager's hands."

"Yes, sir," the control room chanted in unison.

Hanging suspended in the ageless currents of the pacific ocean, Sasha drifted in and out of consciousness. By instinct alone, she continued to hold her breath, never fully succumbing to the effects of the powerful tranquilizer now coursing through her system. In the dark of her mind, the face of the doomed frogman appeared. Blurry at first, but then crisp and clear; the sweat beaded on his brow, the fear in his eyes. *Such conviction, even in the face of death.* Even as he placed the barrel of his pistol beneath his chin. *So shall we go.*

A sharp bump against her midsection caused Sasha's eyes to flutter open. She turned her head and stared into the endless blue-black depths. The ocean called to her, begging her to join it forever. Another bump, this time harder. The pain in her side jolted her to her senses, a spike of adrenaline whipping her back into the present. A cloud of blood puffed out from the wound in her side as the shark's tail fin disappeared in the gloom. She hadn't even felt the bite. A pall of dread descended upon her. The next pass wouldn't be a bump. She'd be missing a limb—or worse.

Sasha's movements slowed to a crawl, and the tissues of her lungs tingled. A faint reminder that she'd have to return to the surface sooner than later. And when she did, Jager and his men would stand ready to recapture her. *Or maybe kill me this time,* she thought. Better that than allow them to brainwash her into being a weapon for them.

From out of the gloom, the hammerhead shark shot in toward her, its jaws wide. Stirred to life by some primal instinct to survive, Sasha wrenched her body to the side, narrowly dodging the vicious attack. Sasha drove her arm to the elbow into the shark's gill slits as it passed. The creature bucked then launched into the depths, dragging Sasha with her. Twisting and gyrating, they descended, leaving a trail of hazy blood in their wake.

Sasha screamed, bubbles streaming from her lips. She clawed at the predator's inner gill lining. With a final savage jerk, she snatched a hole in the Hammerhead's side. Slinging the remains free, she watched as the shark thrashed a few more times, then sank into the deep trailed by a cloud of red.

A pang of guilt struck her in the chest. Never in her life had Sasha wanted to kill any creature simply for doing what came naturally to it. Yet, the feeling washed away as her animal nature took over. A basic instinct: kill or be killed.

Her lungs burned for air. Now free of the shark, her instincts turned to keep her from drowning. Sasha swam for the surface, sweeping greedy handfuls of water behind her. Her vision narrowed, and limbs cramped. Panic swelled in her chest, causing her heart to flutter. The ocean, a place that felt much more welcoming to her than anywhere else, now wanted her dead.

Another bump against her leg. Sasha clawed at the water again, the fear of another shark attack coursing through her. But the bump was gentle, comforting even. A smooth snout slipped under her arms. Sasha's hand found purchase on the dorsal fin of the massive orca as it powered toward the surface.

Sasha broke the surface of the water. With what strength remained, she clung to the back of the large orca. Opening her eyes, lungs on fire, her attention turned to the groaning engines of the approaching *U.S.S. Harbinger*. It was as she feared. Jager was coming for her, and she was too weak to resist further.

The voice of Jager boomed over the PA system and across the water. "*Surrender now, Sasha, and no further harm will come to you.*"

Another gasped breath caused her shoulder and leg to throb. If the pod of orcas left, she may not have the strength to resurface on her own again. Hope drained from her heart, and all at once, Sasha felt as so many cetaceans had over the centuries: hunted and alone.

One of the orcas squeaked to the other. They dipped below the surface and were gone, leaving only the individual, now restless, who propped her up.

The large orca dipped and resurfaced again, making a clicking sound. And somehow, Sasha understood: *follow me.*

"I can't," Sasha gasped. "You go. I won't make it."

The orca chattered again.

"Go, friend," Sasha managed through the lump in her throat. "Thank you."

With a swift thrust, the orca arched its back and dove, and its dorsal fin slipped from her fingers. Slapping at the water, Sasha struggled against the rolling waves. She sank below the surface, sounds and sight muted. With nothing left to give, Sasha gave up and allowed her body to sink into the murk.

But she didn't sink. She moved back to the surface. She felt for the soft flesh of the orca only to find hard, cold metal. A massive form rose from the depths and pushed her up and out of the water. Sasha lay, panting on the deck of a submarine, the word *Argo* stenciled onto the conning tower.

Sasha turned her head to face the huge dark outline of *The Harbinger* powering toward her. The piercing shriek of an alarm rose from the Navy vessel. She didn't know much about naval protocol, but she knew enough to recognize it as a sign Jager's ship considered this new arrival a threat.

A loud hiss drew her attention back to the conning tower. A door opened in its side, and inside stood a man with strong features and clear eyes.

"Sasha, come with us. We can help you," the man shouted.

"Who are yo—"

The screech of a harpoon missile launching from the deck of *The Harbinger* cut her words short. From some unseen arsenal, *The Argo* fired a crackling stream of white fire into the air. *The Harbinger*'s missile locked on the countermeasure and exploded in a deafening blast high above.

Sasha covered her ears and pinched her eyes.

"Sasha," the man shouted. "We have no time. Come with us, or we all perish."

More harpoons screeched into the air, and a cannon pounded away from atop the deck of *The Harbinger. The Argo* sent yet more countermeasures streaking high into the air.

"Sasha!" the man bellowed from the hatch.

Sasha tried to stand but crashed back into the vessel's steel hull.

Two wet-suit-clad people emerged from the hatch and ran to her aid. They grabbed her under the arms and dragged her back through the doorway. Sasha crumpled to the floor and rested on her knees as the door behind closed with a hiss. With a churning jolt of movement, she felt the sub descending.

"Jager … he's coming …" Sasha wheezed.

"The cloaking mechanism is activated by now," one of her saviors said. "We should be off their radar."

A hand rested on Sasha's shoulder. She looked up to see a man of Asian descent, lean and composed, a smile on his narrow lips.

"Where am I?" Sasha asked.

"Forgive me, Sasha," the man said, composing himself. "I'm afraid I've forgotten my manners. Doctor Zhou Murong, at your service." He gave a slight bow. "Welcome aboard *The Argo*, my private research vessel."

Sasha couldn't force a response.

"She's wounded," one of the medics said.

"Yes, of course. Take her," Murong said.

Sasha licked her lips, her mouth unable to form the words.

The two who helped her inside lifted her onto a waiting stretcher.

Too tired to fight, Sasha sank into the fabric.

Murong knelt beside her. "Rest now, Sasha. You have nothing to fear from us."

Sasha pulled the lanyard from her neck and extended it to Murong, the data stick enclosed in a shaking fist.

"What's this?" he said, accepting it from her with care.

Sasha swallowed, her leaden eyelids fluttering. "Evidence," she whispered.

CHAPTER 21

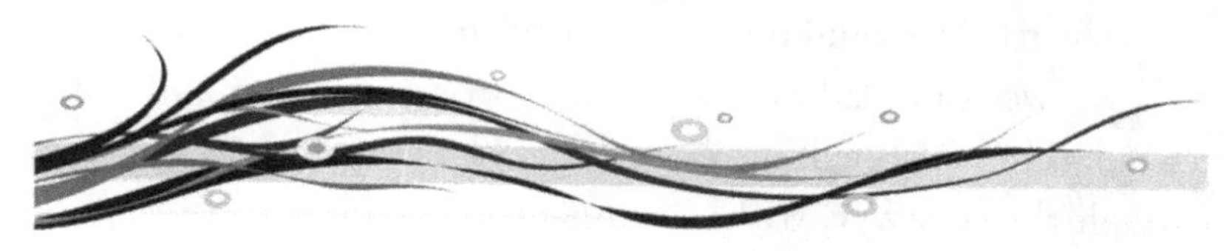

He'd gotten the ominous phone call at 11:09 a.m. It came from the patrol division's sterile-voiced administrative assistant. Short and not very sweet, the message still rattled around in Westfield's head.

Be in Captain Henley's office at twelve o'clock sharp.

Westfield had spent the next forty-one-minute journey to the station brooding. No question his boss had heard about his poking into the disappearance of those kids. He checked watch: 12:10. Ordered in, but now made to wait on a bench outside the captain's office like a schoolchild sent to see the headmaster. The last time he'd sat here, it hadn't gone well.

He rubbed his chin, eyes roving across the newly renovated offices of the admin building—all whites and grays. Sour-faced officers and stressed-out administrative assistants shuffled this way and that, noses buried in open case files. Westfield hated the downtown office. His office was a patrol car, and he liked the isolation it provided. If he didn't like the scenery, he drove somewhere and changed it. But most of all, no one bugged him in the car. Here, in the office, a guy couldn't take two steps before having to explain himself to some fake smile-wearing admin shark with a tie wedged under his Adam's apple, or one of those jerks from internal, always looking down their noses at everyone who wasn't on cannibal duty.

The door to the captain's office cracked open, and a voice that sounded like pebbles grinding beneath a rubber-soled shoe called out from inside.

"Westfield, get in here."

"Damn." Westfield turned the corner and pushed the frosted glass inset door open, taking a tentative step inside. "Ah, you wanted to see me, Captain?"

Henley sat in his large chair, sagging veined jowls framing tired sunken eyes. To Westfield, he resembled a large brown toad perched on a log. "Shut the door an' take a seat," he croaked, motioning to the chairs across from his desk.

Westfield closed the door, turned to sit, and stopped, his eyes landing on the form of Lieutenant Alvin Corley seated in the corner, one leg tossed casually over the other like some playboy on holiday. A jolt of panic-laden déjà vu shot through him.

Just like the last time he jammed me up.

"What's he doing here?" Westfield said, the sinking feeling in his stomach deepening.

Corley smirked. "Sit down, *Officer*."

A wave of toxic hate burned its way through Westfield's chest. He considered a lot of people useless assholes, but Corley took the cake. Maybe it was the undeservedly cocky attitude, or the smug look of superiority he always wore, or the fact Westfield had ten years of experience on him, and the guy still had no respect. Of course, it was more likely the career-altering incident a decade ago when Corley stuck a knife in Westfield's back to save himself. Down into his bones, Westfield hated Corley. *Wouldn't piss on him if he was on fire,* he thought.

Captain Henley motioned to the seat again. "Sit down, Derrick. Don't make this ugly."

Westfield gave one last smoldering glance at Corley before sitting across from the captain—a man he once respected. A few years Westfield's senior, Captain Henley, was a good cop, a good man. But after years of promotional ladder climbing, he now seemed little more than a disconnected bureaucrat who had forgotten his way. He'd lost touch with the grit and grime and desperation of the job and traded it for a big salary, admin hours, and a soft leather chair.

The silence deepened, all eyes boring a hole into Westfield's flushed face. He shrugged, tossing his hands in the air with a chuckle. "Look, I'm not blowing anybody until someone at least buys me dinner first."

"Captain." Corley cleared his throat. "This is exactly what I was referring to. A complete and total lack of regard for authority."

"No, Corley," Westfield shot back. "Just a complete and total lack of regard for *your* authority."

"Westfield." The captain's clipped bark caught his attention. The toad's fat face quivered. "Shut up and listen for a moment."

Westfield offered his best *eat shit* grin and raised his eyebrows. "I'm all ears, sir."

"You're suspended."

Westfield sat there, mouth agape, anger quenched. He looked to Corley, still wearing that damn smirk, and back to Henley again.

"For what?" Westfield asked.

"Interference in an official investigation, insubordination, failure to adhere to departmental standard operating procedure."

"When did I break SOP?"

Corley grunted. "Notice he didn't argue with the first two."

"And why is this cocksucker sitting in on this?" Westfield jabbed a finger in the lieutenant's direction. "He's in the detective bureau. He's got nothing to do with patrol."

"Remember the part about meddling in an official investigation?" Corley said.

"How was I meddling?" Westfield kept his eyes on the captain.

Henley leaned in across the desk. "Derrick, you were involved in a hit and run. You took it personally. Started digging where you shouldn't have and muddying the water for our guys. We can't have that. Remember your position and stay in your lane. That's an order."

Westfield swallowed hard.

"One week, no pay," the captain said.

"A week? For that? Captain—" Westfield started.

"Yeah, a week." Henley interrupted. "Keep your shield and weapon, but you're done poking around this case. Understand?" Henley eyed him.

Westfield said nothing and looked at his lap.

"You'll be glad to know Corley's guys wrapped the Mākaha investigation. Gangs fighting over turf."

The fan squeaked in the corner, dust-covered blades failing to move the stillness in the room.

"Captain, you can't believe that," Westfield said. "Mākaha has never had a gang problem."

"It does now," the captain croaked.

"And the Bodhi kid who was kidnapped during my crash?" Westfield asked.

"The kidnapping was never verified, but yes, there's a good chance it's the same groups. Turf war. Anything goes." Henley sat back and shrugged.

"Okay." Westfield stood from his chair, swinging his arms. "So, this is what? Friggin' amateur hour at the PD? That's what you're saying? Make it go away, so the stats look good?"

"Okay, smart ass. You just got two weeks with no pay. You want more?" Henley lumbered out of his chair, belly heaving, and placed his palms on the desk. "You're a good cop, but you never knew when to keep your mouth shut, and right now, you're on thin ice."

"Great, that's great," Westfield said.

"Look, I'm doing you a favor 'cause we came along together," Captain Henley said between strained breaths. "Don't make me regret leaving you with your badge and gun."

Lieutenant Corley's smirk dripped with unconcealed pleasure.

"Are you receiving me, *Officer* Westfield?" Captain Henley said. "Disregard this order, and it's your ass."

"Whatever you say, *sir*," Westfield said with a dramatic bow.

The shaking gelatinous scowl on Henley's face turned purple. "Get the *hell* out of my office. I don't want to see your face again for at least two wee—"

The door slammed behind Westfield, Henley's words cut short, the frosted glass window rattling. Westfield crossed the lobby and made for the stairs without a word. He hit the push bar on the door to the stairwell with enough force to slam it against the wall. There was bad juju, and then there was this horseshit, and he was up to his eyeballs in it.

CHAPTER 22

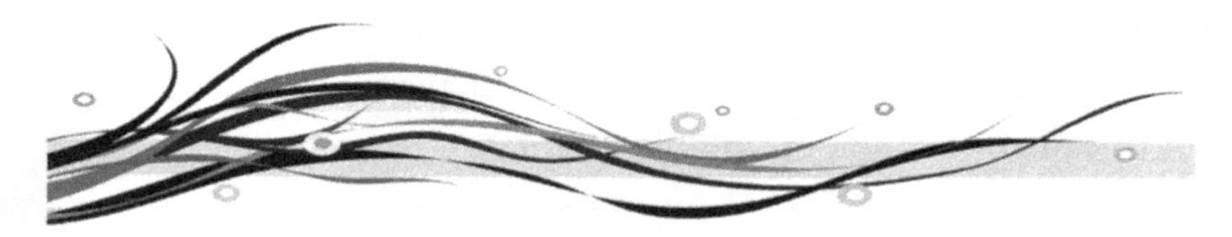

Tal Alvarez dragged one of his injured Strykers into *the box* and dumped him onto a cot next to Dr. Kingsfeld, who stood at one of the stations, peering through a microscope.

"Injuries?" Kingsfeld asked without looking up.

"Multiple fractures, possible internal bleeding," Alvarez said. "There are others, too. On their way."

Kingsfeld looked to the injured soldier. "He can stay right where he is."

Alvarez limped back to the door to help two other men from his team into the room, both nursing injuries. He directed them to separate cots and looked to Dr. Kingsfeld. "What can I do?"

"I need to know what happened," Kingsfeld said, preparing a nearby incubation chamber with a few jabs at its display.

"The Project S.H.R.E.D. asset happened," Alvarez said.

The doctor stopped prodding at the console. "The little girl?"

Alvarez tensed at the insulting insinuation. "Yes. The *little girl.* She's escaped. We tried to stop her."

"Fascinating," Kingsfeld said. "I've tracked her progress since she came in. What I could do with her DNA. Maybe the captain will let me tinker with it soon."

"You don't seem concerned she broke out of containment," Alvarez said. "And was strong enough to take my men apart."

"Should I be? Her levels are off the charts. By sheer accident, she's producing quantifiable results you and your team can't even come close to matching, yet." Dr. Kingsfeld chuckled. "Not to mention she's a hybrid of an orca and a teenage girl, two of the most fierce, unpredictable creatures on the planet. Nothing on this Earth can control something like that."

"Can you help or not?" Alvarez said.

"Of course, I can help." Kingsfeld gave Alvarez a dismissive glance. "I've done some work on an enhancement booster. Strange coincidence, I just received approval to test it on your team, don't you think?"

Alvarez watched as Dr. Kingsfeld approached the wounded Stryker lying on the cot and pressed an auto-injector to his shoulder.

"What does it do?" Alvarez said.

"Reactivates dormant elements of the mutation. Like an immunity boost but for injury. Due to your enhanced biology, your body with heal much faster. When you and your team get injured, it should help." He motioned to the nearest wounded Stryker. "Here, help me get him in the incubator."

Alvarez complied, then watched as the doctor worked. As much as the man was a high-brow asshole, he knew his stuff.

"In about six hours, he'll be right as rain," Kingsfeld said.

"Good. The others, too?"

"They'll have to wait for their turn in the incubator, but yes." Dr. Kingsfeld said, then nodded to Alvarez's noticeable limp. "And you?"

"A twisted knee. It's fine."

"Here." Kingsfeld grabbed a second auto-injector. "You won't need the incubator, but this should help." He pressed the device to Alvarez's shoulder, and a *snap-hiss* followed.

Alvarez grunted his thanks, a little bewildered at Dr. Kingsfeld's friendliness. He limped out of the box, stopping briefly to give assurances to his wounded brothers. As he shuffled into the corridor, a stone of doubt grew in his stomach. *Is Kingsfeld simply a doctor, invested in keeping the United States' best men in fighting shape?* he thought. *Or is he some mad scientist?* The more he considered it, the more the Stryker program felt like a modern Frankenstein retelling.

Alvarez hobbled down the corridor and found the pain in his knee lessened with each step. He rubbed at his eyes, pushing back with the heels of his palms, willing the mounting feeling of confusion and anxiety inside to recede. By the time he hit the stairs, the limp was gone.

"Maria, Tal Jr., Christopher, Kimmie, Vigo, and … and …" Alvarez chanted. "Maria, Tal Jr., Christopher, Kimmie, Vigo, and … *come on, damn you.*" He balled his fists, walking faster, no longer knowing where he was going. His ten-month-old baby girl was the light of his life.

So why in the hell couldn't he remember her name?

Jager stepped into his stateroom, nestled in close proximity to the bridge, and pulled the door shut. The small space contained a bed, a desk, a small sink, and a mirror. He preferred this chamber to the one on the third deck, adorned with all the amenities and extras of a high-end hotel room. Jager didn't care much for luxury or pomp. He'd never sought rank for show or prestige. He followed a single purpose pressed upon him by his father, whether he wanted it or not: find the distant, unattainable frontier of human evolution and discover a way to smash through it.

He stepped across to the thin twin mattress adorned with crisp sheets folded tight as a drum. He unbuttoned his shirt with marked precision, removed it, folded it once, then laid it across the bed. Jager faced the sink, placed his hands on the narrow rim, and stared at his hardened reflection. The inset lights above highlighted the tips of twisted scars that peaked over his shoulders. Every time he moved, the taught pull of keloid tissue crisscrossing the entire surface of his back dragged his mind to a time of pain and fear. Of being nine years old, standing on the threshold of his father's smoke-filled study. He'd just stood there, shuffling on the spot, heart beating in double time. He watched as his father took another long drink of schnapps, the ice in the glass clinking as he set the glass back perfectly centered on the stone coaster.

"Father?" he called to the ominous silhouette in the darkroom.

Without a word, the man lifted a single finger, a gesture young Alric knew all too well. One more unsolicited outburst would get him at best verbally abused or at worst lashed. So, he stood where he was, hands trembling as he held the two sheets of paper. His father took another sip of his drink and adjusted his grip on the periodical pinched between pale fingers. After a moment, he'd rolled his neck and sighed.

"What is it you want?" he said, in his glottal German accent.

"Father, I have what you asked for." Alric's voice was thin, wavering.

"Are you sure?" his father asked.

Alric regarded his list, checking each item.

"Well? Are you sure or not, boy?"

"Yes, Father. I have it here."

The shadow extended a hand.

With slow, intrepid steps, Alric approached the cracked brown leather recliner, his breath held through the smoke-filled haze. He extended the papers to his father, waiting with hands clasped at his waist. An eternity seemed to pass.

A stream of air whistled from his father's lips. "Failure. Again. I suppose it shouldn't come as a surprise."

"Father, I recorded the items in your catalog like you wanted."

"Did you now?" his father said, the tone warning of thinning patience. "Then why is it incomplete? Numbers sixty-seven and two hundred and fifty-four are not here."

"Yes, sir. But I couldn't find them."

An exasperated sigh, like wind hissing through a slit balloon, wheezed from his father's lungs, his hands dropping to his lap. "Alric, you can have excuses, but you can't have results as well. I obviously can't trust you with even the simplest of tasks."

"I'm sorry, Father." Alric's eyes filled with tears.

His father's face become a scowl. "That's right. Cry about it. Like a baby." He'd turned his eyes to the second sheet of paper, his hard gaze taking in the simple crayon-drawn picture with two stick figures holding hands next to a house beneath a sunlit sky. The words, *I love you, Father,* scrawled in near illegible child script at the top of the page.

With military precision, his father sat forward and tapped the picture with his index finger. "What is this?"

"I made you a picture," Alric mumbled.

"You did what?"

"I—"

His father jumped to his feet, his hand shooting out like a striking viper, and snagged the front of Alric's shirt. As his father lifted him from the floor, Alric had barely been able to keep his balance, tottering on tiptoe.

"And this is what you believe to be a good use of your time, boy?" His father spat. "Drawing pictures?"

Young Alric felt the all-too-familiar tingle in his shorts.

"Well, is it?"

The slap came hard and fast across Alric's face.

"No sir," Alric cried, his knees buckling.

His father kept a firm grip with one hand and, with the other crushed the simple drawing. "You created this childish nonsense. Now make it go away." He'd shoved the balled paper in young Alric's face.

"No!" Alric cried, tears streaming down his face.

"Eat it," his father shouted, grabbing his face.

Alric obeyed and his father shoved the paper ball down his throat. But he'd gagged, unable to swallow the jagged bolus.

"Even in this, you defy me," his father shouted, then dragged him by his shirt to the rollback desk. Shoved against it, Alric knew what was to come. He'd felt his father's fingers pull at the neck of his shirt, the buttons popping, the garment tearing free.

"No, Father, please," Alric shrieked. "I'm sorry. I did my best."

"Your best isn't good enough. Your best is an embarrassment to me. Perfection is what I want." He'd pulled open a drawer and lifted out the worn leather strop, clamped his hand around the boy's thin neck, and forced him face-first against the desk. "Failure will not be tolerated."

A knock sounded at the door.

Jager jerked to his senses, the old horrors receding from his mind. He took a moment, then cleared his throat. "What is it?"

"Captain, you're needed on the bridge."

"Five minutes," Jager said, then turned his gaze back to the small mirror before him and listened to the retreating steps. He stared at his worn reflection, the visage of a man possessed of a singular purpose. Reaching for the drawer, his hand closed around the cool leather coil. He returned his cold blue eyes to meet the stare of his own furious reflection—a likeness so damn much like the devil who raised him.

I am on the cusp of greatness, the evolution of the human genome taken in directions no one, not even Father, could have anticipated, he thought. This was his opportunity to best the man whose shadow loomed so darkly over him. To prove the old bastard wrong by taking the man's cherished life's work further than he'd ever dreamed possible. And yet, failure still haunted Jager. Sasha, the most powerful living weapon the world had ever seen, not only escaped, possibly even into the waiting arms of Sentry, but she had also stolen vital secrets related to Project S.H.R.E.D. Secrets that could destroy him.

"Not acceptable. You hear me?" Jager spat at the furious face in the mirror. The strop cracked over his shoulder and into his upper back, causing Jager to grit his teeth. He struck himself repeatedly, willing the swelling pain to relieve him of his imperfection. "Failure will not be tolerated," he said through clenched teeth. Dots of blood speckled the strop as Jager raised it to strike himself again. "*Eat it.*"

CHAPTER 23

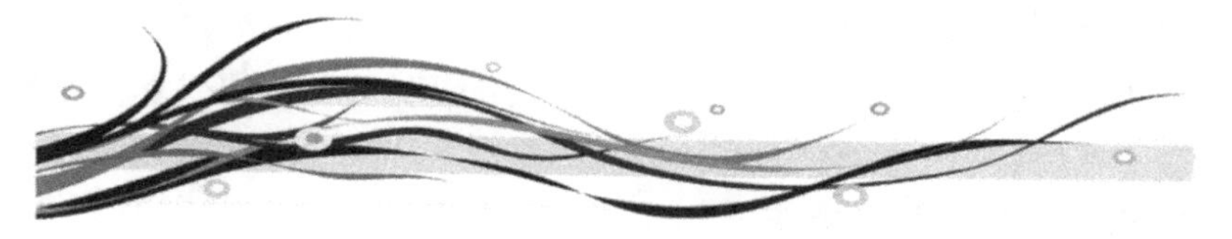

Murong pulled a pair of slim wireframe readers from his shirt pocket. He unfolded them, wiped the lenses with a microfiber cloth, and slipped them over the bridge of his nose. He pulled over the stack of data printouts from the short table next to his seat and scanned the scores of various graphs, tables, and figures detailing their most recent findings on Sasha's condition.

"Simply incredible," he said.

His dark eyes flicked up as the girl stirred on the modified cot. A gentle mist of water cascaded across her skin, and for the first time, he was struck by her youth. His own daughter would be Sasha's age about now … if she were alive. Murong pressed away the thought. *Now is not the time to entertain such notions of familial fantasy*. His was a purpose much more critical to the fate of the world. Yet still, sitting here staring at Sasha, something stirred in his chest.

He looked back to the file in his hands, his index finger gently tracing a path along the lines of text and numbers. He had to remind himself to breathe. Never in his life had he seen such indications of power in a living creature. The void energy had made her more biologically advanced than anything the world had ever seen. *Even now, her evolution may not yet be complete*, he thought. *Who knows what she may eventually become if she were nurtured to stand up for causes already rooted deep in her heart? The ocean. The Earth. The future of all living things. Who would dare to oppose us in fighting for what was right?*

On the specialized cot, modified to accommodate her new form, Sasha winced. Murong set aside the top printout in favor of another. As he raised it, the attending doctor, Katrina Besom, entered the room.

A young, bronzed-skin woman with noble features and an air of absolute professionalism, Dr. Besom was one of Sentry's most avid supporters and had the stalwart reputation of coming through for his people when the chips were down.

"Ah, Zhou. I'm glad to see you here. I'm updating her chart now." Dr. Besom swiped her finger across the screen of a tablet computer.

Murong stood. "And how is our guest?"

Dr. Besom cocked her head. "See for yourself." She handed the tablet over and turned to the sink to wash her hands.

Murong nodded. "Vitals look strong. Is she still in any danger?"

"Well, it doesn't seem that way at this point, but Sasha experienced a significant amount of trauma. She's more than a little banged up but seems to have stabilized after resting a while." Dr. Besom referenced the tablet. "She sustained a concussion, multiple contusions and fourteen penetration wounds from small arms fire and shrapnel, and a small shark bite, not to mention the multi-pronged injection sites on her shoulder and thigh."

"Injection sites? Please elaborate," Murong said.

"I can only assume Jager tried to capture her first since she shows strikes from two tranquilizer darts," Dr. Besom said. "Heavy-duty stuff, too. When that failed, he had his people open fire on her."

"And she took fourteen projectile wounds in the process?" Murong said. "Copper jacket fragments and splash damage, I'm assuming?"

"No, Zhou." Dr. Besom shook her head. "I'm talking about direct hits. At least ten of them. Those security teams are well trained. When they open fire, they hit their target."

Murong held a hand to his chin. "Ten direct hits."

"That's right. Any normal person would probably be dead five times over."

"Have you determined how she survived?" Murong asked.

"Well," Dr. Besom shrugged. "There's this." She reached over and pulled a paperclip from the top of the file on the table. With a flick of her wrist, she tossed it next to Sasha's body on the cot. It landed and began to shudder and scoot across the cot away from her. It reached the edge of the cot, flipped over the edge, and fell tinkling against the floor.

Murong bent to grab the paperclip. This time he flicked the paperclip onto the girl's still sleeping form, but before it could land, it changed direction, hovered back into the air, and sailed onto the floor on the other side of the bed.

"What's that remind you of?" Dr. Besom said, a gleam in her eye.

Murong looked at her. "I'd say it mirrors the behavior of oppositely charged magnetic forces."

"Correct. Now check this out." She gloved up and gingerly pulled on a sagging bandage. As she eased one corner free, something fell from the bandage, bounced off the cot, and dropped to the floor. Besom bent and secured the object using a pair of clamps, raising it to Murong.

"A mushroomed bullet?" Murong said.

"That's right. Look." She pulled on several other bandages, and other rounds, and pieces of copper jacket fell free of the dressing. "She's emitting some sort of low yield magnetic field. That's why

I didn't try to remove any of the projectiles though some of them are close to the surface. After a few X-rays, I noticed something strange."

"Oh?"

Dr. Besom pulled free a bandage on Sasha's shoulder.

Murong watched as a piece of glistening copper jacket slid from the wound, the fissure in the skin sealing before his eyes.

"The bullet fragments are moving back up the wound channels," Dr. Besom continued. "Whatever force is pushing them out appears to also attenuate the potency of incoming projectiles as long as they have certain metallic properties. Nothing penetrated deeper than an inch, so her vitals weren't affected."

"Stunning," Murong said. "Incredible. Imagine the applications for this if we could figure out how to apply it to the medical field?"

"The medical field, yes, but also the battlefield." She gave him a wary glance.

"Naturally. It would alter the course of human history," Murong said, unable to conceal the smile breaking across his face.

Dr. Besom folded her arms. "You mean to monetize it, don't you?"

Murong sobered, scrunching his eyebrows. "Not fair."

"But it's true."

Murong straightened his shirt, feigning injury. "Sentry has to be properly funded in order to carry out its mission."

"Come, let her rest," Dr. Besom said. "She's healing at an accelerated rate. My guess is she should be fine in another four to six hours."

"Truly?" Murong said, struggling to take his eyes off his newly discovered miracle.

He followed Dr. Besom from the room and pulled the thumb

drive the girl brought in around her neck from his pocket. He rubbed the device between his forefinger and thumb. She'd called it evidence. If it was evidence of Jager's activities, their research, it could be a powerful weapon against Murong's old adversary. The time had come to find out.

The gasps came in short spasmodic bursts, his quivering lungs struggling to take in a full measure of breath. Stretched wide, Max's eyes jerked left and right at the faceless people in white lab coats milling about, each operating independently of the others as if endowed with some cosmic preprogrammed purpose. His vision distorted at the edges, made worse by the sterile artificial lights overhead. Max gagged on the rubbery brace working its way farther back between his teeth and into his throat.

One of the lab coats stopped and turned toward him. Her face partially hidden behind a barrier mask, Max could see the faint look of fear in her eyes.

"Helg meh," Max slurred. "Helg meh, pleasch."

The woman swallowed and turned away, back to arranging instruments on a metal tray.

Max flexed his arms and legs against thick leather straps but couldn't move an inch.

"Is the injector cradle ready?" one of the lab coats said, looking to the others.

"It is. Primed and ready," another replied.

Max's stomach roiled. The room moved out of sync with his vision. *Is this a nightmare? Am I dreaming?* A stone sank deep into the pit of his stomach. Memories of his friends, Sasha and Bodhi, his mom and dad, brothers Sam and Cody, plans for a future all swirled together.

"Cradle is primed. Lock it in," someone said.

Pushing against him on all sides, the cool sterile surfaces of the cradle made contact with his bare skin, causing him to flinch. Max squirmed, his limbs cupped in cylindrical-shaped clamps, a brace of pads pressed against his chest and abdomen.

"Power it on and prepare to initiate injection phase."

A machine buzzed with electrical rhythm.

Max's heart hammered against his ribcage as he thrashed and yanked at his restraints. "Helg meh. Helg meh. Helg! Hellllgggg!"

"Stand clear. Initialize."

Max's eyes bulged, a garbled scream pouring from his gagged mouth as a thousand micro-needles pierced his flesh. He shuddered, his muscles spasming, as the machine bracing his limbs hummed louder.

"Serum delivery is complete."

"Good work, people. Remove the braces and reassess the subject."

Max moaned, tears streaming from the corners of his eyes. His body shook with violent tremors, rattling the cradle in which he lay. His gasps came in awkward, spasmed coughs. Max's body sank into a sea of pain that felt as though every nerve ending were set aflame with a white-hot lance.

"Sir," one of the blurry-faced lab coats said. "The subject's vitals are within acceptable tolerance levels. Removing the cradle braces now."

Repeated clunks echoed in Max's ears. He tried to call out for someone to help him, but the sound died in his throat, a whimpered gurgle.

"We're on the clock, people. Let's move," a voice called out.

Beneath him, the wheels of the cart unlocked and began

rolling. Out into the hallway, attendants stood on either side of the gurney ushering it forward down the dull gray painted hall awash with artificial white light. Max groaned, unable to move, unable to speak, his consciousness unable to focus on anything but the pain.

"We've got a short window here. Unstrap him and get him into the second tube in containment one."

"But sir, that's where the other one is."

"Captain's orders. Get him in containment one, now."

A host of hands unstrapped Max from the gurney, removed the gag, then lifted him and passed him to two individuals in crinkled silver bio-suits. A green light on the wall buzzed on, and a door slid open with a hiss.

Max squirmed against the vice-like grip of the faceless people. "What're you doing to me? Why are you doing this?"

With another buzz, the light shifted to red, and a second door in the far wall slid open. The silent foil-suited figures trudged forward, dragging Max into the shimmering green glow beyond.

Max was dumped onto a hard metallic surface. With a mechanical whine, it rose alongside two large tanks filled with glimmering green bubbles rising in lazy arcs toward the surface. One of the silver suits tried to pull a hose-fed mask over Max's face.

With a cry, Max clawed at the rubber. "No."

"You're going in the tank," the man said. "Now, you can go in with an oxygen mask, or you can drown."

Still shaking, Max kept his hands clamped to the rubber mask.

"Your choice, kid," the man said.

Max's posture sagged, and he let his arms drop away.

The mask was pulled tight, and he was pushed into the tank. The warm water caressed his tired skin and lapped at his mask-covered face. "Wait." Max reached out an arm, his voice muffled by the mask. "Please."

With a *shunk*, the hatch in the top of the tank slid shut, and the faceless silver-suited men were gone. He drifted in the tank, the sound of his own breathing loud in his ears. A bright light from below pulled his attention away from the hatch and hopes of escape. There for the first time, his burning eyes landed upon a thrumming multi-sided orb sat anchored with straps at the back of the room. The object shimmered with pulsating waves of emerald light.

The water around him seemed to thicken, his world bending, his grip on reality dwindling. Max looked away. That's when he noticed the two identical tanks across from him. Inside one, the dormant form of a full-grown killer whale, sedated and intubated, floated amidst a curtain of bubbles.

In the other, Max could just make out the form of a man, though he didn't seem to have a breathing hose. Still, Max felt a pang of recognition in his gut. He strained his eyes against the strobing light to get a better look at the familiar form.

"Bodhi?" Max said, his voice foreign, a broken growl inside the mask.

The creature with various odd protrusions, yet with his friend's familiar gangly form, stirred and turned its elongated, eyeless, black face toward him.

A scream of terror erupted from Max's throat.

"No, Bodhi! What did they do?" he cried, clawing at the slick glass walls of the tank. And as he did, he saw the color of his own skin, now turned a terrible rubbery gray.

CHAPTER 24

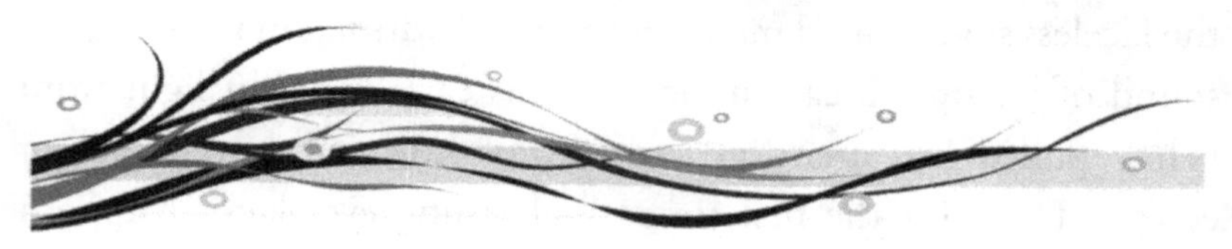

With each jab, cross, and hook, the mounting stress of an undeniably crazy week bled from Westfield's tension-stricken shoulders. The heavy canvas bag, dingy with sweat and use, shook and wobbled under the force of each blow. Adjusting his footing, he bounced to the side, ducked, then rose to strike again and again. Sweat soaked his shirt and dotted the hardwood floor.

Physical exertion, while normally therapeutic, now seemed the only way for him to blow off the dangerous levels of mounting pressure within him. He had to keep from losing his cool. The conversation the day before in Captain Henley's office left him in a funk and produced nothing but a fitful night's sleep. He couldn't swallow it. After all the years of training and indoctrination from the department, where being a bulldog and sticking with a lead until you saw it through was generally rewarded, now he was expected to let this one go because it ruffled the wrong feathers.

He sidestepped with a swear, then pounded the bag with another fast double-jab-cross-hook combination.

Sasha Kino, a nineteen-year-old girl, was still missing. Could there have been an accident, and she simply drowned? Sure, but the girl was a champion surfer. Was drowning still considered likely anymore? But to also have the kid on the bike, Bodhi Li, and the other guy, Max Anderson, also go missing felt off. Not to mention, it all occurred the same night as the Navy's satellite crash. But none of it ever hit the news. All of it stunk to high heaven and brought one unsettling word to mind: *coverup*.

Westfield's phone burst to life playing the theme to *Miami Vice*. He landed one final four-punch combination with a grunt of exertion, then shuffled over to see the caller ID. The name on the screen read *Gordon Kino*.

"Damn," Westfield muttered, then pulled at the Velcro strap of his boxing gloves with his teeth. He really didn't want to talk to Gordon right now. What was he going to say? That he didn't know anything more about what happened to Sasha? That she was exposed to something dangerous? That he was never really assigned the case to begin with and was now suspended? He pulled the second glove off and tossed them both on the floor next to his gym bag.

The ringing stopped.

An older man with a graying beard and the frame of an old-school bodybuilder approached from off to Westfield's left and casually leaned against the wall. Before Westfield could acknowledge the man, Gordon rang again. *The poor guy must be in a panic*, Westfield thought. Looking at the bearded gentleman, he raised an index finger and picked up the phone with a sigh. "Westfield."

"Derrick, it's Gordon."

"Gordon, hey. I was meaning to get back to you. How are you holding up, buddy?"

"I'm uh …" The man's voice shook. "Not good. Have you seen the news?"

Westfield felt himself flush. No. Surely the PD didn't send out the same nonsense they pushed on him.

"Ah, no. What's going on?"

"They're saying Sasha and her friends were kidnapped. That

it's gang-related? Is that true?" Gordon's voice cracked.

"Gordon, listen. You know how the news is. It's all about what's sensational."

"Are you saying it's not true?" Gordon said.

"I'm saying Mākaha doesn't have a gang problem. I'm sure there's a rational explanation for Sasha's disappearance."

"Does it involve kidnapping?"

Westfield pursed his lips. "There's no evidence to prove kidnapping right now, Gordon."

"Yeah, okay." Gordon's voice wavered. "I'm sorry, Derrick. I'm sort of freaking out over here."

"Hey, you don't need to apologize for anything, brother. I'd be a wreck if Janie disappeared and I didn't know what happened. Keep your head up. We'll find her. Okay?"

"Yes. Okay. Thank you, Derrick."

No problem, buddy. I'll keep you posted if I find anything out."

"I would appreciate it."

Westfield said goodbye, ended the call, then wiped little beads of sweat from his forehead with his shirt. He tossed the phone on his gym bag and looked at Curtis, the owner of the gym.

"Hey, Curtis. Sorry. Need something?" Westfield asked.

The man shifted, the musculature of a physique that must really have been something thirty years ago still visible beneath his shirt. "Just listening to you going to town back here and wondering if you're going to destroy more of my equipment."

"You know I won't leave you hanging," Westfield said.

Curtis gave a wave of his hand. "I think we both forget there's a former Army boxing champ pounding away on these bags every week. Only so much they can take."

Westfield nodded and wiped his face and neck with a towel.

"That boxing champ stuff was a lifetime ago."

"Not as long as you think. He's still in there."

Westfield shrugged with a wry smile. "Well, if you see him, tell him to lose some damn weight."

"I'll tell that to the owner of this gym as well." Curtis laughed. "Just came over to tell you this month your membership is up for renewal. No rush."

"Oh, right. Thanks. I'll renew."

"I got you." Curtis waved him off. "Next six months are on me."

"What? Why?" Westfield said, still trying to catch his breath.

"Cause you need the stress relief, and I like having good cops in my gym."

"You don't need to do that."

"I know I don't, but you guys don't get enough love these days."

"Mmm." Westfield glanced at his friend. "Well, thank you, Curtis. I mean that."

"No sweat, my man. I'll see you 'round." Curtis disappeared around the corner into one of the various aisles of glistening chrome weight machines.

Westfield gathered his gloves and wrist wraps, then stuffed them all into a musty gym bag in need of a good airing out. What was he going to do for a week officially suspended from work? Letting things go just wasn't the Westfield way. He shook his head, chuckling to himself. *Guess admin's gonna have to put their foot in my ass. Again.*

CHAPTER 25

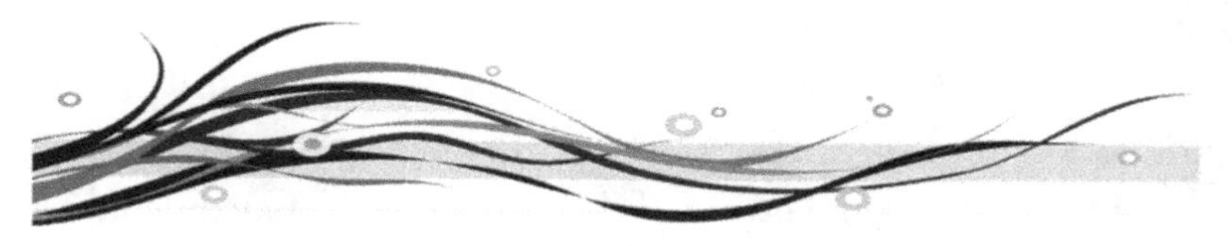

Sasha sat bolt upright and swiped at the nearby woman, sending her crashing into a cart of medical tools. An instant later, two anxious-eyed mercenaries rushed into the room. Vaulting from the table, Sasha landed poised for action, the clawed fingers of her hands splayed open, her teeth bared. "No one else is going to touch me. Understand? I'm done with the tests."

Murong stood from his chair just feet away. "Gentlemen," he said, his voice calm, each word measured. "Miss Kino has been through a lot. Please give her some time to adjust to her surroundings."

The mercenaries shared a look and backed out of the room.

"And you might want to be careful with Doctor Besom," Murong said. "She's the one looking after you."

On the floor amidst a bottle of spilled iodine and a stack of scattered gauze pads lay the woman to whom Murong referred, still on her side, her hands raised to her face.

Sasha flexed her knees, ready to spring into action at the first sign of danger. She glared at Murong, her chest heaving, her gaze bouncing between him and Doctor Besom.

"Sasha, you are safe here," Murong said. "We have done you no harm, and you are free to leave at any time. We simply desired to assess your condition and help you recover from your injuries after your ordeal."

"Who's we?" Sasha said.

Murong opened his arms and flashed a smile. "I am Zhou Murong, and you are with Sentry's critical response team aboard my private research vessel, *The Argo*.

"Sentry." She looked to Murong. "I know you. The fringe eco-preservation group with questionable methods."

"Says the young woman who rammed a Russian whaling vessel with her family's yacht in order to stop them," Murong said with raised eyebrows. "We are no different, willing to do whatever is necessary to protect Earth's innocents."

"And you're the billionaire who runs it?" Sasha asked.

"The one and only," Murong gave a little bow.

"No more tests," Sasha said, almost blurting the words out.

"If you feel strongly about it." Murong gave a nod. "No more tests."

Sasha glanced around the room. "And I can leave whenever I want."

Murong bobbed his head again. "You may, though I should wish you to stay. If only to hear me out."

Sasha took another look around the small medical bay, her focus stopping on the frozen form of Dr. Besom on the floor. Sasha exhaled. "You can get up. I won't hurt you." She turned back to Murong. "Or anyone else as long as I'm not treated like some caged zoo animal."

"Of course, Sasha," Murong said.

Dr. Besom slowly gathered her wits and grabbed some of the fallen items as she stood. "I'm a doctor," she said. "Will you trust me on something?"

Sasha studied the doctor but said nothing.

Dr. Besom bent and retrieved a sealed cup with a single pill inside from the floor. She extended it to Sasha. "You're changing, Sasha. Maybe still changing. Your current condition could be anywhere on the spectrum of that change. It could be finished. It could be just beginning. I'd like to try and stabilize the mutagenic factors in your blood until we can better understand them. Is that fair?"

Sasha eyed Dr. Besom's hand. "What's in the cup?"

"AMGR-760. Originally designed to stop the growth of abnormal cells such as cancer mutations. I think it could help you." She gave the cup a little shake.

"No tricks." Sasha looked at Murong.

"No tricks," Murong said. "Dr. Besom knows what she's doing. I'd trust her with my life."

Sasha took the cup. "Why am I here?" she said, tossing the pill back and swallowing it without water.

Murong pressed his palms together. "You must have a thousand questions, Sasha. Would you like to rest more first, or—"

"I'm ready now, thank you," Sasha said. "And I would appreciate direct answers."

Murong gave another gracious smile. "I understand," he said. "We rescued you after you fled from Captain Jager and his rogue special operations unit aboard *The U.S.S. Harbinger*.

"Rogue? What he's doing isn't official?" Sasha asked.

"No, and that may be what is most frightening about it. There is no oversight, no limit to what he's willing to do to achieve his goal of creating the perfect super-soldier. His vision has ties all the way back to his father's work in Nazi Germany."

"Go on," Sasha said.

"We are up to speed on everything, Sasha," Murong said. "We tracked the Department of Defense's Erebos probe as it entered Earth's atmosphere. We watched it via drone feed. Saw it take you under. I knew then the incident would have unexpected effects on you if you survived." He waved a hand in her direction.

"Understatement of the year," Sasha crossed her arms.

"We also knew Jager would lie to you. Try to weaponize your condition. We wanted to help. It's why I sent my frogmen aboard *The Harbinger* to warn you."

Sasha swallowed. The room hummed with the sound of engines, a constant churning vibration felt through every surface. "All right, let's say I buy you want to help me." Sasha looked to Dr. Besom and back to Murong. "Why put yourself, your vessel, and your crew at risk? Am I worth it?"

Murong pressed his thin lips together. "Sasha, look at you, what you are capable of. I couldn't let you become some mindless black ops soldier for an imperialist government."

Sasha's eyes narrowed. "Get to the point. What's your angle?"

"My angle," Murong said, opening his arms. "Sentry's cause is the cause of nature. For all creatures to survive and thrive in harmony in this our shared world. It is the responsibility—no, the *duty*, of individuals such as ourselves to stand for what is right."

Sasha scrunched her forehead. "And you use force to achieve those ends?"

"If we must," Murong said. "Humankind, though capable of greatness, has shown it is also adept at committing unimaginable atrocities in the name of progress. Force is sometimes necessary to stop these acts."

"But, what is it you people *actually* do?" Sasha asked, her gaze wandering around the lab.

Murong laughed. "That question is a bit more difficult. What we do is multi-faceted. Allow Dr. Besom to tend to your wounds, and I will personally give you a tour of our entire operation."

Sasha looked back at Dr. Besom and nodded. The doctor stepped closer, reaching with a gloved hand to remove the last of the bandages. As she did, small fragments of metal fell from the material and onto the cot. Sasha picked up one of the slivers of blood-speckled copper. "What is this?"

"Bullet fragments," Dr. Besom said.

Sasha's face slackened.

"You were shot, Sasha. At least ten times," Dr. Besom continued. "Look here." She directed Sasha's gaze to a bandage on her side. As she peeled it back, a fingernail-sized sliver of metal slid from the narrow wound and onto the bandage. Sasha watched as the lips of the wound found each other and sealed together, leaving only a small drop of crimson blood the doctor quickly wiped away with a gauze pad.

"I don't understand," Sasha said. "Shouldn't that have killed me? How is my body doing this?"

Murong spread his hands. "You're special, Sasha."

"We've determined you are emitting some sort of low yield magnetic field," Dr. Besom said. "It slowed the incoming bullets enough to save your life, and later, reject the projectiles that struck you, helping your already accelerated healing process to work even faster."

"What does it mean?" Sasha said.

Dr. Besom shrugged. "Well, you're not bulletproof, but you're more bulletproof than most people. That and you'll heal a hell of a lot faster, too."

"Rad," Sasha said.

Dr. Besom smiled. "I'll give you two a moment to talk," she said, then turned toward the door and, with a wink to Murong, stepped out into the corridor.

"I'm sure you have much to learn about your newfound abilities, but time is short," Murong said. "Maybe you will allow my team to help you—train you to use your powers effectively."

"To fight for Sentry." Sasha cut a glare at him. "You didn't want me to fight for Jager, but you want me to fight for you."

Murong gave an understanding dip of his head. "Not fight, Sasha. Defend."

"You're mincing words," Sasha said. "Why should I? For what? I don't owe you anything."

"You don't," Murong said. His look changed to one that was all business. "You mean to tell me you've never appreciated the causes my organization champions? You've never attended a Sentry rally or donated some of your hard-earned cash to help stop the tyranny humankind perpetrates against its fellow animals across the globe?"

Sasha shifted, suddenly uncomfortable. She had done those things. Murong knew it. Activities excused as a teenager's rebellious cause if it weren't for the fact it went much deeper for her. Sasha moved a ropy strand of black braid-like hair from her face. "Okay, you got me. But you're not going to try to control me. You hear me? Jager already made that mistake."

Murong bowed his head in a gesture of deep respect. "I wouldn't dream of anything so barbaric. I'm a businessman, Sasha. I'd rather propose an arrangement."

She pinched her lips. "What sort of arrangement?"

"The sort you benefit from." The enigmatic man checked his fingernails. After a moment, he turned to see her still staring at him. "Your mother is sick. Her cancer is terminal, is it not?"

Sasha clenched her teeth. "I don't see how my mother's health is any of your business."

"Your father wouldn't tell you this, but the insurance company, through his job, is hiking their premiums. He knows he can't afford that *and* put food on the table. He's going to have to drop certain coverages—and with it your mother's treatments."

"He wouldn't ..." Sasha's voice trailed off.

"*The Lorien*, Sasha. Without the boat, he can't afford her care anymore."

Sasha lowered her head. "You don't have to say it like that."

"It's the truth." Murong folded his hands. "Which is why I plan to cover your mother's treatments."

Sasha's head jerked up, tears pooling in her eyes. "What?"

"I'll pay for it. Until she's fully recovered."

"We might not be rich, but we do still have our pride, you know," Sasha said, fighting back the spark of hope Murong had just kindled in her heart.

"Of course, Sasha. I meant no disrespect. This would be no handout. Think of it as compensation for your work alongside Sentry fighting for causes that already lie deep in your heart. It's a win-win situation for you and your family."

Sasha let his words sink in. What did she have to lose? She couldn't help her family, not like this. She looked at the meandering bands of black and white covering her torso. "You said I'd be fighting for Sentry. Against who?"

"Captain Jager and his rogue special operations group, opponents of freedom and natural order, those who would savage the natural harmony of our planet. Together we'll face them all."

Sasha sat in the cot as the weight of the proposal hit her. "You're talking about fighting against the United States Navy's Special Projects Division. They'll destroy us."

"Not as easily as you might think." Murong stooped and grabbed a few remaining items from the floor. "Jager has much at his disposal, but it is limited. There's only so much support he can request without drawing too much attention to the illegal and unethical work he's doing. On top of that, Sentry uses advanced technology and guerrilla tactics, subterfuge, espionage. Rarely do we meet challenges head-to-head. We pick them apart one piece at a time. Plus, we have you—the most powerful biological weapon on the planet."

"I'm not sure I can control it," Sasha said, the screams of the men she'd killed ringing in her ears.

Murong took a step forward and touched her elbow. "You can, Sasha."

"I was afraid you'd say that." She clasped her hands to her chest, mulling the situation over. "I'll help you on two additional conditions."

"Name them," Murong said.

"You guarantee the safety of my family from reprisals, and you help me find and protect my friends Max and Bodhi."

"Tricky, but I'll do everything I can," Murong said. "Jager will not relent on his search for you. If anything, he will double down. He must have you to finish what he started." He raised the data drive collected from her when she first arrived.

"What's on it?" she asked, the breath caught in her chest.

"Enough," Murong said. "And I know just who to share it with. But what concerns me most is what Jager will try to do with your newly deformed genetic code. You've already seen his Strykers."

Sasha nodded.

"What he's doing may soon take a turn for the worse."

"Worse? How?"

Murong's features grew placid, his eyes far away. "Jager is playing god. And now he's in possession of the Erebos, which is still emitting dangerously high levels of morphic void energy, according to our data. I fear his next artificial leap forward may lead to something … quite monstrous."

CHAPTER 26

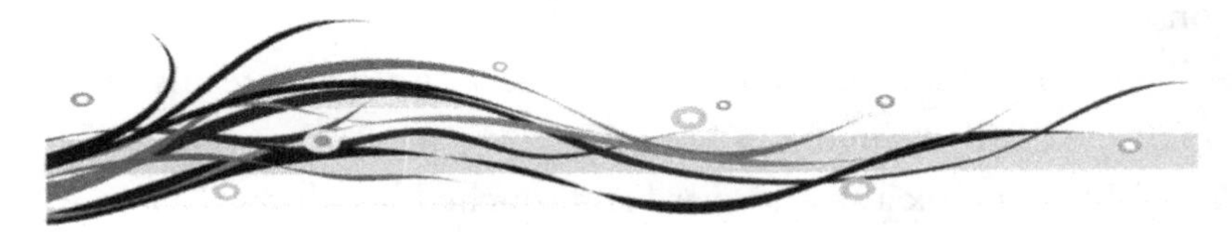

Hot black emptiness burned his eyes. He let out a huff of breath, warm against his bare chest, and worked his tongue back and forth inside the foreign form of his jaw. A wheezing itch tickled in his lungs, the feeling like he needed to cough. He felt sick down in his guts. He needed mother. Mother always took care of him when he was ill.

"Is he secure? I'm not getting close to him if he's not," a faint voice said.

"Don't be a coward. He's sedated. Look at him."

Bodhi turned his head, the blackness clearing only enough to reveal the gray outline of a shadow. A disturbed pool of inky liquid. The sickness swarmed in his brain, searing and smothering. *Not at home. Something's wrong. Where am I?* His brain struggled and strained for answers that wouldn't come.

More noises echoed from the shimmering pool of black. Outlines emerged, soft imprints of figures, standing or moving without color or definition. His eyes rolled, opening wide, unblinking. A shiver of pain rolled across his body. He flinched, his breathing quickening as cool gloved hands pressed something together around his neck with a snap and a chime.

"The collar is on."

"Read out is good to go, vitals are steady."

Bodhi tried to speak, to ask the voices what was happening, but only a wet gurgle emerged in his throat. His heart rate gained momentum. Frustration rising, Bodhi tilted his head up, the mass of bone and flesh connected to his neck, far too heavy to be his. He strained his voice to call out to the shadows flitting back and forth, dancing gray specters against the black.

"Wwhhaarrgg …"

A chill descended upon him at the sound. The movement in the room stopped, faces turning to stare. He pulled upward on the restraints, his arms shackled to the chair. Heart pounding faster, he suddenly jerked against the shackles, his right arm breaking free in a squall of snapping metal."

"Get back."

"Look out, he broke the restraint."

"Give him another injection of etorphine. Hurry."

"We did already—"

"Well, give him another, look at him."

Without warning, a needle slid into his left thigh, the muscles stinging with the force at which the fluid pushed into the tissue.

Why are they doing this? Why can't I remember?

"Mmuuwwhhaarrrggg!" Bodhi pulled his left arm, trying to free it, but his limbs ached, filled with an incredible heaviness. His head sunk forward, hot breath on his chest once again. Fear grew inside him, mixing with a burning hate for the shadows that gawked and gasped, his terror and fear pooling together in little gathering streams of misery and confusion.

"Make sure he's heavily sedated and secured at all times. Is everyone clear on that?"

"Yes, sir."

"Obviously, he's capable of snapping steel restraints. Triple up on them for now until we determine a better way."

"Sir, what about the collar? Can't it incapacitate him if we get in trouble?"

"We don't know yet. They had to firm it up and crank the voltage it can produce after the incident with the female."

Quivering, Bodhi shook as he pulled against the hands fastening his right arm to the chair again, but his strength had left him. The ghostly figures whispered and pointed, their hazy outlines bleeding into the charcoal black that filled his vision.

Fragments of memories, images of a different life, flashed in his head. Only the face of his mother could he see. Gentle, smiling.

"Mmmuuuvvvaaaarrr." A final ugly plea escaped him. And then he was gone, adrift in a dreamless void.

Four sharp raps on the door had Westfield on his feet in a flash. Winking the sleep from his eyes, he fumbled for his service weapon on the nightstand, a worn and beaten Springfield Armory 1911 operator model in matte black with tiny pinprick green night sights.

"Who is it?" he called out from the edge of his bedroom doorway.

He waited for an answer, a sound, anything that might betray the identity or purpose of the individual at his door. Another knock. Westfield swore. Nobody ever came to visit, and his buddies at the PD knew better than to come knocking this early in the morning.

He crossed the length of the hallway, weapon at the ready, snapped the lock, grabbed the handle, and sidestepped as he jerked open the door, leveling the Springfield at the man on his doorstep.

The fellow gave a squeak of terror, dropped a package at his feet, and turned to run. Westfield lunged forward and seized the man by the collar of his shirt. After a sharp glance in both directions down the breezeway, he gave the man's dirty shirt a twist.

"Pick it up," Westfield said.

Nodding and whimpering, the man licked his peeling lips and grabbed the package at his feet.

Westfield jerked him into the apartment and slammed the door shut with a *clunk*. He shoved the blithering man against the wall and placed the barrel of the pistol against his cheek. "Who are you? What do you want?"

"I ..." the man stuttered. "I'm nobody, man. A guy on the street offered me five hundred bucks to deliver this to an Officer Westfield, man. Meant no harm, bro. It was easy cash."

Westfield gave the man another shove. "What did the guy look like?"

"Who?" the man squawked.

"Santa Clause. Who do you think, genius? The guy who gave you this." Westfield grabbed the package and pushed it in the face of the terrified man.

"Uh, oh man, I'm not real good with that sort of stuff, man."

"Try," Westfield said, the words forced through clenched teeth.

"Uh, yeah, uh dude was like, he had like dark hair."

"That's it? That's what you can tell me? Are you stupid?" Westfield said, then shoved the package into the man's arms and stepped back, both hands now on the 1911.

The cowering man shrugged, the package clutched to his chest now wrinkled and distorted from his death grip.

Westfield composed himself. "Open it. If it blows up or something, you die first."

"Aww, man." The man's bony fingers pulled at the top of the package. "What kind of mess have I got myself into this time?"

"The serious kind," Westfield said. "Now open it."

"Aww, man. *Damn, man.*" The guy whimpered, squinting as he tore the top of the package open. He stood there for a moment, frozen stiff, eyes blinking.

"For the love of St. Peter, you really are as dumb as a bucket of hammers." Westfield sighed. "Pull out whatever is in there." He waved his pistol at the still-shaking man.

The man reluctantly reached his hand in and extracted a single microdata drive, extending it to Westfield in a trembling fist.

Westfield grabbed the drive from him. "That it?"

"Yeah, man, and a note." He extended a small slip of white paper. "I can go now?" He released a goofy laugh shook the package upside down.

Westfield glanced at the note.

Confidential. Eyes and ears everywhere. You know what to do.

"Anyone know you came here?" Westfield said to the cowering man.

"Naw, man, I'm over it, bro. I need a fix, man. Just wanna get high an forget all this, ya know?"

"No, I don't know." Westfield snarled. "Get out of my place, and if you ever come back, I'll shoot you in the face and feed you to the sharks."

The man gasped a short cry as he fumbled with the doorknob, flung the door open, and bolted from the apartment.

Westfield shut the door and re-engaged the deadbolt. He leaned against the frame with a sigh of relief and gave a hoarse chuckle, remembering the terrified look on the poor guy's face as he'd opened the package. Couldn't much blame him. Westfield looked again at the thin black data drive. *Why would someone send me a data drive?* He sure as hell wasn't stupid enough to plug this thing into his personal computer. A little field trip was in order.

An hour later, Westfield crossed the lobby of the Ewa Beach Public Library at full stride. Dressed in plain clothes, he still looked like a cop—it was a look that went much deeper than simple attire. Tactical style khaki BDU pants, a black 511 polo, and a pair of black and gray Salomons. Beneath his untucked shirt secure in a concealed Kydex holster sat the Springfield accompanied by his shield, a micro tac light, an extra magazine, and a Spyderco lock blade knife. They'd suspended him, but cops didn't take off days or leave work at work. They changed out of one uniform and into another, but the mindset stayed the same, twenty-four-seven, three-sixty-five until they either bit it on the job or dropped dead from years of critical stress. That was the job, and it didn't take breaks.

A quick survey of the quiet space revealed total privacy. Ewa Beach Public Library, a quaint place with nice helpful staff, was a bit run down. Nothing like the mega public libraries downtown with the crowded booths that made you feel like everyone was looking over your shoulder. Taking a seat at one of the computers, he checked his phone, opening his personal and work emails to scan them for anything important. Nothing on the personal front outside a save the date reminder for his nephew's upcoming wedding stateside. Then, he looked at his work emails. Numerous Power DMS updates told him he was late catching up on two hundred unread policies. Westfield rolled his eyes. *What are they going to do? Suspend me?*

Fishing into his cargo pocket, Westfield extracted the slim microdata drive and looked it over. "Here goes nothing." He pushed it into the compatible slot on the computer.

Project S.H.R.E.D. initializing ...

"Project S.H.R.E.D.?" Westfield muttered.

The screen jumped to life, multiple windows opening filled with photographs, data graphs, and charts. Overwhelmed, Westfield sat back, his mouth ajar. Project S.H.R.E.D.: Super Humanoids for Reconnaissance, Espionage, and Defense.

Westfield scanned the various documents, files, and photographs, a deepening feeling of dread creeping over him. He focused on an image of a humanoid female, lithe and powerful, with jutting fins and sweeping paths of black and white covering her naked body. The caption read: *test subject alpha: Sasha Kino.*

Westfield placed a hand over his open mouth. "My God, Sasha. What have they done to you?" He jerked the drive from the computer and twisted in his chair to scan the library behind him. With sudden clarity, he knew the drill, why Len was so afraid of this. Jager's group was playing God.

Westfield made for the library's exit and didn't stop when the librarian at the front desk asked if everything was all right. Hitting the parking lot in stride, the fingers of his right hand hooked under the edge of his shirt where his concealed weapon lay. By accessing the S.H.R.E.D. file he'd just gone from a nuisance to priority number one. *You dumbass. You've really done it now.* Approaching his truck, he veered left. He thrust his hand into his pocket and grabbed his cellphone. With a heave, he threw it off into the brush. Leaving his truck where it was, he retreated into the nearby park to take cover and wait.

Ten minutes passed. Along the beach, a young man in board shorts threw a Frisbee to a deliriously happy retriever. In the other direction, an older couple walked hand in hand. Holding a crouched position, Westfield's calves and lower back began to ache.

He started to feel foolish. Irritation swelled at the idea he might have overreacted, and his phone was now somewhere beneath the creeping bacopa ground cover. He stood from behind the low stone wall just as a blacked-out government sedan whipped into the parking lot in front of the library. Westfield dropped back behind the wall and watched two men in black BDUs exit the vehicle, then pointed in the direction where he'd thrown his phone. One of the men headed for the bushes while the other entered the library.

They'd marked him.

Westfield put as much distance between them as possible, staying low and bounding from one point of cover and concealment to the next. He had to get clear and contact his guy with the bureau, or he wasn't going to live long enough to make it off suspension.

CHAPTER 27

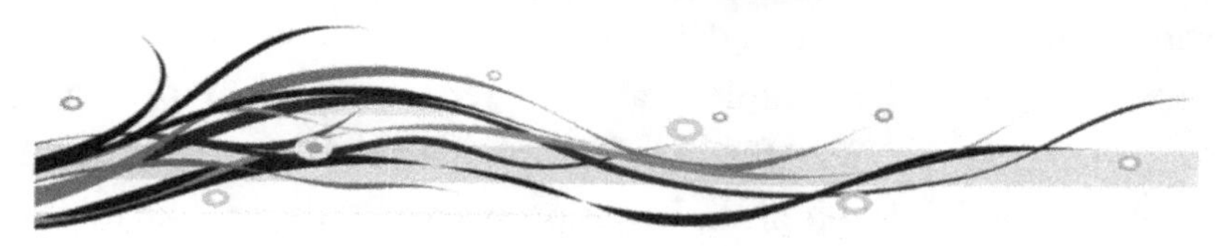

Captain Alric Jager stood stock still, a grim fixture upon the bridge of *The U.S.S. Harbinger*. His knurled fingers clenched white against the ceramic mug, a final sip of bad coffee at the bottom. He leveled an intense gaze into the wash of endless blue before him. Leaning forward, he put down the mug and placed his hands on the cluttered table. A faint wince spread across his weathered face. The half-healed lash wounds scored into the meat of his back scratched against the fabric of his shirt.

Two days and still nothing on Sasha's whereabouts, he mused. The Department of Defense wanted their device. Time was running out. At first, he'd been able to stall them by stating the recovery operation took longer than predicted. They weren't buying it anymore. Just this morning, he'd received a formal request from the DOD stating in no uncertain terms that their representative would need the appropriate clearances to come aboard *The Harbinger* and oversee the recovery of the Erebos. That was unacceptable. He needed more time with the device. He was so close, he couldn't allow these simple-minded idiots to complicate things now.

Jager ground his teeth, then raised his chin as another figure in crisp blue camouflage Navy uniform stepped onto the bridge.

"Commander Atcheson. What do you have for me?" Jager said, not even turning to face the ship's XO.

"Some developments you should be aware of," Atcheson said.

"Such as?" Jager said. He felt for the cigar in his shirt pocket and fingered it but left it in place. He fired a withering glance over his shoulder at Atcheson.

"Captain." Atcheson swallowed. He looked around to the various stations and consoles filled with sailors bustling here and there. "Might I have a word? Privately."

A sour look enshrouded Jager's face like a rippling tide working its way from his broad forehead, down the bridge of his long prominent nose, and into the taught muscles of his neck. He gave a curt nod and marched for the door past the XO. Down the hall he pivoted into the briefing room, now empty and silent.

"What is it?" Jager said, his voice hollow.

Commander Atcheson shut the briefing room door behind them and turned to face the Jager. "Captain, I've served with you a long time. You know you can trust me. So, I'll speak frankly here—right now, this operation is falling apart." Beads of sweat glistened on Atcheson's forehead.

Jager eyed him coldly, the way a great white might eye a hunk of cow meat.

Atcheson swallowed and glanced at his shoes, polished to perfection. He met Jager's arctic glare again. "What you're doing with project S.H.R.E.D. will be exposed sooner or later. How long until the public gets wind of what's happening here? How long until one of the men breaks their silence? And that's not to mention the DOD. You can't—"

Jager lunged, grabbed him by the shirt, and shoved him against the wall. In a moment of shock, Atcheson grabbed at Jager's fist with both hands. Jager, in response, slammed him against the wall again.

"Get … your hands off me," Atcheson said, flailing.

Jager's slap hit him hard across the jaw, buckling the XO's knees. Atcheson's legs quivered, his grip on Jager's hand slipping.

A second slap struck him in the same spot. Atcheson gasped as Jager shoved him back against the wall a third time.

Jager closed in, his snarling face inches from the XO. "It sounds like you've forgotten you're in as deep as the rest of us, Atcheson. It's not what I'm doing, it's what *we* are doing. I spoke to you about this at the start and you assured me you were on board. You gave me your word. As a *man*."

"I didn't realize—"

"That you'd lose your nerve so easily?" Jager finished the XO's sentence, his lip curling in disgust. "Neither did I. If this operation is failing, that failure falls on your shoulders, too. Is that what you want? To bring discredit and dishonor to yourself in ways you never believed possible?"

"No, Captain," Atcheson said.

"Then fix yourself," Jager snapped. "You're the XO of this ship. Act like it."

"Aye, Aye, Captain."

"If you become a liability for me, Atcheson, I'll have you thrown in the brig for acts of treason."

"Treason?" Atcheson said meeting Jager's gaze, his mouth opening to speak again.

Jager silenced him with a withering glare. "Exactly what I said. This is a matter of national security, and you're either with me or you're not."

Jager released Atcheson, then helped stand the man upright. He brushed the bunched wrinkles from the XO's shirt with a few gentle flicks of his fingers. A dour smile stretched across the Captain's face, a posture more akin to a lion preparing to take his prey than a gesture of peace. "We're not finished yet, Atcheson. There's still work to be done and we still have the might of the United States Navy at our backs to see it through." Jager fingered his cigar. "What are we looking at and how do we fix it?"

Atcheson, licked his lips, touching at his tender jawline and neck. "Sir," he said, then stood straighter.

Jager waited in silence for the XO to speak.

"The Gorgon asset that escaped containment is still unaccounted for. It appears she was recovered by Sentry during the incursion we had with their stealth sub. As of yet we have lost them and have no actionable intelligence on her whereabouts."

"That's not new information. Continue."

"Sentry will try to reprogram her behavior, use her negative experiences here to make her a weapon against us."

Jager cracked a bitter grin. "Of course, they will. We're talking about Zhou Murong here. The crazy bastard will no doubt try to use her as he sees fit."

"What will we do, sir?"

Jager studied his XO, a man bewildered and quite out of his depth. "Buck up, Atcheson," Jager said. "We'll draw them back out of hiding and recapture the asset. There's still time yet to wrap this up nice and neat."

"How?"

"I have a few ideas." Jager looked at his watch. "What else have you got? I don't have all day."

Atcheson rubbed his hands together.

Jager squinted at the lieutenant commander. "My God, Atcheson, pull yourself together. What's wrong with you?"

Atcheson's flesh seemed to drain of all color. He wet his lips. "We recently received a security alert. Someone plugged one of our secure data drives into a public terminal off site. When it hit the Wi-Fi it sent us a ping."

Jager's body drew still, a coiled adder waiting to strike. "What are you saying to me?"

"Sir," Atcheson rubbed his hands again. "The drive pinged as 0764, the same drive missing from the console where Sasha escaped. She must have grabbed it when she fled."

Jager ingested the information, his mind on fire. Only the faintest tremble in his limbs gave any indication of the fury boiling inside.

Atcheson spoke first, breaking the awful tension. "Sir, the activation source IP leads to the Ewa Beach Public Library in Honolulu."

"A public library? Are you joking?" Jager said, his face flushing hot.

"It may have leaked onto the net," Atcheson said. "But … we know the identity of the person who accessed it."

Jager stepped forward, his eyes wide.

"It's the same Officer Westfield I told you about. His truck was at the scene of the activation. We believe he's working with Sentry."

"How about that," Jager said. "He just made himself an enemy of the United States of America."

"Captain, he's a police officer—"

"Remove him from the equation." Jager spat the words. "Make sure it looks random. Give the job to our boys on the island. They'll be more than happy to come off surveillance and do some real work."

Atcheson blinked and swallowed.

"This Westfield have any close family?" Jager said.

"An adult daughter," Atcheson said, his eyes glassy.

"Have our boys pick her up. A little insurance in the event this stubborn asshole wants to play hardball." Jager tapped his chin. "Come to think of it, I want Sasha's father and sister as well. Can't ever have enough collateral."

Atcheson coughed, barely able to nod in response. "Aye, aye, sir."

Jager swore, inhaling to compose himself. He ran a worn hand across his salt and pepper high and tight.

"What is the status of the other S.H.R.E.D. subjects?"

Atcheson rubbed his hands, fumbled with a personal tablet in his pocket. "I'm told the first one, the kid named Bodhi, is stable and in good condition." Atcheson powered the tablet on and double tapped the S.H.R.E.D. file on the background and scrolled the data. "The bigger one, Max, will be an excellent candidate if they can get him to stabilize—"

Jager waved the XO off. "Ready the first subject." He extracted the cigar from his pocket and ran its length beneath his nose, appreciating the musky scent of dried tobacco leaves. After a brief inspection he wedged it in the corner of his mouth. "Ensure he's conditioned to attack Sasha on site and set him loose near Honolulu Harbor at eighteen hundred hours. We're going to cause a little old-fashioned mass hysteria."

"Captain …" Atcheson almost dropped the tablet. "There's nothing subtle about—"

"Of course, there isn't, Atcheson. That's the point. We can still spin this however we choose—with Sentry and their wacko agenda at the center of it."

Atcheson blinked. "But Captain, Honolulu Harbor on a Friday night … there will be families on the pier …"

"That's right," the captain said. "We'll have control of the situation."

"I don't understand," Atcheson said, his face a mask of terror. "Why?"

"Stop sniveling like a child, Atcheson. Desperate times call for desperate measures. We're out of time." Jager pulled the cigar from his mouth. "And we need to summon a Gorgon."

CHAPTER 28

The sun dipped low into the western edge of the Pacific Ocean, rays of orange and red, turning pink before bleeding away into the starry expanse above in tones of purple and midnight blue. The ink-black DF-16 Barracuda throttled down, the bulk of the multi engine attack vessel sank in the swells of the darkening sea. At its stern, a steel-infused titanium cage sat facing to the rear of the vessel.

Inside the cage, Bodhi sat slumped against the bars, his monstrous form jerking with each hitched breath. He raised an elongated black snout and snuffed at the air. His head cleared, the warmth and heaviness of the drugs they'd pumped into him day in and day out, fading from his system.

A muffled groan escaped him and he thumped a muscled arm against the metal of his prison. The men around the cage clad in midnight BDUs stepped back, their weapons trained on him. Like him, their bodies had been manipulated to serve a purpose. He could smell it.

"*Stand,*" a voice said, the sound emanating from the collar fastened securely around his neck. He'd tried to pull it off once before. That was a mistake.

Bodhi grunted, pulling his knees under him. The growing terror and anxiety drove a blossoming fury in his chest. *They can't keep me like this,* he thought. *And who are they anyway? Why can't I remember?*

The endless hours of flashing images and audio commands he'd endured rattled around in his head. Voices barking orders at him in a dizzy drug-induced haze. He'd tried to focus on the face of his mother. It offered little comfort.

"*Stand up.*" A chime sounded from the speaker at his throat. "*Do it, or you will be motivated.*"

Bodhi looked over his shoulder. Hazy, featureless, spectral gray figures pointed their weapons at him.

Motivated. Like a kicked dog.

The collar crackled, the stinging jolt knifing him in the throat. Bodhi screamed and climbed to his feet, his webbed hands grasping at the bars.

"*Initial boost injection authorized. Standby,*" the voice in the collar said.

Bodhi flinched as a needle within the collar stabbed at his neck. Fluid pushed into his tissues and set his blood ablaze. Bodhi bawled again, and pulled on the bars. He felt the muscles of his back bulging, and the titanium alloy cage bend in his hands.

"Keep him covered," one of the men called out.

"I've got him," another shouted.

A cattle prod pushed through the bars and jabbed Bodhi in the ribs with a crackle of electricity. He shrieked and lurched away against the opposite side of the cage.

"What the hell is this thing?" A fresh-faced man said, the fear in his young face palpable. "Some sort of dolphin-man?"

"Orca," another replied. "Apex predator, man."

The first man swallowed. "Chief, are we really releasing this thing near Honolulu Harbor?" he asked, looking to the lights of the harbor's shopping district.

The man named Alvarez paused for a moment, then seemed to struggle with the right words. "Both of you stow it." He squared his bull-shouldered physique. "Our orders are to release it here. That's the mission. We have assurances from command that civvies aren't in danger. Stay in your lane, Sailor."

"Yes sir." The young sailor's eyes bulged from his head.

Alvarez motioned his men forward. "Everyone, stand ready."

"*You will go to Aloha Tower.*" The speaker at Bodhi's neck buzzed. "*You will follow all given directives.*"

"God help us," one of the men muttered.

"Cage locking mechanism deactivation in three, two, one …"

With a *shunk* the lock disengaged and the bars of Bodhi's cage separated.

With a grunt, Bodhi flung himself toward the opening. He crashed into the bars and they swung wide. He tumbled forward and plunged into the sea. Bodhi rose to the surface, watching and waiting for instruction. The cold waters of the Pacific caressed Bodhi's skin, calling something deep inside him back to life. But he felt wrong. Whatever they'd injected him with made his insides feel hot, threatening to release something volatile and furious.

The lead Stryker keyed his mic. "Zero to command. Jackknife deployed."

Bodhi duck dived beneath the waves, his sleek form knifing through the water.

"*Proceed to the pier. Do not deviate,*" the voice in his collar said.

He didn't want to do what the voice said, but if he didn't, they would hurt him again. Maybe until he was dead this time. A coil of dread found its way from his spine and into his brain. *No choice. Have to go.* With a sweep of his webbed hands, he shot through the currents like a dart, gliding with deadly purpose toward the shimmering lights of the crowded pier.

CHAPTER 29

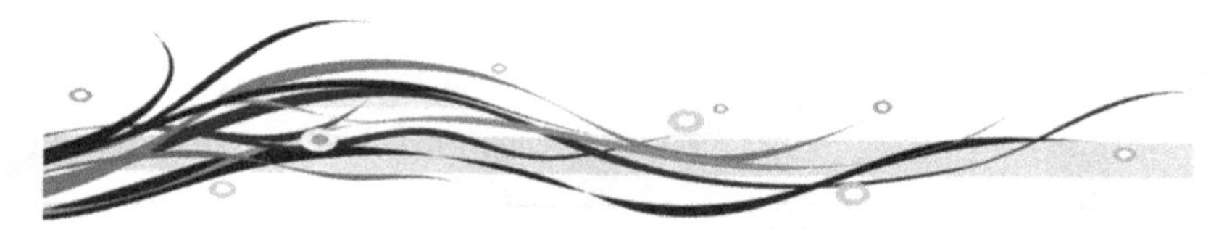

"Look guy, I appreciate the effort," Westfield said, elbow-checking the Springfield 1911 concealed beneath his shirt for the third time, "but relax with the line of questioning. I didn't book this ride to tell you my life story."

The car service driver glared at him in the rearview mirror. "Sure thing, asshole."

Westfield shrugged. "You're right. I'm an asshole. Let me out." He grabbed for the handle. "This is Nuuanu Avenue anyway." He pitched a handful of crumpled bills into the passenger seat.

The driver slammed on the brakes and twisted in his seat. "Hey asshole, you … I don't take cash. Use the app. Hey! Don't be a total—"

Westfield slammed the door as he exited the sedan. He hated having to catch a ride with a service especially under these circumstances but there was no way he was going back for his truck now. He watched with mild amusement as the driver animatedly thrust his middle finger in an upward motion then pulled away from the curb with a bark of rubber.

Westfield took a moment to check the busy downtown street. Sparse palms lined the road, their fronds catching the shifting island breeze as it navigated its way through the busy sector. The dim fire-orange glow of the setting sun reflected off the glass and steel above. Only a few blocks from the pier, foot traffic would be significant here on a Friday night. The towering high-rise apartment building loomed ahead, his eyes wandering to the lit sign out front. This was it, Honolulu Park Place, where a two-bedroom two-bath apartment cost upwards of six hundred thousand. Westfield gave one last look around and, satisfied no one was following him, made for the service entrance where a white van sat backed in.

The screech of tires on Nuuanu behind him sent his right hand instinctively to the 1911 concealed on his hip.

"Hey, watch it man. Are you trying to get run over?" The driver of a baby blue BMW yelled at a pedestrian far too absorbed in his phone.

Westfield grunted, the initial spike of tension fading away. He'd been on the move all day. No phone and no truck, he used the cash he had on hand to complete a few necessary tasks. Avoiding his own place and the usual haunts, he'd looked over his shoulder so much he'd started to feel like a transplant in a bad conspiracy movie. Hunted by black clad military men with an interest in keeping this top secret S.H.R.E.D. project quiet. *What's the end game here?* Westfield didn't like not having an answer—which was why he'd called in a favor to Reggie in dispatch and got the home address for Len Mitchell. If anyone had the answers it was the FBI man. And this time, Westfield was going to get the answers he wanted.

Stopping at the white panel van labeled Mike's Dry Cleaning, Westfield opened the passenger door and plucked out a navy-blue shirt with the company's monogrammed logo, which lay crumpled on the passenger seat. He slipped on the shirt, buttoned it, and moved to the back of the van where he grabbed a bunch of dry cleaned garments on hangers covered in plastic. Up the concrete stairs at the base of a rollup door, sat a tired evening security officer in a faded brown shirt with mustard stains on the front.

"Another delivery? I thought the first guy said there were only two?" The security officer watched him as Westfield approached.

"Yeah, one more. My guy called down and said he forgot this one. Uh, name on it is ..." he pretended to check. "Mitchell."

"Mitchell," The old man squinted his bushy white eyebrows. "Don't know them."

"The address I've got says 1037?"

The security officer shrugged. "Tenth floor. Take the service elevator on your left."

"Thanks partner," Westfield said.

"Uh huh," the old man mumbled.

Westfield tabbed the button and waited for the metallic doors of the service elevator to open. Entering, he hit the button for the tenth floor and waited as the elevator shifted upward with a slight bounce. He'd try the delivery thing, but if it didn't work? *I'm gonna, what? Bust the door in get some answers from this guy?* Westfield swallowed. "God, what is happening to my life?"

With a ding the doors slid back and Westfield stepped out onto the tenth floor with purpose. The hangers held forward, he whistled, eyes scanning the apartment numbers as he strolled past. He nodded, offering his best smile to a thin woman in running tights and reflective everything, as she exited her apartment and jogged down the hall.

Westfield stopped at the navy blue door marked 1037. He paused, checking over his shoulder to make sure the jogger was out of sight, then knocked. Unsecured, the door creaked as it pushed open an inch.

"Son of a bitch," he said. Westfield hung the dry cleaning on the door across the hall, then pulled a pair of latex gloves from his pocket and snapped them on. Another quick look back and forth down the hall and he drew the Springfield from its position of concealment. With a gentle nudge the door opened. Westfield stepped into the apartment, weapon held at the low ready.

The space looked like it had been hit by a hurricane. The sun-streaked interior beyond was adorned with tossed furniture and strewn items that littered the floor. Shards of glass glinted in the light of the retreating sun and cracked beneath his shoes. Westfield swept his weapon back and forth across the entryway.

"What the hell happened here?" he said. "Len?"

A groan reached out to him from deeper inside. His heart rate accelerating, Westfield side stepped the small kitchen until legs came into view. Then he saw the blood stretching its way across the white tiled floor. Another step to the side and Len Mitchell came into full view, clutching a center mass gut wound.

"Len, it's Derrick."

The FBI man, pale from shock and blood loss didn't even raise his eyes. He took a shuddered breath.

"Where are they?" Westfield said.

Len managed to shake his head.

Westfield completed a quick sweep of the wrecked apartment and found it empty. He returned to his old acquaintance lying propped against blood-stained cabinets in the kitchen. Taking a knee next to him he assessed Len's wounds. The guy was tuned up and had both knees shot out. They'd interrogated him. Westfield's scalp tingled. The whole thing had the mark of an operation carried out by a single group of ruthless mission focused soldiers.

He put a gloved hand on Len's shoulder and gave a gentle squeeze. "What can I do?"

"Tried to tell you, stupid bastard. But you … you …" Len coughed.

Westfield lowered his eyes. "I'm sorry, Len. I didn't mean to drag you into this."

"But you did, anyway." Len shook his head, bloodless white fingers clawing at the hole in his midsection. "You don't understand. They don't just come for you," he said, a tear streaking down his pallid cheek. His hand dropped from the wound, bloodied fingers smearing across the cracked glass of a framed photograph. An image of Len smiling, his arm around his wife, their three grown children standing around them.

"Your family. Are they safe?" Westfield asked.

The FBI man's stare grew long, his lips trembling. "It's too late for us," he said, the light leaving his eyes. "You too …" A shuddered exhale, and the FBI man was gone.

Westfield jolted upward onto his feet, adrenaline surging in his veins. He turned and rounded the edge of the kitchen. A deep boom sounded in the distance, the sound setting off a chain of barking alarms and sirens down on the street.

"What now?" Westfield said, stepping over a broken chair toward the large glass windows overlooking the city and harbor. Between the buildings a column of black smoke rose into the air.

He grabbed the empty pocket where his phone usually sat. "Damn." He spun, his eyes searching for a phone. He walked over to Len, checked his pockets, and found the government-issued smart device. Westfield sucked his teeth and shook his head, then finally tabbed the initialize button and allowed the device to scan the dead agent's face.

"Sorry, brother."

"*Agent Len Mitchell,*" The device said. "*Confirm?*"

Westfield swore. He grabbed Len's lifeless hand, wiping the hand clean before placing all four fingertips against the glass of the device.

The phone blipped and the screen showed a wave, an indication of active listening.

"Phone." Westfield said.

"*Phone,*" the device repeated.

The screen blinked and showed a digital dial pad. Westfield lowered Len's hand and punched his Janie's number into the phone, then hit the green call button. It didn't even ring.

"Hi, you've reached Janie ..."

"Come on," Westfield clenched his jaw and hung up. Jabbing 911 into the keypad, he raised the phone to his ear.

"Nine-one-one, what's your emergency?"

"Oh, thank God. Reggie, it's Derrick." Westfield said.

"Derrick? What phone are you calling from?"

Westfield paused. He didn't want to give away too much. "A friend's. Look, I came over to visit him and found him shot. His place was tossed. Maybe a burglary gone bad. I need medics."

"Okay, hang on. What's the address?"

"Honolulu Park Place, number 1037," Westfield said.

"Yeah, the place I got the address for you. Injuries?"

"One patient. Multiple gunshot wounds. You're going to need a coroner. Listen, Reggie, I can't stay on the line. I need you to set up a welfare check for me. Separate location. I can give you the address as well."

"Derrick, I'll get someone over the shooting as soon as possible, but ..." The seasoned 911 operator paused, a tremor of stress in his voice. Westfield could hear the chaotic bustle in the background as operators tried to calm stacked phone lines full of hysterical callers. "Something bad is happening down at the harbor. We're getting a bunch of crazy calls pouring in. People saying a monster is on the loose."

"Reggie, I'm talking about real bad stuff going on here, not fairytales," Westfield said through his teeth.

"I'm serious. I've never heard anything like this. All the lines are full and I've got every available unit headed there. The welfare check isn't happening right now. I'm sorry. Gotta go."

The line clicked off.

Westfield pulled the phone away from his ear and stared at it. His gaze returned to the rising finger of black smoke coming from the pier. A second boom, and beyond it, intermingled with the wail of alarms rose the chattering sound of gunfire.

Monsters? The images from the project S.H.R.E.D. file flashed in his mind. A chill of gooseflesh peppered his arm.

"What the hell is happening?" Westfield said, slipping the open phone into his back pocket and grabbing Len's Suburban keys off the counter. No more time to waste. Janie was in serious danger. He had to get to her.

"Again." Lemeaux said.

"Again?" Sasha's chest heaved. "We've been at this for two days."

The able bodied Frenchman steadied his feet and squared his shoulders. "Yes, again. It takes thousands of repetitions to create true muscle memory." His toes squeaked as they gripped the padded blue mat flooring of the training room. The space was long and narrow, not roomy but well equipped for the purpose of sparring.

Sasha smirked, "What do I need muscle memory for when I can knock you across the room?"

Lemeaux lowered his kick shield. "Okay. Knock me across the room."

"I was kidding," Sasha said.

"I wasn't. Do it—if you think you can." Lemeaux's body

tensed.

The smile faded from Sasha's face. She raised her fists, the muscles of her legs twitching. Shooting forward, the kick shield slapped her in the face, temporarily obscuring her vision. She swiped at the pad, tearing the stuffing from it in a flurry of drifting foam. Driving forward, Lemeaux was gone.

The punch landed hard against her left ear, causing her to falter.

Swinging back with a closed fist, her teeth bared, she hit nothing but air. Rising in front of her, the world champion kickboxer slammed her in the ribs twice with such speed, she couldn't track the movement of his legs. Dodging another wild swing, Lemeaux bobbed to the other side of her guard, this time punching her below the opposite ear. Both ears ringing, her ribs aching, Sasha screamed, driving Lemeaux off his feet and to the ground. She raised a clawed hand to finish him then paused, her teeth bared. The Frenchman simply raised his hands in submission.

"Good, but now you see," Lemeaux said. "Your anger makes you reckless."

Sasha released him and stood, rubbing her rib cage.

"Still believe you don't need skill?" Lemeaux got to his feet.

Sasha didn't answer, her gaze smoldering.

"Sasha, you are powerful, but you have to learn how to harness that power. I'm only a man. Given, a man who trained his whole life in Silat and Muy Thai, but still. You must always be ready for the odds to stack against you."

"Meaning?" Sasha huffed.

"It means with a little training, I was able to out maneuver and out strike you, for a moment at least." He opened his hands in a gesture of peace. "But what if I was one of Jager's experiments? What if I was as strong as you? Or what if you have to take on a whole squad of Strykers at once? Trained killers, all of them. They'll pull you apart if you don't clear your mind and act with some precision."

Sasha placed her hands on her hips. "Okay, how do I do that?"

"Breathe." He smiled and tossed the shredded pad to the gym's padded floor. "Calm your mind and hone your body. Make it a weapon, one that you have complete and total mastery of." He raised a fresh kick shield. "Again."

"Sasha."

Sasha and Lemeaux turned to see Dr. Besom standing in the doorway to the training room. "Murong needs to speak with you. Follow me, if you please."

Sasha and Lemeaux gave each other a knowing look before following Dr. Besom out into the narrow corridor.

"What's going on?" Sasha asked.

Dr. Besom shook her head. "You'll have to ask Murong. I'm just the messenger. But I think something big is happening."

They passed a technician in the hallway who stepped aside to give them room. "So shall we go."

"So shall we go." Dr. Besom and Lemeaux responded in kind.

Sasha scowled. "That's not cultish or anything."

Dr. Besom laughed. "Cultish?"

"I don't know, chanting a peculiar phrase to one another in passing?" Sasha watched the technician return to his duties. "Yeah, cultish."

Lemeaux chuckled.

"Your people certainly believe it. What does it mean anyway?" Sasha asked as they took a ladder up to deck two.

"I'll take this one," Lemeaux said. "*So shall we go* is simply a way of acknowledging that we, all of us, have a duty to adhere to and protect the fate of our world. Just as all things begin, end, and renew again, so must we. Yin and Yang, light and dark, good and evil. Balance in all things."

Sasha blew out a puff of air. The stark image of the lone Sentry frogman uttering those cryptic words as he took his own life, still echoing in her mind. "That's deep. Might need some time to get my head around it."

"Indeed." Lemeaux gave a dip of his head. "Birth, death, and renewal, all things must follow the cycle. You most of all, are a perfect example of this, Sasha."

Sasha said nothing more as they approached the control center, her mind captivated by the meaning of Lemeaux's words. *Is there anything I believe in so strongly that I would give my life for it?*

Stepping through a hatch and into the control room, a wash of chatter, radio traffic and general busyness greeted them. There in the middle of it all, like a rock amidst the crashing of the surf, stood Murong. Posture relaxed, hands clasped behind his back, the man seemed to display an uncanny ability to master himself under any given circumstance. He turned to see Sasha and the others.

All movement slowed and a hush fell over the group. Sasha tried to conceal her growing embarrassment at the many stares. She was, after all, naked as a jay bird, and though her new form wasn't as stark or bare as most human nakedness, it still took some getting used to.

"Sasha." Murong brought his hands together. "How are you feeling?"

Sasha shrugged. "Outside of strange cravings for raw fish at all hours of the day and night? Pretty well."

Murong looked to Lemeaux. "And how is her training going?"

"She shows great potential," Lemeaux said.

"René's the absolute best there is," Murong said.

Shoulders back, Lemeaux stood straight, his face full of pride.

"I've interrupted you due to a matter of critical importance." Murong pursed his lips and waved to the command center. "While you've been preparing yourself for the coming storm, we've been busy following the movements of *The Harbinger* and deciphering radio traffic across the entire encrypted spectrum. Moments ago we intercepted priority radio traffic on Honolulu public safety's main channel."

"Yeah?" Sasha managed.

"Traffic going out from first responders on the scene at Aloha Tower are calling all cars. The officers on scene are saying a monster is wreaking havoc on the pier."

Sasha's breath caught in her chest. She struggled to find the words. "A monster?"

Murong nodded.

"Jager can't have ..." She looked at the wizened face of her benefactor. "He can't have created something that fast, could he?"

"I'm afraid anything is possible," Murong said. "He has your DNA as well as the Erebos probe that altered you. Your transformation took place in hours. He has the ability to re-create the environment necessary to do something terrible—if he's crazy enough to do it."

"We both know the answer to that," Sasha said. "What's the play?"

Murong took a turn around the control center his hands clasped behind his back. "It is undoubtedly a trap, designed to draw you out of hiding. Prudence would suggest we do nothing."

"But there are families on the pier." Sasha said, finishing his thought. "And I'm the only one who can stop whatever Jager unleashed."

Murong took a step forward and gave a slight bow. "My sentiments exactly, Sasha."

"How far out are we?" she asked.

"Ten minutes. We'll insert you at the mouth of the harbor." He paused, looking her over. "Are you ready for this?"

Sasha took in a breath and held it for a moment, all stares resting on her. "As ready as I'm going to be," she said, exhaling and extending her thumb and pinky in a hang-ten gesture. "Let's do this."

CHAPTER 30

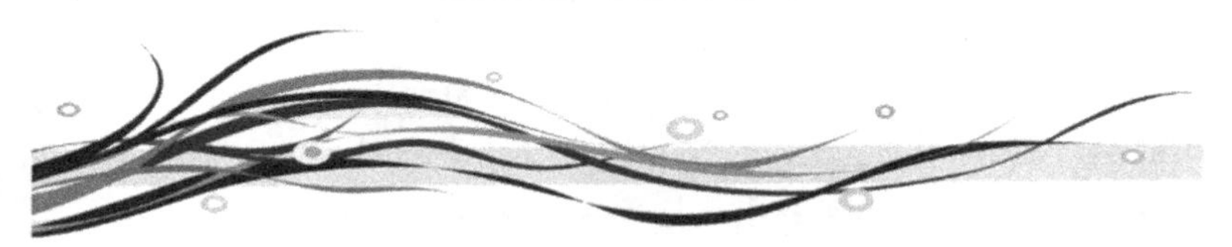

Gordon Kino, wearing only his shorts, sat on the end of his bed and checked his father's antique, cracked brown leather strap wristwatch. Seven fifteen. Too late to do much, too early to sleep. *Sleep? After everything I've been through this week?* He released a loaded sigh, then shuffled to the small kitchen of the simple one-story home and began pulling plates from the steaming dishwasher.

He pushed a plate too warm to handle with bare fingers up onto the counter with a curse, shook his hands, and looked through the small window at the evening sky. The sun sat low and orange on the horizon and a light breeze rustled the palms in cascaded waves. The sound was almost comforting if it weren't punctuated by the incessant barking of the Cooper's German shepherd at the end of the row.

"Oh, Sasha," Gordon said, leaning against the kitchen counter, acutely aware of how old and tired his voice sounded. "Please be okay."

The tinkling sound of jostled windchimes—not blown by the wind—made him frown. A moment later the sound of breaking pottery came to him from the open patio door at the rear of the residence. He froze, listening.

One Mississippi, two Mississippi.

Nothing more.

The breeze must have knocked something over.

Gordon walked to the open back door and peered around the

yard.

He stepped out and stopped short. Mika's hand-painted clay pot lay broken and protruding from a small heap of black soil directly below the hanging planter. Gordon shook his head and crouched to pick up the shards.

"Don't move," a voice said from behind.

Gordon froze. He considered flinging himself in the direction of the voice, hoping to get lucky. *I could take him. Never mess with a pissed off dad.* His body coiled, ready to do something ridiculous and reckless.

"Do anything but what I say, and your daughter dies. If you understand, nod your head."

Gordon's blood ran cold. *Sasha.* He nodded slowly.

"I've got him. Bring the van up," the voice behind him said.

Gordon shifted hoping for a glimpse of the man.

"Don't look at me. You want your daughter to die?"

"Of course not," Gordon said.

"Where's your youngest? Inside?"

"No, she went to stay with a friend."

"Are you lying to me?" the man asked.

"No, I wouldn't. You can check," Gordon said, his flesh now crawling. "It's just me here."

Two figures in black, hats pulled low to conceal their faces, rounded the corner, pushed past him and entered his home. From within the sound of doors slamming, cabinets being ransacked and chairs flung to the floor rang out. Time passed at a crawl. For the first time in his life Gordon wished his backyard didn't offer such total privacy and kicked himself for not trimming the hedges back farther.

The two in black reemerged shaking their heads.

"Nothing. He's alone."

"You took care of those Sentry clowns on surveillance?" The voice behind him said to the others.

"That's right. Never knew what hit 'em."

"All right let's go," the voice said. "Listen up, Mr. Kino, do anything stupid and your whole family pays. Understand? Your whole family."

"I won't do anything stupid," Gordon said.

The rear end of a narrow gray Dodge Sprinter backed into view past the edge of his house.

"Walk to the back of the van," the voice said. "We're going for a ride."

Gordon moved to the rear of the van and the doors swung open. He peered inside the gloomy interior and found the outline of a woman, her hands and feet bound, and a strip of black duct tape stretched tight across the width of her mouth. For the briefest of moments, a flicker of hope kindled in his heart. "Sasha?"

The woman murmured and shifted, her face now more visible.

Gordon's hope died. "Janie?" he croaked. "Oh god, please don't hurt her. Derrick was just helping me out. This has nothing to do with them. Please—"

Something cold and hard smacked against the base of Gordon's skull. He faltered with a groan, grabbed for the door, tried to turn. The second blow struck him in the side of his neck, and his knees gave way. The ground fell away beneath him and a rush of air filled his ears. He had the sensation he was flying, soaring upward and away into the great beyond on wings outstretched like a bird in the wind.

The blacked-out fed-issued Chevy Suburban swerved from the parking garage and out onto Nuaanu Avenue, its tires trailing black skids. Westfield jerked the wheel and mashed on the horn. The large SUV jumped the curb, causing startled pedestrians to dive for the grass.

"Move!" Westfield honked the horn, and wrenched the wheel again to avoid a baby stroller.

Another boom sounded only blocks away, the fading echo of some distant explosion. His sense of duty pulled him strongly toward the gathering wall of smoke down at the pier, but he kept the car pointed on its current heading.

"You're suspended, Derrick," he said aloud. "Going there isn't going to help Janie. Your meddling got her caught up in this. She needs you."

Bouncing free of the sidewalk, Westfield left the road altogether, and piloted the Suburban across the open grass of the adjoining Nuaanu park. People abandoned their blankets on the grass. A half-full soda in a flimsy wax paper cup smacked against the windshield, splattering and rinsing the glass in a film of cola-colored liquid.

"Come on, dammit," Westfield said, fumbling with the wipers. Under normal circumstances he wouldn't have gotten this far driving like a deranged idiot. HPD was far too good for that. But right now, with all assets diverted to the harbor, no one could stop him.

He pulled Gabe's phone from his pocket and raised it to call Janie again. As he looked at the transparent glass of the smart device, his reflection stared back and it occurred to him just how deep in he was. He'd unlawfully entered an FBI agent's apartment, tampered with a murder scene and stolen the man's government-issued smart device and vehicle. Not only was he going to get busted by his command for this, he was going to get labeled as a suspect. If things went bad, it could mean jail time and the end of his career.

"Crap." Westfield muttered.

"*I'm sorry, I cannot do that,*" the phone said.

"Ah, crap. Um …"

"*I'm sorry, but I am unable to crap,*" the phone repeated.

"Recent calls, damn you." Westfield said, pinching his lips.

"*I do not understand 'recent-calls-am-you.'*"

"Useless son-of-a-bitch," Westfield said, as the SUV crashed through a short, wrought-iron fence and slid into oncoming traffic with a squall of smoking tires.

"Recent. Calls," he shouted.

"*Recent calls,*" the phone repeated.

He tabbed Janie's number on the screen and turned it to speaker. Again, it didn't ring. Instead, the sweet voice of his daughter's recorded message piped through the speaker of the phone.

"*Hi, you've reached—*"

The smart device flew from his hand as a black sedan slammed into his left flank. Westfield's head struck the driver's side window, and the car shuddered to a halt. With a groan, Westfield grabbed the wheel with both hands bracing his shoulders in an attempt to stop the swimming in his head. He blinked and gazed around the interior. The glass where his head had hit, splintered in a spider's web of sunlit cracks. A dribble of blood streaked from his forehead, dripped over his eyebrow, and spattered the khaki fabric of his pants.

Westfield jammed the accelerator to the floor, the large police package 5.3 liter V8 lurching in response. He checked his rearview mirror. The sedan that had hit him, crushed front end and all, swerved in behind him.

A second blacked out sedan, similar to the first, accelerated alongside.

"Okay, who the hell are these guys? FBI?" Westfield raised one of his hands off the wheel in an act of submission. "Take it easy, boys."

The sedan on his left dodged around a motorcycle before swerving dangerously in toward him.

"Oh, come on!" Westfield shouted.

The sedan on his left crashed into the driver side of his Suburban, forcing it against the interstate guardrail. Simultaneously, the other car giving chase slammed into him from behind, throwing him against the steering column.

"No," Westfield groaned, unable to maintain control of the vehicle as it ground to a halt, its mangled front end wedged beneath a guard rail twisted in coils.

Rising like dark mechanical agents of doom from the crashed sedans, men in black, wearing balaclavas, emerged from the vehicles. From their sides they raised stubby black MP-7 submachine guns.

A spike of awareness lanced through Westfield. *This isn't an arrest. It's an execution.*

He thew himself sideways toward the passenger side floorboard as a hail of gunfire smacked against the armored body and windshield. Westfield's jaw clenched.

"Get some of this," he said through gnashed teeth. Westfield shoved his hand down onto the gas pedal, and the SUV jumped forward, eliciting a piercing scream from one of the men as his lower body pinned between the two vehicles. Westfield righted himself in time to see the pinched man clench the trigger and spray two of his comrades with a burst of automatic gunfire.

Westfield grabbed a flashbang grenade from a pouch on Gabe's outer carrier vest still wedged in the passenger seat. He clenched the spoon in the web of his hand and yanked the pin. Drawing the Springfield from his hip, he threw the door open and tossed the flashbang forward of the SUV.

With the deafening concussion of a thunderclap, the distraction device detonated. Westfield exited the SUV, spun to the rear of the vehicle, and fired one round straight through the forehead of an approaching assailant. Two more double tapped rounds felled a second man approaching from the rear. Bullets raked the front glass.

Westfield spun and dropped to a knee, the impact of bone against concrete causing a spike of pain to flare through his leg. One last man rounded the front of the car, his gait unsteady. Westfield fired three rounds in quick succession. The heavy jacketed forty-five ACP hollow point rounds punched holes in the chest of the masked man and staggered him back against the sedan. He slid to the ground, still fumbling with a spare magazine.

Standing with a wince of pain, Westfield held the Springfield at the ready and approached the downed man. His shoes scratched atop broken glass and empty brass shell casings. A small crowd gathered on the highway, crouched behind their vehicles.

As Westfield approached, the man pulled his balaclava free from his head. For an instant, a twinge of anguish spiked in Westfield's chest at just how young the man looked, boyish even. The assassin spat blood, his breathing ragged. The tactical carrier he wore had no armor in it, blood running freely from the trio of holes in his chest. They'd planned for an assassination, not a gunfight.

"Who are you with?" Westfield said, checking over his shoulder again.

"You hear that?" The assassin groaned, ignoring Westfield's question.

Another *boom* in the distance followed by the *rat-a-tat-tat* of sporadic gunfire.

"What did you idiots let loose on the harbor? One of Jager's experiments?"

The assassin gave a wheezing chuckle, the sound of lungs filling with blood and fluid. "You're done, traitor."

"I'm not the one who looks done, kid," Westfield said.

The downed assassin reached for his weapon.

Westfield's face hardened. "Don't do it."

"Your daughter," the assassin said flashing blood tinged teeth. "You'll never see her again."

"Where is she?" Westfield asked.

The assassin grabbed for the sub-gun.

Westfield fired a round directly between his eyes, knocking him back where he rolled to the side, dead.

Westfield double checked his weapon and performed a tactical reload, removing the magazine still loaded with a few rounds and replacing it with a fresh one from the Kydex mag holder on his left side. He checked the assassin's body but found no identifying information, phone, or any other items of interest. He reached into the Suburban and grabbed Gabe's tactical body armor with a placard labeled *FBI Agent* attached to the back. He slipped it over his shoulders and cinched the straps down, then moved toward the sedan where an unconscious half-crushed man was still pinned to its side. After entering the driver's side, he slammed the door.

He took a moment to survey the interior of the vehicle, his mind a whirl. Desperation gripped his heart. *What if I can't find Janie? What sort of barbarism are these bastards willing to inflict on her?*

"Come on," Westfield shouted, raking through the contents of the vehicle with trembling hands. Papers, a file containing a dossier with his picture and bio, and various locked electronics scattered. He had to get his mind right. *Don't make it personal,* he thought. *That makes you sloppy, and sloppy gets you dead.*

"Okay, girl, where would they take you?"

Westfield tabbed the touch screen and watched as it winked to life. He touched the button labeled *navigation*. A map materialized on the screen, showing his present location. He touched the button labeled *options*, followed by *recent places*.

"Come on, be this stupid," he murmured.

He blinked at the screen. The previous location was Gabe's address at Honolulu Park Place on Nuuanu. They'd known where he was going. He eyed the previous entry. A spike of realization sent a wave of relief washing over him. The warehouse and shipping district on the far side of the harbor. Quiet. Secluded. It's where he'd take her if he were them. *There's still hope. I can do this.* Westfield jabbed at the screen and the mapping system plotted the course to his destination, a holographic arrow hovering above the dashboard.

"Hang on, Janie," he said, throwing the sedan in drive, the back tires barking as he pulled away onto the open, smoke-shrouded highway. "I'm coming, honey."

CHAPTER 31

"Are you clear on everything?" Murong asked. His words seemed to pick up an echo, a dim reverberation that hummed at the mouth of one *The Argo*'s smooth bore launch tubes.

Sasha looked from Murong to Lemeaux and nodded, pushing her fear down deep inside her. Now was not the time to show weakness.

"Take this." Murong held his hand out to her. Pinched between his fingers was a small black nodule the size of a pencil eraser. Snaking from it was an ultra-thin hair-like thread attached to a small bulbous piece.

"What is it?" Sasha said, glancing at the technician next to her as he opened the door to the launch tube.

"A micro radio com-link device with video capabilities. Submergible and impact resistant, it transmits communiques via vibrations affecting the small bones of your inner ear. Pop it in and loop the wired camera over your ear. You can continue to communicate with us and we can see what you see. You won't even know it's there." He looked to a woman holding a tablet computer.

"I've got device audio and the video feed is strong, sir," the woman said.

"Excellent." Murong looked back to Sasha. "Will you try it?"

"Yeah, okay." Sasha took the small device and inserted it in her ear, wrapping the filament thin wire over the top of her ear. "It doesn't have the ability to hurt me does it?"

Murong squinted, almond-shaped eyes narrowing in confusion. Then a look of realization crossed his features. "You're referring to the collars Jager uses. No, of course not. It's only audio and video."

Sasha managed a nervous smile. "Had to ask."

"Remember," Lemeaux said, "you have no idea what we're about to face. Jager will do whatever he can to throw you off and overwhelm you. Be smart. Think of it as a game of chess. Each movement, each counter movement must be skillfully considered. Your life and the lives of innocents may depend on how you respond."

"I got it," she said, grabbing the bar above the chute and sliding her feet in.

"A hammerhead assault vessel will be standing by to provide assistance if needed." Murong pushed the hinged door halfway closed. "Stay true, Sasha. There are many who are counting on you."

The hatch above her head shut with a clunk, the bolts in the locking mechanism sliding into place. With a whoosh, water filled the pitch-black chamber. Sasha relished the salt-laden scent of the ocean as it piled up around her head. A final breath and the tube gushed full around her. With a peep, the opening at the far end slid open. Sasha, expelled in a jet of water, shot from the belly of *The Argo* and into the mouth of Honolulu Harbor.

Continuing her momentum, she took a few more strokes. Her webbed hands grabbed handfuls of the surrounding sea, as her lithe body slid through the dark currents like a wraith in the burgeoning night. Rising to meet the chaos above, her head broke the surface of the water. The sharp crack of gunfire raked at her inner ears. Beyond the chaos, a sunset drew long drifting currents of color across the horizon, melting from shades of dark pink to purples that stretched like an oil canvas into the starlit sky above.

Muzzle flashes flickered across the pier. The rhythmic blinding strobe of activated police lights. At the end of the docks a delivery truck burned out of control. Everywhere people ran, scattering in all directions or cowering in terror behind whatever barrier offered the safest refuge. A discordant scream filled the air and echoed across the water, the ugly sound causing a sensation of dread to crawl across Sasha's skin.

The tall, twisted silhouette, of what Sasha could only describe as a beast, shifted between her and the burning truck. She watched in shock as the large creature strode on two long legs toward Aloha Tower, its gangly alien features and sharp angled protrusions casting eerie shadows in the flickering light. The way the creature moved was so foreign and yet, so familiar.

"Oh my god, Jager. What have you done?" she whispered.

A new volley of gunfire cracked from the HPD officers crouched behind their police cruisers, warning lights strobing. The creature screamed again, a terrible shrill sound, and sent a cruiser tumbling into the water. Sasha watched in horror as it advanced on the petrified officers.

"*Sasha, what have you got?*" Murong said over her earpiece.

"I see it—or I did." Sasha gasped, water lapping against her face. "It's on the move. And it's big."

"*You must intercept it. Lives are at risk.*"

"Okay." She tried to control the tremor in her voice. She took another gulp of air and dipped below the surface of the harbor, the banging of her heart a bass drum in her ears. With each stroke of her arms, each kick of her legs, her body knifed faster through the darkening waters of the harbor. She gave one last powerful upward thrust and shot from the water like a sub-launched missile. Flying high into the air, water streaming from her body, Sasha tucked backward into a full gainer. She twisted in the air and landed with perfect form between the monster and the stunned crowd.

"Everyone, hold your fire!" a police officer called over the megaphone from behind her.

Sasha rose to face the beast.

The creature's brawny pale white torso stood in sharp contrast with its jet black limbs. An elongated head revealed dagger shaped white teeth and a roiling pink tongue bathed in the frothed spittle. The thing was much taller than her, it's lean torso and ropy appendages rippling with dense muscle.

Sasha studied the twisting bands of black and white, the same as her own. This thing had been made with an orca too, maybe even using her DNA. Genetic material Jager stole and repurposed. But that also meant the creature used to be somebody.

Sasha held up her hands, her palms open. "Can you understand me? My name is Sasha. I want to help you."

The creature snuffed, its tongue pushing between tusk-like teeth. It turned its head regarding her with little black eyes.

"I don't want to fight you. But I can't let you hurt these people."

"Stand down or you both will be fired upon," the police officer with the megaphone called.

"No, wait. Just wait." Sasha turned her a palm toward the police cruisers behind her.

"Hashaaa," the thing moaned placing its clawed hands against its face. "Nohashaaa no."

"Murong, it looks scared. What should I do?"

"*You see the collar? It's like the one Jager forced you to wear.*" Murong's voice buzzed in her ear. "*Talk the creature down if you can. If you can't, submit it. Then remove the collar. Sentry can help, but first you have to get that collar off.*"

"Stand down or you *will be* fired upon!" the officer shouted again.

"Wait, dammit!" Sasha half-turned.

The sound of a small chime dinged. The beast jerked to life, snuffing and groaning as it paced. Sasha heard a small voice. She took a step forward. Two more chimes. They came from the collar. She knew that sound.

"*Destroy her, now,*" the voice in the collar said.

Bright and fast, a series of electrical shocks snapped from the collar against the neck of the thing. The beast shook its broad head and groaned, clenching its fists, then locked on Sasha. A strange look of distress and recognition washed across its sloped face.

"Hashaaa," it gurgled, as it advanced on her, its claws flared open.

Sasha faltered. *Is it saying my name?*

"Hang on, don't—" Sasha started.

"Fire!" the police officer boomed through the megaphone.

"No!" Sasha screamed, the rippling string of gunfire cutting her words short. She felt the piercing sting of a bullet as it struck her low in the back. Then another, in the back of her leg. She ducked to escape the hail of small arms fire, but by then, the beast was upon her. A vice-like grip encircled her neck, squeezing with impossible strength.

"*Fight, Sasha,*" Murong's voice said, distant and hazy in her ear.

Sasha gasped, hands clawing at the slick webbed fingers around her throat. The creature's stinking hot breath, the smell of rotting fish, huffed against her face. With a grunt the beast flung Sasha through the air, and sent her crashing against the stacked stone base of Aloha tower. The monster screamed raising its ropy arms to the sky. It came for her again, stomping forward amidst the whizz and pop of flying projectiles.

Sasha raised herself from the ground, pulverized stone rolling from her shoulders. A grim look of defiance spread across her face.

"Well come on, then." Sasha coiled and sprang forward her body colliding with the beast. Together, they twisted in mid-air and fell back to the ground. Sasha ducked a swipe of the creature's hand and rose to the outside with a hard punch to its ribs and a swift roundhouse kick to the midsection.

"*Hands up, Sasha. Focus your strikes on its snout,*" Lemeaux said in her ear.

"I'm working on it," Sasha said, dodging another swipe.

Deflecting its attack, Sasha slipped sideways and punched the creature square in the end of its snout. The creature stumbled and went to all fours. As it moved to stand again, Sasha encircled its neck with her arms, locking it in a choke. The beast grabbed at her arms. And in that moment, within the ink black skin of its shoulder, she could see it: the outline of a spiky tribal tattoo, a design she knew well.

Sasha's grip loosened. "Bodhi?" she whispered.

With a grunt, the beast slung Sasha against the ground.

"No urt Hashaaa," he groaned.

The collar chimed and the white hot electrical currents snapped against his neck driving him back to his knees, a look of wild terror and desperation in his face.

"*You don't know her. She is your enemy,*" the voice in his collar said.

Sasha raised herself to a knee, and reached for her friend, a lump in her throat. "Bodhi, what did they do to you?"

Bodhi screamed and came again.

"No, stop Bodhi, please," Sasha said.

Rolling away to her feet, Sasha evaded Bodhi's fist as it

pulverized the concrete.

"I don't want to hurt you." As she dodged another blow, something toward the end of the pier caught her eye—the glint of firelight on glass.

"*Sasha, we have eyes on a sniper.*" Murong's voice tickled in her ear. "*They're going to try to tranq you again.*"

"Yeah, I see him," she said, breathless. "Get ready to provide an extraction. I've got an idea."

Bodhi screamed, slashing wildly at the air as he came. Sasha ducked his melee then spun, and vaulted into the air. Touching off the side of Aloha tower, she bounced high, then allowed herself to fall fast toward her opponent. Balling her fists, Sasha slammed them against the top of Bodhi's snout. He roared and stumbled back. Sasha grabbed Bodhi around the torso and twisted his back to face the end of the pier, just as the sound of a rifle crack filled the night. An instant later, the sniper's tranq smacked against Bodhi's flesh.

Sasha held Bodhi there, pinning his arms to his side. He struggled, but already his strength faded under the effects of a powerful tranquilizer. She felt his balance break and used the opportunity to lower him to the ground. Then she grabbed the collar around his neck with both hands, and pulled. She screamed long and loud, the collar distorting under her fingertips. With a squall of rending metal, Bodhi's restraint collar shattered and came free. She hurled it off into dark.

A second snap of the rifle followed. Sasha leaped to the side, narrowly dodging the whistling tranquilizer round as it flew past.

With a snarl, Sasha rocketed toward the end of the pier. Landing with a thud before the Stryker who had already chambered another round. Sasha seized the gun barrel and bent it downward in an L shape.

The Stryker smirked. "Gotcha."

The muzzle of the pistol blasted inches from her torso. Sasha screamed in pain as the Stryker advanced on her with gun and blade, fighting with the fury of a trapped animal. She evaded another shot, the round zinging wide. She grabbed him by the neck and braced his gun hand. An electrical jolt lanced through her body as the Stryker electrified his own skin.

Sasha heard a commotion behind her, and glanced back. Strykers had descended upon Bodhi's crumpled body and draped him in a net.

With Sasha momentarily distracted, the Stryker before her pulled from her grasp and torqued his hand free. Sasha sidestepped as he fired his weapon far too close to her face. Her head rang with the concussive blast. Knocking the weapon from his grasp, she lost the path of his knife. The blade slashed deep across her midsection. A gasp escaped her. She caught the Stryker's knife hand and, with a single jerking motion, dislocated his arm from its shoulder socket. The man screamed as Sasha flung him from the pier and into the water.

"Murong, they're taking Bodhi. I need some help over here," Sasha said, her chest heaving.

"*Bodhi?*" Murong said.

"My friend. No time to explain," she said. "Get us out of here, now."

"*Standby. Support incoming.*"

A Sentry hammerhead burst from the water. A turret swiveled and fired a battery of white flares high into the air. At the same moment a crew of frogmen led by Lemeaux climbed onto the pier and opened fire on the Strykers, sending them falling for cover. Beyond, the police, overwhelmed and underprepared, could only watch from behind the cover of their vehicles.

"Go, Sasha," Lemeaux said.

Sasha leaped across the distance in a flash. Landing next to Bodhi, she kicked the legs out from under one Stryker and sent another tumbling with a crushing punch to the jaw. Grabbing the edge of the net covering her friend, she made for the water.

"Lemeaux, get ready to get your men out of here," Sasha said. "You can't hold off those Strykers."

"Get your friend to safety," Lemeaux shouted back, his submachine gun rattling.

With a groan Sasha marched toward the water, the motionless body of her deformed friend still snared in the net. The hammerhead extraction vessel wasn't far. She could make it. She cast another look back as Jager's super soldiers bounded expertly from cover, laying down suppressive fire on Lemeaux's group.

"Lemeaux!" Sasha shouted.

Sasha plunged into the water with a gasp. Net secure in her fist, she dug at the water with her free hand. "Lemeaux, come on!"

The seasoned merc met her wide-eyed stare with a knowing look and a dip of his head. "So shall we go."

Emerging from behind cover, Sentry's mercenaries, led by the valiant Frenchman assaulted the Stryker force, driving them back with a barrage of gunfire. Tears formed in Sasha's eyes as her brave new friend clashed with the lead Stryker, and the super soldier's knife buried deep in Lemeaux's chest.

CHAPTER 32

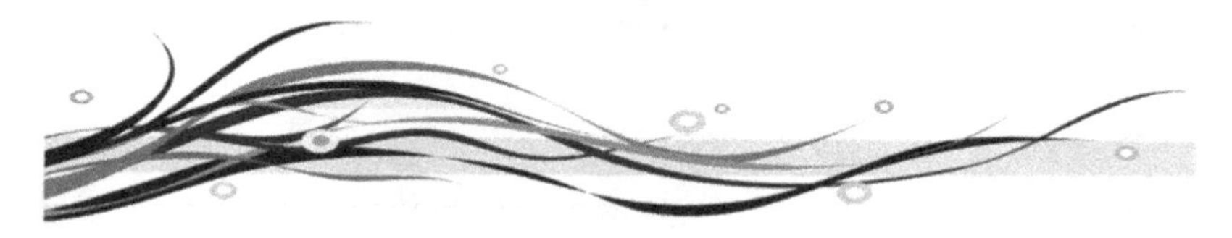

Night fell, gliding across the sky from its heavenly perch, descending and covering the windswept horizon in a blanket of stars. The short jump deck of *The U.S.S. Harbinger* buzzed with activity. Jager stood, arms crossed, watching the ongoing frenzy with renewed interest as Stryker team zero, led by Alvarez made it to the deck and headed in his direction. Jager moved the unlit half-chewed Dominican to the opposite side of his mouth. He'd bitten the damn thing so hard it was almost cleaved it in two.

This debacle meant another major loss. What seemed like a sure-fire way to reclaim the S.H.R.E.D. program's primary asset, had taken a turn for the disastrous. Now a second asset had been lost, and Sentry had control of both of them. All he had to show for it was a handful of dead Sentry mercs and a beat-up squad of Strykers.

He eyed the small elite squad as they drew near. They'd taken a thrashing, some of them supporting broken limbs and gunshot wounds. *Super soldiers,* Jager thought with a grunt, *beat up by a child.*

"Captain," Alvarez said. "I've got others in my chain of command asking questions, but we came straight to you."

"I am your chain of command, Chief," Jager said, his voice firm. "You report direct to me. Now, give me a SitRep."

"Roger that, sir." Alvarez handed off the wounded man to another Stryker. "We made a silent approach and staged according to the mission briefing. Everything was in position." Alvarez paused for a moment. The man appeared to have difficulty forming the right words.

"Go on," Jager said.

With a grunt Alvarez continued. "It went south, Captain. My marksman had a tranq shot on Gorgon and he took it, but the Jackknife asset was struck instead. With Jackknife disabled, my team was compromised. We had to engage."

"And you got your asses kicked. In public," Jager said with an ugly smirk, "by a girl and a bunch of half-rate mercs."

The senior chief clenched his jaw but said nothing, luminescent eyes staring.

Jager grinned. "At ease, Chief. Are any of your men critical?"

Alvarez shook his head. "No, sir. I've got one with a dislocated arm and a few with minor GSWs and frag."

Jager gave a sharp nod. "Get your men to Dr. Kingsfeld and get them patched up. I need your team back on the ready, ASAP. Once they're good to go, get those that can fight up to speed and ready to rock."

"Another serum dose, sir?" Alvarez asked.

"Something a little different this time." Jager winked. "Should make you boys just shy of invincible."

"Aye, sir," Alvarez said, turning and gesturing for his squad to follow.

Jager stood for another moment, watching as the flight crews and mechanics prepped and checked a handful of F35-V Lightning III jets standing ready on the jump deck. His request for support had been approved after he'd reported the initial incursion with Murong's stealth sub. Nothing moved fast through the upper command's decision-making process, but mention the word terrorism even now, eight years after a dirty bomb detonation in

San Diego, and the kneejerk reaction from the brass was still strong.

According to his official report, Sentry, led by the fanatical Zhou Murong, a Chinese national, had engaged Navy assets and provoked an incident off the coast of Hawaii. His people responded with force. In addition, he'd reported his intel unit received information Murong's group was performing illegal genetic experiments and was releasing the unstable mutated subjects in the area of American civilian populations. Jager described Sentry as subversive, aggressive and highly volatile—a terrorist entity whose destruction was of imminent importance to the protection of the United States of America and its people.

In a matter of hours, assets from the 7th joint battle group, a nuclear sub and a stealth destroyer, were authorized to assist them. The men and women in these groups, operating under the belief they engaged a terrorist entity, would be all too ready to throw themselves at his cause.

Leaving the hustle and bustle of the jump deck, Jager made his way down the narrow stairs and cramped gray corridors toward the labs on deck four. As much as he didn't want to admit it, Atcheson was right; the operation was belly up. If Sentry cultivated further assets, they would have the potential to develop a fighting force the likes of which no standing government could contend with. With the snap of his fingers Zhou Murong would have the power to topple nations and fill the power vacuum that ensued. It could mean World War III, not to mention a bitter end to his career and his precious life's work.

Over my dead body.

Then there was Sasha Kino. This volatile, headstrong, and highly capable young woman had become a real thorn in his side. When Sasha finally made the connection the creature she'd engaged on the pier was her friend Bodhi, and discovered her friend Max was likely still under *The Harbinger*'s control, the tables would turn in Jager's favor. With a doggedness he'd come to expect from the girl, she would come after the *Harbinger* in an attempt to rescue her friend. But Jager would be ready for her this time. On his own turf, the petulant child would face the full might of the United States Navy.

Scanning his keycard at the entrance to the lab, he followed it by placing his palm on the biometric scanner to the right of the door.

"*Welcome Captain Jager,*" the synthetic female voice said as the door slid open. Jager's eyes fell on the disheveled lead scientist, a man who appeared to be coming apart at the seams. Pacing the floor with restless strides, he muttered something to himself about improbability and conflict with natural law. His eyes flicked to the captain. A dread at seeing him registered on the man's face like the discovery of a terminal illness.

"Dr. Hanson," Jager said in a syrupy sweet tone. "Tell me things are progressing with the second test subject."

"Well, ah …" Hanson scanned the room nervously.

Jager cleared his throat. "Let me see him."

Dr. Hanson swallowed. "Of course, sir. Follow me."

Through another room, this one requiring dual authentication, Hanson jabbed at the tablet clutched in the crook of his arm. Ahead, a wall of steel slid back to reveal a chamber holding a cylindrical bubbling containment and conditioning tube in the center. Inside the glass the monstrous inhuman thing hovered, suspended in the water amidst a curtain of silver-tinged bubbles. Jager observed the dormant, even peaceful-looking, black and white creature with its heavy musculature, fins, and claws.

"Oh, father." A sigh escaped the captain, the wheezed release of some ancient pain. “I wish you could be here to see me outdo everything you ever achieved, you old son-of-a-bitch.”

“Sir?” Hanson asked.

Jager cut his eyes at the lead scientist. “Is it ready?”

“Ready?” Dr. Hanson’s eyes flared wide. “No sir, of course not. It’s not nearly far enough along in the cerebral conditioning program, not to mention this specimen, while physically perfect, shows dangerous levels of aggression. No sir, I would have to say it most definitely is not ready.”

Jager eyed the top secret folder on the table before him. “What do you call this one?”

“Breach,” Hanson adjusted his glasses. “We call him Breach.”

“Outstanding. Get the beast ready. It’s showtime.”

Hanson’s tablet fell from his hands and bounced on the corner of its rubberized protective case and flopped against the floor. He stood there gawking. His watery eyes glanced to a tech wearing a hazmat suit and mask inside the enclosure, checking the various wires and hoses leading to the tank.

“Sir, we can’t,” he squeaked. “It’s not ready. We can’t control it—”

Jager grabbed the bumbling scientist by his lab coat and shoved him backward, causing him to bump into a wheeled cart.

“Do it,” Jager said with a snarl. “Or I will.”

Hanson whimpered, his face full of terror. He plucked the tablet from the floor and with great hesitation, jabbed at the screen. In response, a whooshing sound filled the air as the tank before them drained. A malicious grin stretched across Jager’s face as the room drew quiet, the various scientists, sailors, and techs, stopping to watch the process in silent, fearful, awe.

CHAPTER 33

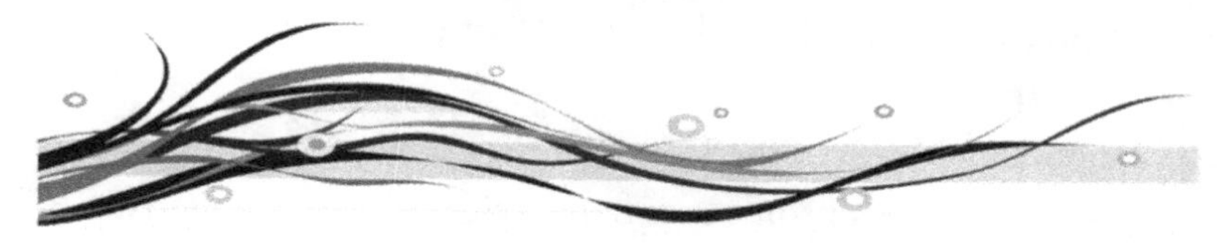

The wheels of the unmarked, heavily damaged, black sedan screeched to a stop across the empty parking lot. A steady stream of smoke drifted from beneath the crumpled hood, the engine trilling and knocking like a percussion set. Westfield emerged, and scanned the row of dark warehouses for suspicious activity, vehicles, anything that may give him a heading. The sedan's engine clunked and choked out. A stillness descended, emphasizing the faint beep of a forklift in reverse somewhere in the complex. The only other sound, the continuous shifting of a restless pacific wind. A storm was coming.

Westfield conducted a series of combat breathing reps, trying to slow the jack-hammering of his heart. It was then he heard it, a little sound that could have easily been lost in a place like this. A muffled cry, followed by the hushed murmuring of angry voices. The sound of a struggle.

Ducking back into the car, he made sure the battery was keyed on and tapped the red triangle button on the console.

"*Summon emergency services to your GPS coordinates?*" the automated voice said. "*If yes, press the initiate button again.*"

Westfield pressed the button a second time and leaving the door open, ran with a limp, his knee already swelling with a throbbing ache, across the empty parking lot. Crossing between two large warehouses, he scanned, looking for any sign of the disturbance. There, on the ground several feet away was a still-locked padlock, but the bar had been clipped and lay distorted. He moved to the nearby door and pressed his ear to it. The hushed voices of men reached out from inside. Westfield tried the handle, and teased the door open just enough to get a narrow visual of the space.

Past the shelves cluttered with parts and dormant conveyor belts crisscrossing like tangled serpents across the open space, he could just make out several figures in black fatigues standing around two figures sitting bound to chairs. Beyond them, a dormant forklift sat rusted and unused, cloaked in shadow.

"You spoke to that HPD Lieutenant, right?" one of the men asked. "We don't need any random business checks over here that force us to kill another cop."

"Yeah, everything's set. Guy's a weasel, too, selling his own guy out like that."

"Corley." Westfield clenched his teeth so hard he thought they might break. *I'll kill you, you dirty son of a bitch.*

"How long do we wait?" one figure said, stepping off to the side with a man with chiseled features and board-straight stance. *Clearly the squad leader.*

"Give them a few more minutes," the squad leader, said. "Their last transmission said they'd engaged the target on the interstate while the police were tied up at the harbor."

"But shouldn't we have heard something from Bravo by now?"

"They're busy popping smoke. We stick to the plan," the squad leader said.

"I don't like it. The sooner we can get these two extracted and out of here, the better."

"I'm with you, but the boat isn't here, so we hold for now," the squad leader said. "Go keep an eye on them."

The men parted ways.

With his field of view clear, Westfield could see the two hostages for the first time. Even though he'd feared the worst, actually seeing Janie strapped to that chair caused his stomach to bottom out. Westfield bit his lip and focused on the second individual, a broad-shouldered man with long dark hair that drooped across his face and the duct tape that covered his mouth.

"Gordon," he whispered. "I've got you, brother."

Westfield turned his attention back to the men holding them. He'd already identified the squad leader. Westfield's gaze bounced to the others. Unmarked military style black BDUs. Pistols secure in tactical holsters. *How in the hell have military assets been deployed to kidnap American citizens on American soil?*

Westfield paused and pressed his back against the corrugated metal wall of the warehouse. With a bump of one ankle against the other, he confirmed his five-shot backup piece, still strapped to his lower leg. He drew the Springfield from its place on his hip and did a brass check, easing the slide back to get a visual on the thick forty-five round already nestled in the chamber. The safety clicked off with a snap.

"God," Westfield's eyes flicked up to heaven. "I don't know if you're listening, or if you're even out there at all." He swallowed. "But if you are, help me go the distance here. For Janie. For Gordon. I'm begging you, please ..." He tried to swallow again, the saliva thick in his throat.

He waited until the men in the room turned away, preoccupied with their duties. In one move, he pulled the door open and slipped through the gap and into the outer edge of the darkened warehouse. Staying low and using every available element of concealment, Westfield made his approach to within twenty feet of them. From here he could better see the disheveled form of his daughter. Chest heaving, face streaked with running mascara as she sat in an old metal chair with her hands secured behind her back. Her tangled blond hair drooped over a bruised face, her clothing torn. She'd put up a good fight. She moaned a small sound of desperation. A sound that made the fibers of Westfield's body pull tight. *These bastards took my little girl, and for that they're dead men.* The veteran officer steeled himself, his muscles tensed, ready to spring forward. It was then that the cold steel of a weapon muzzle pressed against the back of his head.

Sasha paced the cramped steel confines of *The Argo*'s medical bay. The terrible sensation of a doomed fate grew inside her. She eyed the ugly, twisted form of one of her best friends in the world, laid on a gurney. The trauma nurse, using a set of clamps, extracted the last bullet from a nasty wound in Bodhi's abdomen and applied a compress dressing to it.

"He took a lot of punishment," the nurse said, glancing to Sasha. "He doesn't have your magnetic properties which means he took the full brunt of each bullet. Amazing he was still standing by the end."

Sasha reached out, her fingers touching the cool slick flesh of his arm. "Is he going to be all right?"

The nurse shrugged. "Only time will tell. Murong gave the order to off load him onto a hammerhead for transport to one of our facilities. He needs better care than we can provide here."

"I'm sorry, Bodhi." Sasha cast her eyes to the floor. "This is my fault."

"Sasha," Murong said, looking to her from a table where Dr. Besom and her assistant worked furiously to save an intubated Lemeaux's waning life.

Sasha ignored him, a budding fury in her chest.

"Sasha," Murong repeated.

"Where does it end?" she said, her jaw set.

"You want the philosophical answer? Because this," Murong stood straight and motioned to the injured in the room with a certain coldness, "this may not ever have an end. Not as long as we fight back."

"You know what I mean," Sasha said. "We have to do something."

"We are doing something."

"Yeah." Sasha flushed. "We're getting people killed." She swung her arm at Lemeaux whose thready pulse now barely registered on the heart monitor. "René's a good man, he didn't deserve this. I should have stayed behind to fight those Strykers."

"His pulse is arrhythmic," Dr. Besom said. "Standby with the defibrillator."

"René is a hero and a champion of our cause. He knew what he was doing." Murong took a half-step toward Sasha, and pointed to Bodhi. "If you stayed, they would have reclaimed your friend there. You'd be dead or recaptured, and Jager would have moved his pieces into position to execute an uncontested checkmate."

"Checkmate?" Sasha raised her voice, the words frail as glass. "This isn't a chess game. My best friend was experimented on and shot to pieces and René is dying."

"I can see that," Murong said, his typically composed demeanor fraying at the edges. The billionaire activist, stepped away from the table and straightened his jacket. "René understood what he was fighting for. Do you? The world needs you. It needs us all to be prepared to give our lives in its defense."

Sasha balked. "That's supposed to make this okay?"

"Zhou," Dr. Besom said, turning, blood smeared across the

front of her apron.

"What?" Murong kept his eyes on Sasha.

Dr. Besom shook her head. "I can't save René. He's lost too much blood." She looked to the faint series of diminishing digital humps steadily blipping across the heart monitor. "He won't hold on much longer. We need to put him in stasis. Let him go peacefully."

Sasha's mouth hung open, her lungs devoid of air. "You're going to let him die?" she whispered.

"Have you been present for this?" Dr. Besom said. "You think I want to let him die?"

"No, but—"

"That's what you said," Dr. Besom shot back.

"Stop, both of you," Murong snapped. He waited for the room to quiet, his narrow eyes flicking between the two of them. "Sentry can save him. We have the tech, the knowledge to save him."

Dr. Besom turned. "Please share how you plan to do that, Zhou."

Murong clenched the fingers of his right hand, a fist which he placed against his lips. "We have active genetic material from Sasha. We can do a comparison against the properties found in Bodhi's DNA to make sure it's viable. The rejuvenating properties alone could sustain his life, even heal him."

A look of shock and disgust crawled across Sasha's features. "You would do that? How is that different from what Jager is doing?"

"Hang on Zhou," Dr. Besom said. "That's taking major ethical liberty, even for us."

"I don't see any other path forward," Murong said. "Not if we want to preserve the life of our friend. We must do whatever is necessary."

Sasha stumbled back toward the hallway. "Experimenting on him without his knowledge?"

"It's not experimentation. It could save his life, Sasha."

"But you can't make that choice for him," Sasha said.

"I believe I will," Murong said, snapping his fingers to gain the attention of several of his crew. "Stabilize him. Do whatever you have to in order to keep his brain and organs alive. Off load him with Bodhi. We'll go from there."

"Yes sir," the crew said, moving to assist a resigned Dr. Besom.

"If you're willing to do this without René's consent, what are you willing to do with Bodhi? Or me? You like to think you're different from Jager, but you're not. You want what you want and nothing will stop you."

"I'm nothing like Jager." Murong's countenance flashed with anger. "I'm the only one here willing to do what's necessary. René signed an agreement when he joined up giving us the power to medically treat him as we saw fit, in the event he couldn't decide for himself. Moments like this require decisive action. Every second we waste is one they don't have."

Sasha raised her hands to her face. "I'm not sure you realize what you're saying."

"I know exactly what I'm saying. It's you who is lost."

Sasha pinched her lips. "Well, I guess Zhou Murong always gets what he wants, no matter the lines he crosses." She turned and stormed from the medical bay.

There were few places a young girl could hide aboard his ship, and as he suspected Sasha had chosen his fully stocked library. A small room of paneled hardwood and priceless works of art, it never failed to inspire a sense of peace in him. He approached the doorway, leaned against the frame and watched the girl. Her webbed hand raised, she allowed her fingers to graze the spines of works by Aristotle, Galileo, Darwin, and Newton, Einstein, and Sagan.

"I lost my composure." Murong cleared his throat. "Unusual, I assure you. I apologize."

Sasha cast a sideways glance at him. "That makes it better?"

"No."

Sasha lowered her head. "It's hard to get away aboard a submarine."

"You picked my favorite room to try," Murong said.

Sasha continued scanning the titles. "Have you read them all?"

"Every single one," Murong said. "One cannot discern the future if they are blind to the past, to the wonders, myths, and legends preceding one's own existence. Not to mention the scores of folly and catastrophic failure others have experienced and recorded."

Sasha nodded but did not turn.

"Did I ever tell you why I named this vessel *The Argo*?" Murong asked.

"No."

"I loved mythology as a child." Murong took a step into the library, eyeing the wall of books. "Chinese, Greek, Persian, the incredible stories of adventure and of heroes and fearsome monsters, they captivated me. But one of my favorites was the story of Jason and his Argonauts. The perils they faced in search of the fabled golden fleece? So exhilarating, sailing the open seas aboard *The Argo*.

"I was inextricably drawn to the idea that I too one day might enjoy my own grand adventure. Have the opportunity to be a part of the myths and legends future generations will speak of." Murong tucked his chin to his chest. "Maybe it was the influence of a foolish boyhood dream which caused me to name my vessel *The Argo*. Although, I can't help but sense a feeling we are here, with the chance to do something worthy of the old stories. I've spent my life and my personal fortune standing in defense of what was right, searching for that moment, and here it is. We have a duty to our world, Sasha. We must stay the course, even when all seems lost. Even if it costs us everything."

Murong opened his hands.

Sasha regarded him, a glimmer of hope lighting her face.

"Sasha, I know you don't always see things the way I do, but it doesn't make me your enemy. And even if it did, the enemy of your enemy is still your friend. Jager is out there. If we don't stop him, this ugliness is only the beginning. Together, we have the power to succeed."

"Together? I don't really know anything about you, who you are."

"Of course, you do," Murong replied. "I was honest with you about my intentions."

"I don't mean that." She tilted her head, her eyes questioning. "I mean who you are as a person. Where you came from? If you have anyone who hopes you'll come home someday."

Murong's cheeks reddened. He half turned away.

"I'm sorry," Sasha said.

"No, it's a fair question. One I'm ..." Murong faltered, a hand moving to rub at the center of his chest. "I'm not sure I'm ready to answer."

Sasha looked hard at Murong, a deep look of worry crossing her face. "You may be mysterious, Zhou, but I'm not. My life is an open book. Everything I know is threatened right now. I've never dealt with anything like this before. What am I supposed to do? Jager is out of control. If I press him, he could hurt my family."

"He could," Murong said. "Which is why I have assigned squads of my best to try and ensure their safety."

"And what about my friends? Jager had Bodhi all this time. I'm sure he has Max, too. You said you'd help me protect them. You promised me."

"I did, and I will," Murong said.

"You've done a lot for me. But I'm not sure I always agree with your methods. Hell, half the time I don't even know what your methods are."

"You have the power to make a difference," Murong said. "I have seen it. But you must decide where you stand."

Sasha regarded him with wet eyes.

"If we don't take him on, Jager will destroy everything, and I mean *everything* we hold dear," Murong said. "This is the tipping point. Now is the time for action—which is why we can't stop. We have to press the fight."

"So, we, what? Go after *The Harbinger*?" Sasha asked.

"Exactly, but we're talking about facing off with a rogue faction of the United States Navy. We need strategy, we need sound tactics if we are to succeed. Not only our lives and the lives of those we care about are at stake here. Many of those sailors working for Jager, as well as my crew aboard this ship and others, are simply following orders. All of us believe what we're doing is right."

"So, we try not to kill anyone unless we have to?" Sasha asked. "That would mean just killing Jager, and maybe his Strykers—if they won't back down."

"Easier said than done. Jager won't show the same restraint. Are you willing to bear the responsibility for the sort of violence necessary to see this through? Even for casualties that may not be intended? Because that's the price we must be prepared to pay."

Sasha pinched her lips. "If I have to. Like you said, it must stop."

Murong tented his fingers in front of his face with a sigh. "Whether the captain has your friend Max or not, he will be ready for us. It's a play designed with one purpose—to lure us in and destroy us."

"He'll try." Sasha lifted her chin, her eyes flashing silver in the artificial light.

"Such an indomitable spirit." Murong smiled. "I knew it would guide you true." He held up an index finger. "Might I make a suggestion as to how we proceed?"

"You're the tactician."

"I've was thinking about something. It's a bit outside the box, but Sasha, you are far more powerful than any of us could possibly understand. Even now your powers are still evolving. You're stronger now than you were just days ago." Murong started pacing. "Consider this: what if your localized magnetic field was not only a defensive boon for you, but also an offensive tool for you to exploit against *The Harbinger*?"

Sasha crossed her arms. "Okay, what are you saying?"

Murong's eyes narrowed to mere slits as a mischievous look broadened across his chiseled face. "This is all highly theoretical, of course."

CHAPTER 34

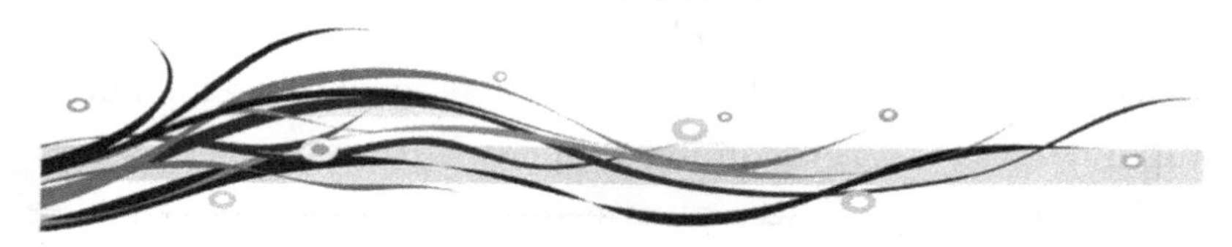

Tal Alvarez took a second bite out of the side of the still wriggling tuna. His jaws worked mechanically as he stood dripping wet, starring at his reflection in the mirror. He didn't remember his eyes looking so yellow before. He leaned closer, noting the way the pupils stretched upward and downward creating a slit that gave his eyes a cat-like appearance. He finished masticating the tough glob of meat, bones, organs, and scales, licking a bit of clear jelly from his lips.

It's in my head, Chief. I can feel it. Telling me what to do.

Just days ago Bobby said these words to him.

Alvarez thought about those words a lot recently. All of his guys said the same stuff. Strange desires. Instincts they'd never felt before. Now he could feel it, too. He looked at the tuna he'd caught moments ago with his bare hands. The urge to eat the wriggling flesh of a struggling fish came upon him with such power he'd felt like he'd come apart if he didn't do it.

So he'd walked to the outer rail on deck three, pulled off his shirt and boots and dropped over the rail. The thrill of the hunt filled him with a vigor for life he scarcely remembered ever feeling so strongly before.

He'd never forget the looks of the men on deck as he'd climbed back aboard soaking wet and holding a huge, thrashing fatty tuna in his hands. He'd taken the first bite right there in front of everyone just to watch their mouths drop open.

"Maria ... and ..." His voice trailed off, unable to remember the next name, that of his eldest son. A muted sensation of guilt passed over him. What did it matter if he couldn't remember a stupid name? He was becoming a super-man.

Eyeing his appearance, it was as though even now he could see the advancements happening in real time. The little rows of gill slits along the sides of his neck, the broadening forehead, the jutting teeth. Man, he felt jacked. Electrical. Alive. Like he could bench press a house.

Ever since getting the most recent Stryker 2.0 injection from Dr. Kingsfeld, his instincts were in overdrive. The future was suddenly bright with possibility. He and his team were now unstoppable. The exploits of the United States Navy's Stryker Team Zero would be legendary.

And the first place they'd focus their efforts would be stopping this fanatic, Zhou Murong and his group of wacko eco-terrorists. They'd start with the girl, Sasha. The rogue asset Captain Jager called, Gorgon.

Little bitch.

She'd been given plenty of chances and she'd chosen her side. If she wanted to ally with some radical nut job, that was on her. She was no match for a platoon of hardened special operations soldiers using tactics and teamwork. *Or is she?* Tal Alvarez slung the remnants of the tuna into the corner, gnashing his teeth, bits of blood and white meat pushing between them.

At every turn this Gorgon ran roughshod over them, tossed them around like rag dolls. Reckless, undisciplined, yet still capable of uncanny strength and breathtaking damage.

No more, he thought. Next time they met, it would be on his turf, and she'd get more than she bargained for. She was a terrorist. An enemy of the United States of America, and if Tal was anything, he was a patriot. There wasn't anything he wouldn't do for his country. There wasn't anyone he wouldn't kill for it. A soldier had to believe in the mission, and Captain Jager, though a bit unorthodox, had yet to lead him astray.

It was time for the good guys to gain some ground. It was time for a reckoning.

CHAPTER 35

"Move and you're a dead man."

Westfield stood and raised his hands slow and deliberate.

"I caught him over here trying to sneak in," the man behind him said.

Others approached.

"What did I tell you?" the squad leader said. "He's a salty old street cop. I knew he'd come." He nodded at Westfield. "Take the armor off of him."

With a ripping of Velcro, his body armor was pulled off and thrown to the side. One of the other men took Westfield's sidearm from him, cleared it, and tossed the gun in a corner. "Dumb as hell, coming here all by yourself, cowboy."

Westfield's heart sank at the notion he'd followed a trail of breadcrumbs meticulously placed for him.

"Nothing to say?" The man behind him seized a handful of Westfield's hair and gave it a savage jerk. He moved the muzzle of the gun to his temple. "What happened to our guys on the road? Huh? You kill them?"

Westfield swallowed and licked his lips. His eyes flicked to Janie. A subtle twisting of her wrists suggested she was already exploiting her captor's preoccupation.

"Listen to me," Westfield said as evenly as possible. "Your command is wrong. Your orders—what you've been asked to do, on American soil, is wrong. You took an oath—"

In one smooth motion the team leader whipped his pistol across the bridge of Westfield's nose, splitting the flesh. Westfield's knees buckled, a red stream running off his chin. An arm snaked around his neck restraining him as the pistol pressed against his head again.

"Don't tell us about our oath, traitor," the team leader said.

Westfield clenched his blood-soaked teeth. "Is that what they told you? I'm a traitor?"

"You're working with Sentry. Preparing to conduct terrorist operations on American soil."

"And you believe that?" Westfield asked.

Behind them, Janie had one hand free, the steely look of determination hardened into her tear-streaked face. Beside her Gordon looked from her to the commotion, eyes wide.

"Listen to me. We're not different. I'm you," Westfield continued. "Corporal Derrick Westfield, United States Army, eighth military police brigade out of Fort Shaftner. Served eight years. Honorable discharge. Decorated police officer for almost twenty years. I understand duty, but this … it's crazy. It's *criminal.* Please don't hurt them. Don't throw your lives away like this."

The man behind him gave another sharp jerk of his hair. "I'm supposed to listen to you run your suck hole about duty after you killed my brothers?"

Westfield winced at the tension on his scalp. "I had no choice. I didn't want this fight, you did." He strained to look forward, a sense of relief filling him as Janie freed herself and stole away like an alley cat into the shadows.

"Well, remember this, old man, whatever happens next, you brought it on yourself," the team leader said.

"Yeah," Westfield sighed. "I usually do." He let the silence deepen for a moment. "Say, you guys lose something?" He thrust his eyebrows up, his chin toward the empty chair across the dusty space.

The crew of men seemed to jolt, two of them turning, scanning back and forth in sudden panic.

"No."

"Where'd she go?"

The team leader turned to look, and Westfield heard a whispered curse escape the lips of the man behind him, the grip on his hair loosening.

"There's a saying," Westfield said.

"Shut up," the man behind him said.

"Beware the old man, in a profession where men die young."

Westfield flung his head backward, a sting of pain arcing through his skull as it smacked against the nose and teeth of the man behind him. Another backward strike of Westfield's skull against his captor's face and he felt a trickle of his own blood run into his collar. The grip on his hair tightened like a vice.

Jerking his arm down on top of the man's gun hand, he held it fast between his palms, and extended the weapon forward, his finger overlaying that of his foe. The men before him spun, their hands grabbing for their weapons as each muzzle blast illuminated the twisted pain on their faces. Again and again the weapon recoiled, sandwiched between their palms. Men crumpled and folded, lifeless piles of clothes heaped in the musty dark.

The man behind Westfield screamed something unintelligible, driving him into a stumbling trot, his legs tripping and slipping beneath him. The weapon clenched in their hands fired again, the flash blinding, the round pinging off the metal wall of the warehouse. Another blast from the pistol sent a round zipping off the concrete floor at their feet as his opponent wrenched the weapon down.

Scrabbling for control of the gun, they fell against the operator controls for a nearby conveyor belt. The line jerked to life with an electronic buzz, and amber lights began to strobe.

"I'll kill you!" the man screamed.

A hook punch struck hard against Westfield's ribs, followed by another that landed with a sickening thud. With a groan, Westfield forced the man's gun hand between the rotating gears driving the conveyor belt. The assassin's hand disappeared into the machine with a wet crunch. His captor shrieked, flailing wildly as he tried to jerk his mangled hand free.

Westfield twisted to the side and fell to his back, for the first time noticing the blood-soaked fixed blade knife clenched in the assassin's free hand. Pulling his ankle back to him, Westfield unsnapped his backup weapon from the triad holster on his boot and yanked the Smith and Wesson thirty-eight snubbie free.

With a cry the assassin tore his useless hand free from the gears, the flesh hanging like strips of jerky. Raising the knife he threw himself forward as Westfield's revolver cracked five times in a blitz of gunfire. Westfield's chest heaved, the empty revolver smoking and quivering in his hand. In the darkness, the assassin faltered, a lost look on his face as he stumbled and fell face first onto the moving belt, the toes of his boots squeaking across the floor as it carried him away.

Westfield groaned, grabbing his side, a flaming hot brand of pain boring a hole through his midsection. Pulling his hand away he found it wet, blood pooling in the depression of his palm. The realization he'd been stabbed, not punched, floored him.

"Janie," He wheezed pushing himself to his feet. "Janie, are you okay—?"

The crack of a gun echoed, the sound reverberating in waves

off the metal-walled space. Westfield staggered and fell back against a nearby shelf. With a gasp his eyes dropped to his upper chest, a crimson stain spreading outward from the neat hole in his shirt.

"I got you, you tough old bastard. I got you." The squad leader wheezed as he struggled to stand, handgun outstretched, his free hand clenching a gunshot wound in his side.

Westfield wheezed, his eyes squinted, waiting for the final blast.

With a shriek, Janie lunged from the shadows, and slammed a steel bar down across the wrist of the squad leader. The man cried out, and the gun clattered against the floor. He threw himself upon her, strangling her with his bare hands. He struck Janie in the face with his fist, once, twice, her body sagging as she fell away from him. He grabbed for the pistol at his feet, and raised it.

Shocked back to life, Westfield gave a scream of fury as he shoved off the wall, his lead-filled legs pumped clumsily beneath him. But he'd never get there in time. A lurid sneer stretched across the squad leader's face in the face of imminent victory.

With a muffled groan Gordon shoved to his feet, the strapped chair hanging from his rear end. He dropped his shoulder into the squad leader, bowling him forward, the pistol flashing in the dark with a blast of fire. The man turned into him and a second report caused Gordon to scream.

Westfield connected with the squad leader, tackling him low. The blow sent him sprawling against the ground as the gun slid into the dark. In an instant, both men clamored to their feet, blood on fire with the deadly effects of fear, hate, and adrenaline. The squad leader lunged for Westfield, who side slipped the grasp and belted the man with a tight jab-cross-hook combination that sent the younger, stronger man, staggering.

The squad leader swung again, hard, a haymaker from

downtown. Westfield ducked, hammering him with another cross and two shots to the body, followed by an uppercut to the jaw. Screaming, the team leader forced himself upon Westfield, digging probing fingers deep into the bullet wound in his chest. Westfield gasped, his consciousness fading.

With a final savage cry, Westfield grabbed the man by the neck and forced him back. Stumbling and flailing, a train of furious energy, the team leader shrieked as a large metal spike lanced through the meat of his chest. He hung there for a moment, bewildered, moaning. His fingers clawed fruitlessly at the impaling foreign body. After a moment his eyes glazed over, and his body sagged to hang from the front of the forklift.

Westfield faltered. His breath gurgled in his chest, an all-consuming lake of fire welling in his lungs as his consciousness faded.

"Janie," he slurred, reaching for his daughter. His body pitched forward onto the floor.

"Daddy!" Janie cried, crawling toward him. She clamored to her knees and rolled him to his side.

"My girl," Westfield said, a crimson pool spreading out beneath him. "I'm sorry, honey."

"Don't be sorry, Daddy. You did just fine."

He reached with bloodied fingers to touch her face. "I never deserved to have something so good in my life."

Janie sniffled, wiping at her tear-streaked face. "Don't you quit on me." She sobbed, reaching into his pocket and dumping the contents of his wallet onto the floor. She grabbed a credit card, tore his shirt open and pressed the flat of the plastic down hard over the bubbling froth of the sucking chest wound. With her free hand she pulled a section of her shirt and clamped her teeth down, tearing it free. Wadding it up, she rolled him toward her and applied a firm compress to the stab wounds in his lower back.

Free of the chair, Gordon stumbled over and fell beside them, his fingers clenched over the dripping gunshot wound through his forearm.

"Hang on, Derrick. Just hang on, buddy," Gordon said, his face pale with cold sweat.

"Do you hear us Officer Westfield?" Janie shook him, looking for a response in his glassy eyes. "You don't get to give up. Not ever."

"I love you, Janie," Westfield wheezed. A tear streamed from the corner of his eye and across his stubbled cheek.

"I love you, too, Daddy," Janie sobbed. "Hang on, your boys are coming. They're coming."

Westfield shuddered as she held him close, the dark interior of the warehouse soaked in the pungent coppery smell of blood and cordite. And in the distance, the sound of approaching sirens rose in the night like a gracious eternal chorus of angels, riding on the wings of the endless island breeze.

CHAPTER 36

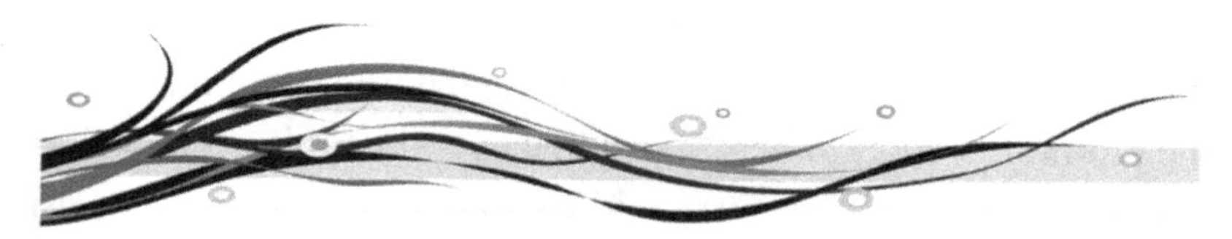

Jager strained his eyes searching an inky black horizon, the turbulent surf intermittently illuminated by branched chains of jagged lightning. The storm, a wall of churning black, would be upon them in minutes. It would only make the coming hours more troublesome. Jager glanced at his watch: 0130 hours.

Off the starboard side, Jager could see the sharp angled outline of *The U.S.S. Corrigan*, a state-of-the-art Zumwalt class destroyer with stealth capabilities, tasked with watching their six. Beneath the waves, patrolling the depths in search of *The Argo*, was the recently commissioned *U.S.S Dallas*, a Virginia class fast attack sub, also with stealth capabilities. Murong didn't have the firepower to go toe to toe with them. And Sasha, even for all of her enhanced abilities, was only an emotional child.

His Strykers, dosed with the newest evolution of the Stryker program would be unstoppable. Jager rubbed the light stubble of his chin. He had something she wanted, and he couldn't wait to give it to her. Now it was a waiting game. Before sunrise, the Gorgon would either be recaptured or dead. At this point, after all the trouble the little bitch caused him, he was starting to prefer the latter.

Jager glared with unconcealed contempt at Lt. Col Atcheson. Sweating profusely, the man appeared a nervous wreck, his hands fumbling over themselves in tumbled circles. Jager gnashed his teeth, the muscles of his jaw flexing.

"Sir? I've got something," a young sailor said.

Jager approached the console where the fresh-faced girl sat staring at an undulating series of blue digital waves rippling across the monitor in front of her. A hush fell over the bridge. The sailors under Jager's command were told that contact with the terrorist group Sentry was imminent and that this volatile entity had the ability to attack them with sophisticated technology and genetically modified super soldiers. None of them had any real details about what they faced, or why.

"What am I looking at?" Jager said.

"There's a biological anomaly in the readings here, sir," the woman said.

Jager grunted. "And?"

The young sailor wiped a bead of sweat from her temple, hands trembling. "Well sir, um." She swallowed. "Sir it looks like the same magnetic signature the lost Gorgon asset emitted."

Jager slammed his fist on the tabletop, causing the sailor to jump. "She's not lost, dammit. She defected."

Not a soul in the room stirred.

Jager felt the crawl of desperation along his spine. A looming madness. Just like his father. *How long has it been since I took my meds?* He struggled to compose himself, hard gaze cutting like a saber through every person in the room before looking again to the frazzled young woman. "How sure are you it's her?"

"It's not like radar. It doesn't say exactly where she is, only she or something similar to her specific magnetic properties is within a current three kilometer radius of our position." The sailor's eyes widened. "Wait. Two kilometer radius, sir."

Jager said nothing, his gaze narrowing as he stared at the screen.

"One kilometer."

"Not possible." Jager snarled. "The equipment is wrong.

Nothing in the water is that fast."

A deep *boom* resounded in the depths of the ocean like the sounding of some ancient drum of war.

"Captain," the radio operator said. "We have a distress signal from the Dallas. They're reporting something struck them in their rotors. They're dead in the water. They're asking if we've got anything on our screens."

"It's them," Jager said.

"Sir, the signature is moving again," the young sailor said.

"Get me a target location, now," Jager said through clenched teeth.

The console operator shook her head. "Sir, there isn't—"

"Captain." Commander Atcheson stepped forward, his finger extended toward the horizon. "Enemy sub just broke the surface. Port side, eleven o'clock."

"Get a weapon's lock on them and get *The Corrigan* on the horn," Jager said.

"I've got two more vessels advancing on the surface," an ensign with night vision binoculars called out. "Ten o'clock and twelve o'clock, sir. They're using cloaking tech."

A smile spread across Jager's face as he watched *The U.S.S. Corrigan*'s powerful modified 155mm Mark 51 turret mounted Advanced Gun System pivot in the direction of the Sentry vessels. "See you in hell, Murong."

A tiny shadow fired from the water between *The Harbinger* and *The Corrigan*. Jager squinted, watching the human-sized object as it arced through the air and connected with one of *The Corrigan*'s Mark 51 turrets. A blinding flash of light and the concussive boom of an explosion caused him to flinch. Jager faltered, his mind paralyzed. He watched as the shadow dashed with astonishing speed, crashing into a second bow turret with a concussive flash-

boom.

"All hands! General Quarters! Get those birds in the air!" Jager screamed across the bridge. "We're under attack!"

Atcheson clenched the console before him and braced. He vomited onto the floor, straightened, then grabbed a water bottle and poured its contents directly across his face.

"Hit them with everything we've got. Defend this ship!" Jager shouted, fumbling with a handheld radio as the sirens wailed. "Get ahold of yourself, Atcheson, you've got the bridge."

Jager stormed past the still vomiting XO with the radio pressed to his lips. "Sound general quarters. Get me Alvarez. Now!"

The radio squawked. "And the Breach asset, sir?"

"Load him up," Jager said, brimming with adrenaline and expectation. "It's time for a little reunion."

CHAPTER 37

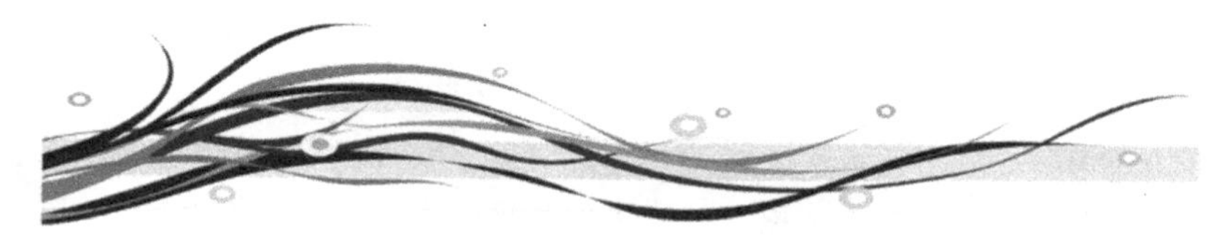

Sasha landed with the grace of a gymnast on the deck of *The U.S.S. Corrigan*, her chest heaving from the exertion. She could scarcely believe it. Murong was right after all. Something about her speed and power combined with her constant magnetic properties made her a surgical weapon, capable of punching through ships the way a sharpened pencil might lance through a single sheet of paper. Murong's theory worked to devastating effect on the turret-mounted weapon systems. The real test though, was still to come.

Two F35-V Lightning III jets screamed overhead, loosing a directed barrage of 25mm machinegun fire against the Argo and two other Sentry vessels.

"*Incoming EMP Sasha. Keep up the distraction,*" Murong said.

From the deck of *The Corrigan* Sasha watched a fusillade of countermeasures fly into the air, followed by a rocket that burst from *The Argo* and screamed high into the night sky. A wave of blackouts rippled across the ships, lights winking out in choreographed unison. The two F35-Vs fell from the sky, twisting and crashing in a spray of foam into the dark undulating waves.

"*Keep moving, their emergency systems will bring them back online in no time.*"

Smoke billowed in plumes from the disabled destroyer, rising and dissipating amidst the snapping of a turbulent storm-laden wind. The fast moving squall line would be upon them in moments rendering the small battle group ineffective. Sasha strained her eyes, searching for the black outline of the micro carrier through the hazy smoke-laced night. *The Harbinger* was out there somewhere waiting.

"*Sasha, if you can read me, they have a lock on* The Odyssey. The Corrigan*'s weapon systems are still active,*" Murong said.

With an ear-splitting crack, the last of *The Corrigan*'s Mark 51 AGS fired, the fireball flash-frying her vision. Sasha flinched and shielded her face. An instant later a secondary explosion greeted her ears. A rolling column of fire burst upward from one of Sentry's assault vessels, *The Odyssey.*

"*Sasha, where are you?* The Odyssey *is down. There's a lock on* The Argo. *We can't dive in time.*"

Sasha launched across the deck, the crack of small arms fire in her ears. She cursed her thoughtlessness, the oversight of having missed just one AGS already a fatal blow against Sentry's forces. Innocent lives, lost.

Grabbing the giant barrel of the weapon she wrenched it to the side as it fired a second time, the blast wave causing her bones to ache and her ears to ring. An explosion cascaded in the night, illuminating *The Harbinger*. The heavy 155 millimeter round punched through the upper levels and tore a massive gaping hole in the jump deck, the last F35-V Lightning III jet rocking on its side. With a shout, she slammed her balled fists against the barrel of the AGS distorting it downward and rendering the massive guns inoperable.

With *The Corrigan*'s main weapon systems out of the fight and Jager's stealth sub disabled two hundred feet below the surface, she now focused her attention on the flame lit outline of *The Harbinger*. Murong seemed to read her mind, his voice suddenly in her ear with a crackle of static.

"*Excellent work, Sasha. We're initiating evasive action. Make your move on* The Harbinger *now.*"

"Wish me luck," Sasha said.

"*You won't need it.*" Murong's voice was calm, confident. "*Do what you were made to do.*"

Sasha ran for the rail of the destroyer, even as a gutsy group of *The Corrigan*'s sailors attempted to close on her, their weapons raised. Tucking over the rail in a full dive, she rocketed toward the dark waters below and plunged beneath the waves. The cold water bathed her skin, stoking a desire in her to leave all the madness behind. But she couldn't leave others to fight her battles. *No, this fight started with me and it will end with me. One way or another.*

Diving deep, Sasha swept in an arc drawing back toward the surface. She flashed through the water in a trail of swirling bubbles. Above her, the hull of *The Harbinger* stood outlined against the dark by the flash of lightning and the flickering of fire. With a groan, she sped upward, her momentum mounting. A final push sent bubbles streaming from her lips. Fists extended, her body rocketed toward the hull.

Sasha collided with the bow of *The Harbinger* with the explosive force of a next generation Mark 48 torpedo. The blast wave buckled the hull and tore a gaping hole through the belly of the giant ship. Sasha pierced through the metal at an upward angle, knifing through the side wall of the great ship like a high-velocity armor-piercing round. Her body flew free and crashed back into the white-capped waves.

Sasha broke the surface gasping. Her hands and arms throbbed with excruciating pain. She took in another breath, the waves slapping her face as *The Harbinger* gave a shuddering crack, its back broken. Water chugged into the belly of the ship, dragging it under.

"*Well done, Sasha. Now finish it.*" Murong said over her earpiece.

Sasha pushed her fear and doubt away into the dark hidden corners of her consciousness. *No time for that.*

Moving fast, she scaled the shattered hull, climbing her way up to the jump deck by way of a nasty split in the ship's side. Below her, fuel spread out across the surface of the water, a glistening purple sheen in the light of the growing fires. This place was a powder keg. She had to find Max.

Making the top of the seam, Sasha vaulted into the air and cleared the side of the ship. The growing storm of wind and rain whipped past, covering her lithe form in a glistening crystalline glow. Sirens shrieked and lights flashed across the deck of *The Harbinger*. A screaming hiss scratched at the air.

Struck with the full force of the whining 66 mm rocket, the projectile caught her in mid-air, catapulting her across the deck and sending her sprawling amidst a pile of strewn metal transport crates. She lay there, unmoving, smoke wafting from her back, blood smeared beneath her nose.

"So, the Gorgon bleeds after all," Jager said, dumping the shoulder-fired M72 LAW on the deck and taking a fresh one from one of the Strykers beside him. At their fore, Alvarez stood, arms crossed. These weren't the soldiers Sasha faced before. Jager did something to them. She eyed their swollen, imposing frames, as they flanked their captain with furious faces and balled fists.

"Don't bother getting up," Alvarez said. "You're surrounded."

Sasha groaned, stirring. Bringing her elbows beneath her, she tried to raise herself. Her eyes lolled in her head. A thin trickle of blood streamed from her left nostril.

"*Sasha you've got to finish this. Get up or they're going to kill you.*" Murong's voice buzzed in her ear.

"I gave you the chance to do something of immeasurable value for your country, to be someone, and you threw it in my face." Jager's eyes shone with madness. "You think Murong is your friend? He's using you to enforce his agenda."

"*Sasha, you have to resist,*" Murong said.

She pushed herself up, a hiss escaping through pinched lips.

"Come now, Sasha," Jager said. "Don't be foolish. I have your father. Continue to go against me and he's dead."

"You're a coward. Leave my family out of this," Sasha said. Rising, her head swimming, she shoved to her feet and lunged at Jager, her teeth bared.

The second M72 rocket hit her squarely in the chest, bursting in a fireball that flung her across the deck and into the side of a crashed F35-V Lightning. Sasha tumbled to the ground, limp and unmoving, the white bands of her chest and abdomen singed black.

"Sasha, Sasha." Jager sucked his teeth. "See, I had this epiphany. You may be bulletproof, but you're not rocket proof. Your body, however advanced, is still affected by a close quarters detonation of high explosive."

Sasha groaned, trembling as she tried to raise herself.

Jager stood over her, a coldness descending upon his features.

"*Sasha …*" Murong's voice hissed through a garbled wash of static.

"I didn't want this, but you're too much of a liability. I can't leave you to your own devices." Jager pulled the earbud from her ear and dropped it on the ground, crushing it beneath his boot. "See, that is always the trouble with cowards like Murong. Unwilling to engage himself, Murong wants a girl to do his fighting for him. He's a weak, pathetic, typical Chinese. When you're dead, we'll hunt him down and destroy the last remnants of Sentry. And you know how?" Jager asked with mock sweetness. "We're going to use someone near and dear to you to do it."

Jager glanced at Alvarez. "Get her on her feet."

Dragging her to her feet, a pair of Strykers on either side held Sasha firm by her arms. Little streams of blood ran from her nose and pooled in her ears. She coughed, her head hanging as they held her upright and she struggled to regain her senses. Rain lashed from the rumbling sky in waves, sweeping the deck and whipping sideways with each gust of wind. *The Harbinger* groaned, shuddering, and with a series of cracks, shifted beneath them.

Their vessel doomed, the Strykers looked to Jager, but he showed no acknowledgment. His gaze remained locked on his captured prize, the object of his obsession.

"Send him up." Jager touched his ear and smiled, a rekindled insanity dancing in his eyes. The lift whined as it rose inch by inch carrying a dark, shifting monstrosity. "Sasha, you remember your friend? Or … was this one more than a friend?"

"Max." Sasha whimpered, a black void of hopelessness swelling in her chest. "No …"

The hideous beast snorted as it came into view, pulling on its chains, a thick pink tongue flailing among pointed teeth.

"This is all because of you, Sasha," Jager said, pausing with a finger raised. "If you'd stayed, I wouldn't have had to resort to this. Now look at what's become of your dear Max. Allow me to introduce to you the United States Navy's newest super soldier. Codename, Breach."

The long sloping black head of the beast came into view. Snuffing and growling, its muscles bulged as it pulled on the manacles that held it chained fast to the deck. It was massive, at least twice the size of Bodhi, and fitted with a titanium control collar like the one they put on them both.

"No," Sasha said, straightening, the Stryker's grip on her

tightening. "You did this to him … to us. This is all you, Jager." Her eyes narrowed. "And I've come to stop it."

Jager sobered, jabbing a finger at his Strykers. "Hold her fast. Don't let her—"

Stepping forward, Sasha dropped her weight flinging all four Strykers forward of her position.

"Kill her," Jager shouted, stepping back.

"Come on!" Sasha bared her teeth.

Senior Chief Alverez and his Strykers rushed her, shooting forward with a heightened level speed and agility. Sasha tracked them as they came, her eyesight so acute, every twitch, every movement, a dagger pulled, a handgun produced, seen all at once. Driving forward, she met them head on, colliding with the first man, catching him under the chin and thrusting him from the ground with an uppercut. Veering to her left, Sasha landed a push kick to another's midsection, doubling him over. A reverse spinning elbow strike caught a third man across the neck, sending him stumbling to the side.

Alvarez came at her. She dodged a swipe of his combat knife, swinging her fist in an arc toward his face. With a smack, it landed hard in Alvarez's palm. Sasha flung her free arm upward to brace the knife as it came stabbing toward her chest. Her eyes flared wide at the sudden strength of the lead Stryker.

"I know, right?" he said, a grin of satisfaction on his camouflaged face. "We got an upgrade."

Sasha groaned, wrenching her hand free to brace the knife and press it away. She attempted a knee strike to his groin, but he twisted his hips to the side at the last moment.

"You're about to find out what happens to terrorist scum," Alvarez hissed.

"Jager's lying to you. Don't do this."

Alvarez punched Sasha in the ribs with his free hand as another Stryker kicked the back of her knee, buckling her legs. The man behind her grabbed a fistful of her thick hair strands, and yanked back. Sasha cried out as the knife continued to press in.

"Max, I know you're in there. Don't let them control you," Sasha said.

A bolt of lightning streaked across the sky, illuminating the muscled form of Max. He craned his neck with a snarl, pulling on the chains.

"Don't let them do this," Sasha said.

A punch thrown from one of the Strykers snapped her head to the right. Sasha tried to rise as she was struck again, the other men crowding around.

The Harbinger tipped dangerously back and forth with the rising storm, rain cascading like drifting curtains across the broken deck.

"Let's make this interesting," Jager said, holding the weatherproof control tablet he'd taken from Hanson. Scrolling through the menu he punched with his finger at the rain splattered screen. A hiss rose from Max's collar as a concoction of stimulants injected into his bloodstream. A bloodcurdling shriek erupted from Max's throat, his chest heaving, black eyes dodging back and forth. White foam gathered in the corners of his gaping jaws.

"Leave him alone!" Sasha shouted, her grip on the knife aimed at her chest slipping.

"You can't stand against all of us." Alvarez bared his teeth. "We'll never stop. Gonna kill you like we killed those terrorist friends of yours."

Sasha twisted with a scream, thrusting the knife into the chest of the Stryker behind her. Stepping beneath Alvarez's arm, she forced it down across her shoulder, snapping it at the elbow joint like brittle plastic. Alvarez shrieked and fell, the knife clattering from his hands. Another Stryker lunged forward, a pistol blasting at close range. Sasha knocked it from his hands and with an action born of sheer fury, leaped into the air, landing a flying punch that folded the gunman's face inward in a spray of blood. He pitched over and fell against the deck, the contents of his skull mixing with the splashing rain.

The remaining Strykers converged on her, howls of rage upon their lips at seeing the death of their brother. Jager stepped well back, stopping next to an open case marked FGM-148 Javelin. Looking at the tablet, his finger hovered over a pulsating red button. One last look at Sasha flinging his best across the deck, and Jager's finger dropped against the screen.

With repeated clacks, the heavy chains securing Max's wrists fell free. He howled, holding his heavily muscled arms high in the air.

"That's it. Now do what you were made to do," Jager said.

Max swung his head in Jager's direction and gave a snort.

"Destroy her." Jager tabbed another button.

Electricity snapped in widening arcs across Max's thick neck, eliciting a bestial scream. He grabbed at the collar and received another much more sustained shock.

"You will obey me!" Jager screamed.

Stomping forward, Max closed on Sasha. He rolled his shoulders, flexing open the talons on his huge, webbed hands. He snarled, spittle drooling through his teeth as he approached.

"Max, it's me. It's Sasha. You know me. I ..." She swallowed. "I love you."

The giant creature stopped, and snorted, swiveling its elongated head back and forth, appraising them all.

"Kill her," Jager shouted across the deck.

Alvarez struggled to his feet clutching his disfigured arm. "What are you waiting for, get on with it or you're next." He leveled a carbine rifle with one arm at the hulking form of Max.

Blood sprayed into the air as Alvarez stumbled back, the meat and bone of his chest cavity draped open in a crimson curtain. He coughed from his mouth and toppled to the deck. Max crouched over Alverez, snarling, blood and meat dripping from his clawed hand.

Sasha slammed into the closest Stryker and the blow from her shoulder sent him sprawling.

"Son of a bitch," Jager screamed, mashing on the tablet.

White hot arcs of electrical current snapped against Max's flesh. He screamed, grabbed the collar with both hands.

"That's it, Max," Sasha said as she landed another solid blow. "Fight it."

With a roar, the collar cracked and tore free. Gripping the shattered thing in his hand, electricity twisting up his arm, Max hurled it away into the dark.

A Stryker opened fire with a Squad Automatic Weapon. The bullets streaked across the deck, striking Max as well as the fuel tanks of the F35-V Lightning III behind him, sending jet fuel spraying across the deck. Pivoting into the Stryker, Max knocked the weapon from his grasp, grabbed him and broke the stunned man's back over his knee.

Max grabbed two more Strykers. Holding each by the neck, he swung them upward toward each other, their heads exploding together in a plume of blood and bone. Max gave a victory cry as he and Sasha turned back to back. The last remaining Strykers flung themselves upon them with gun and knife.

Jager dropped the tablet with a curse, his hands feverishly digging through the crate for the Javelin anti-tank weapon system.

"You've ruined me. Everything I've worked so hard for. My legacy. I will kill you all."

He braced the Javelin launcher over his shoulder and acquired a lock on the largest target, the lumbering form of Max. A wicked smile spread across the captain's worn rain-soaked features as he eyed the jet fuel spraying against the deck beneath Sasha and Max's feet.

"Get some of this," he said, firing the weapon system. The missile fired straight up into the sky. Jager dropped the Javelin and ran, his feet plodding and slow as he made for the edge of the ship.

"Oh god, Max," Sasha said looking at her fuel soaked feet and pointing at the missile. It arced over in a graceful bend, streaking down with a whistling shriek as it came.

Max lowered his head sniffing the rising fumes of jet fuel and raised his black eyes to track the condensation trail of the missile. He opened his mouth to speak. A grinding of broken words raked across his ruined vocal cords. "Leabe meih … Ewe gho … Pleach." His massive, clawed hand touched Sasha's shoulder.

Sasha stared at him. "What? No, Max, don't—"

Surging forward Max crashed into the remaining Strykers, digging his claws into them as they retaliated, sinking their knives deep into his body. He screamed, bringing his full strength to bear against his foes.

"Max!"

Sasha turned her gaze upon the missile as it shot earthward, angling toward him. Locked in on his heat signature. Sasha's body stiffened, the air caught in her lungs. Max couldn't survive a direct hit. But maybe she could. Sasha clenched her teeth, her eyes narrowing to mere slits. "So shall we go." Flexing her knees, she crouched then thrust upward into the air, her fist extended, a powerful scream upon her lips.

A blinding flash lit the sky as Sasha collided with the Javelin. The concussive blast wave sent Max and the Strykers hurtling in all directions tumbling like rag-dolls thrown from the deck of the carrier. The rippling hellish inferno streaked forth, sending arms, ammunition, and fuel popping and exploding upward in a giant rolling fireball that raced from one end of the ship to the other and set the water around *The Harbinger* ablaze.

Reaching the edge of the jump deck, Captain Jager clawed at his ruined face, his fingers sinking into the swollen blistered flesh as smothering flames enveloped his body and sank into his lungs. A high-pitched shriek erupted from his throat, even as his body tumbled from the deck of *The Harbinger* in a brilliant streak of fire.

CHAPTER 38

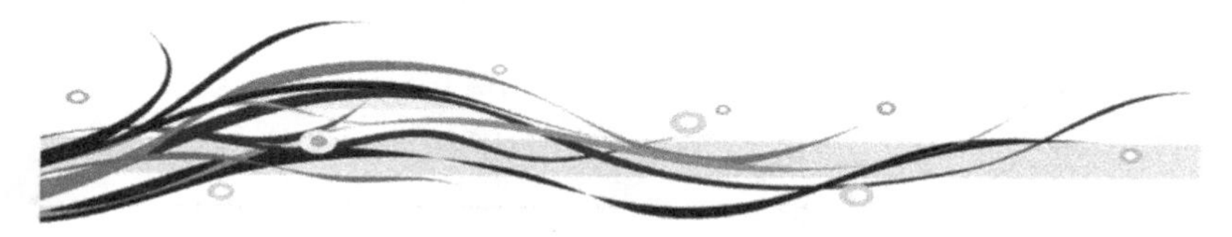

Soaking wet and buffeted by cascading gusts of wind, Zhou Murong scanned the surface of the water from his position aboard the back of a trolling Sentry Hammerhead assault vessel. He swung his arm back and forth in dramatic arcs, a handheld radio pressed to his lips, as he directed Sentry assets and pointed out individuals in the water in need of assistance. These men and women had raised arms against him, but that didn't mean he was willing to let them all drown.

"That group of sailors there. Get a life pod in the water."

"Yes, sir," a merc said, raising a forty-millimeter launcher. With a snap, the compressed round fired from the large barrel, sailing across the rising waves and inflating with a whoosh. Sailors from the burning *Harbinger*, wearing their personal flotation devices, helped one another into the life raft with gasps of relief.

"You know," the merc said, loading another quick inflate raft into the breach of the launcher. "No one will ever know that we tried to help these people." He fired and the raft inflated with another swell of compressed air. "Even if they talk, no one will believe them."

Murong wiped the rain from his face and eyed the rumbling storm set high above the flaming *U.S.S. Harbinger*. Bubbles chugged forth from the hull as it rolled sideways, the bow elevating high as it sank.

"That's not why we do it," he said, pointing to yet another

group of sailors huddled together amidst the waves.

The merc's launcher fired again.

Murong turned to the helm where he looked to a weary-faced navigator, eyeing a set of screens. "Anything?"

"Yes, sir. Team two recovered the other test subject, the one they called Breach. He's unconscious and badly injured. They're asking for permission to sedate, stabilize, and extract."

Murong nodded. "Get him to sea base Delta. Make sure he is treated well but kept secure for now."

"Affirmative."

"And Sasha?" Murong leaned into the cab, his eyes roving the various screens. "Anything on her?"

"We're registering her magnetic signature, sir. But we don't yet have a location on her or any indication of her condition."

Murong eased out a disappointed sigh. "Keep searching. I want her found."

He pulled a set of glasses from his pocket and pushed them up the bridge of his nose. He tabbed the power button and the glasses winked to life showing a list of available commands scrolling before his eyes. "Archive footage. Surveillance drone four." An instant later the lenses of the glasses flickered and an aerial image of the smoking deck of *The Harbinger* popped across his vision.

"Playback," Murong said.

He'd already seen this live and it was difficult to watch the first time. He had no desire to witness it again, but something told him he might gain some insight from viewing the footage again. He watched the seconds tick by, the fight playing out as Sasha and Max took on Jager's forces together. They'd each tried to save the other, and in the end, both were blown into oblivion by Jager's final act of malice. Max survived, but he'd been on the deck. Sasha, however, took a direct hit from a Javelin missile—ordinance designed to pierce and destroy tanks.

Is there any chance she could have survived?

Murong shook his head disabling the image on the glasses and placing them back in his pocket. Everything inside him wanted to find her, but he had other pressing matters to attend to. A foul presence remained on the rain-laced wind, a feeling of ominous dread he couldn't put his finger on. By all reasonable accounts, Jager should be dead. Though they'd yet to recover a body. Murong felt sure the man couldn't have survived what happened aboard *The Harbinger.* So why the growing feeling of doom inside his chest?

The Erebos probe, still emitting dangerous levels of void energy, was last known aboard *The Harbinger.* As Sentry wasted precious time trying to help the survivors of this senseless conflict, the most dangerous, volatile, mutative device on the planet was sinking to the bottom of the pacific amidst a giant hunk of twisted steel. This more than anything terrified him, for who could say what atrocities might later spawn from the depths.

All he could say for now was the world was a little safer for what Sasha and Sentry alongside her had done. As long as mankind existed, so too would the destruction and perversion of the natural world. It must be contested, and with or without Sasha, he would face it.

Murong rubbed his face and watched with apprehension as the flickering flames of *The Harbinger* extinguished with a hiss, and the bow slipped beneath the waves in a foam tinged spray of air.

CHAPTER 39

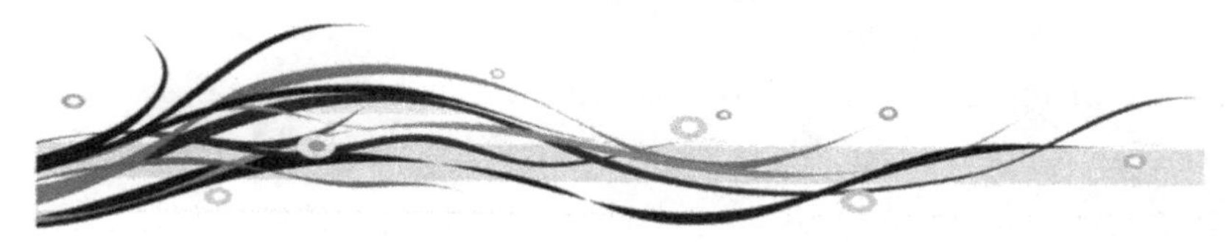

In a sterile white hospital room inside Queen's Medical Center, Derrick Westfield stirred beneath the thin sheet draped across the less than comfortable pre-positioned medical bed. A host of little pips, beeps, and other various medical chimes greeted his ears. A slow strained wheeze whistled from his mouth. With remarkable slowness, his right hand raised from beside his body, touching at his beaten features, swollen eyes, and the flexible oxygen hose snaking away from the underside of his nose.

Afraid to probe further he lowered his hand, his mind foggy with pain killers. One painful moment at a time, the madness of the past few days returned. The last thing he remembered was his daughter's sweet voice in his ears.

"Janie," he croaked. "Where's my Janie?"

Next to him, a form stirred awake, sat forward and cupped his face in slender angelic fingers. "I'm here," she said, her tired face, complete with black eye and split lip, still framed by picturesque blond locks.

"My girl ..." Westfield's voice trailed off. "You okay, honey?" His hand, taped with an inserted IV, grazed the broken skin of his daughter's lip.

Janie's eyes welled and she sniffed. "Yeah, Dad. I'm okay. Mr. Kino, too. We're going to be okay." She regarded him with a knowing look. "You almost weren't, though."

Westfield grunted. "How bad?" He motioned for a cup of

water at his bedside.

She handed it to him. "You were on the table for seven hours and took twelve units of blood. Those knife wounds missed your liver by a hair, Daddy." She patted his arm, pinching her lips and swallowing back a sob. She struggled to smile for him. "Thought I might lose you."

Westfield said nothing patting his daughter's hand. An overwhelming sense of gratitude filled his heart. Tears welled from beneath his swollen purple eyelids, fell and caught in his bearded cheeks. "I think I might want to try going to mass again."

Janie's face slackened. "Did you hit your head?"

"No," Westfield said. "I was stabbed and shot and I'm still alive. Maybe I should stop neglecting that part of my life."

Janie smiled, wiping away another tear. "I'll go with you. How's that?"

"I'd like that," Westfield said. "Keep the priest from asking too many questions." He wheezed a laugh.

Janie gave his arm a squeeze. "Can I show you something?" she said and picked up the remote from a bedside stand. The small TV in the upper corner of the room blinked on.

"The federal investigation into the leaked file on a covert Navy special operations group took an interesting turn today when the Justice Department in cooperation with the Department of Defense and the U.S. Armed Forces high command, arrested more than thirty individuals for crimes ranging from conspiracy and illegal genetic tampering, to attempted murder and beyond."

Westfield watched the polished young news anchor delivering the news. He curled his finger at Janie. "Turn it up a little." Janie pointed the remote at the TV.

"The commander of this unit, Alric Jager, said to have orchestrated this vast conspiracy that had deep connections all the way back to

Operation Paperclip as well as previous Nazi attempts to create a new breed of super soldier, is believed dead at this time. Authorities stated he may have perished aboard The U.S.S. Harbinger, which sank off the coast of Hawaii two weeks ago during an incursion between Naval forces and a known group of eco-radicals, called Sentry."

"Two weeks …" Westfield mumbled. "I've been out that long …" He watched as a picture of him in uniform flashed on the screen. Westfield stiffened. "Here we go …" he mumbled.

"In a series of dramatic incidents, authorities believed to be related to the conspiracy, hero Police Officer Derrick Westfield, was gravely injured while trying to save innocent lives near Honolulu Harbor. In a statement released by the police commissioner, Officer Westfield selflessly intervened in a series of well-orchestrated criminal incidents that involved multiple kidnappings and the murder of an FBI agent. The FBI, alongside the Honolulu Police Department, claim that Westfield exposed himself to catastrophic danger in an attempt to save innocent lives. Though gravely wounded, Officer Westfield is expected to make a full recovery. The mayor's office stated that he will receive the city's highest award, the Medal of Honor, for his courageous actions."

"Turn that garbage off," Westfield groaned.

"My hero." Janie rubbed his arm and clicked the TV off.

"Stop it. I defied direct orders and put a lot of people in danger. The city would never have done this if it weren't such a media frenzy. They're afraid of it blowing back on them."

"Okay, grumpy grump," Janie said. "How about be thankful you're alive to receive a medal."

"Yeah." Westfield sighed. "There is that." He looked at the television, now gone dark and silent. "I hope those kids are okay," he said, the unknown looming over him like a great shadow. He might never know the answers to the questions that started this whole mess.

"What kids?" Janie asked.

"Don't worry about it." He forced a smile that turned into a wince of pain.

Janie paused for a moment before nodding at the now dark TV. "That leak, the one that opened up the whole investigation. That was you?"

"Insurance. Sent direct to the FBI as well as the major networks in the event something happened to me."

"Well played." Janie smirked. "So, this is going to come as a shock, but something happened to you."

"You don't say."

"Oh." Janie gave him a little nudge. "Someone sent these." She reached onto a side table and pulled over a bouquet of flowers. Attached was a small card. Westfield pushed it open with his finger.

Thank you for your service. Your medical bills are taken care of. When you get ready to retire, give me a call. I've got a job for you. ~ ZM

Westfield wheezed a chuckle.

"Who's ZM?" Janie asked.

"A friend," Westfield said.

Janie gave his arm a pat and stood, making for the doorway. "I'm going to get some coffee and let the nurse know you're awake."

"How long do I have to stay here?" Westfield groaned.

A petite nurse with olive skin and dark curly hair rounded the corner and stepped into his room. "Oh, don't start that already. Have you seen yourself?"

Westfield gave an exasperated huff. "Hey, Emily."

Janie winked at him and slipped from the room.

Emily looked in her direction and back to Westfield. "She hasn't left your side. You're a lucky man."

"I don't deserve her," Westfield said.

"You are correct, sir." Emily smiled, then silenced a beeping heart monitor.

Westfield tried to look sideways at Emily. "You requested to take care of me?"

"I did as a matter of fact."

Westfield managed a pained smile.

"You did this you know?" she said with a gentle tap of her finger on his arm. "You said next time you saw me it would be with a gunshot wound."

"Mmm." Westfield's face darkened. "I did, didn't I."

Emily turned to him, her face serious. She laid a hand on his arm. "I'm glad you're okay, Derrick."

Westfield swallowed a lump in his throat. "Thank you, Emily." He paused and breathed deep, a mischievous smile gathering at the corners of his mouth. "So, what are the chances you might get coffee with an old rogue when he gets released from the hospital?"

Emily bent, holding his gaze. She reached over and grabbed his hand with a squeeze. "Make it dinner." She winked. "And drinks."

CHAPTER 40

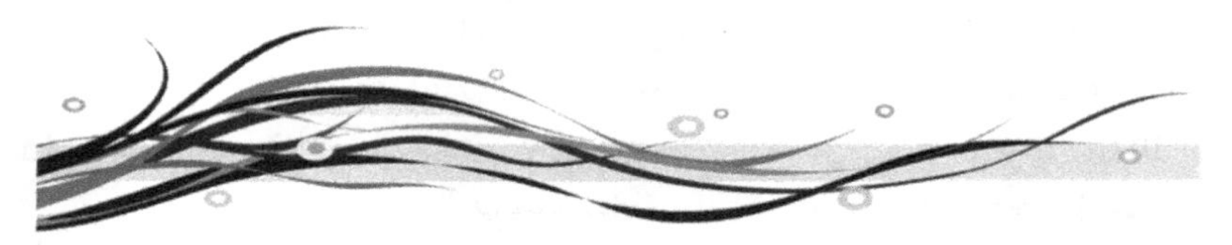

The deepening scarlet twilight seemed to stretch on in infinite broadening colors from one horizon to the other in a seemingly endless expanse. Beneath it, the two men sat at the edge of the pier along an isolated stretch of Mokulē'ia Beach on the north shore of Honolulu. They sat in silence, their presence at odds with the occasional fisherman patiently working the length of the pier. To anyone watching they appeared to simply be two friends admiring the brilliant sunset.

Derrick Westfield, still looking rather bruised and beaten, but freshly shaven, turned to Gordon Kino whose left arm lay held in the crook of a sling.

"Think she'll show?" Westfield asked.

Gordon pressed his lips together and shook his head, swallowing back his uncertainty.

Following the incursion with Jager's rogue unit, Zhou Murong contacted them both and told them the story of her heroism. Weeks passed, and Gordon began to think he might never see his little girl again.

Then he'd received an anonymous message telling him to meet at this remote location at nightfall today. *It's her. I know it is.* He glanced at the grease-stained brown paper bag on the bench next to him, her favorite treat.

They watched as a tired looking fisherman with a weathered face like the leather palm of a catcher's mitt shuffled past. Fishing pole in one hand and a small cooler of bait and cheap beer in the other. No doubt in a hurry to get home and finish tying one on.

"You saved Janie's life," Westfield said staring off into the brilliant horizon. "I'm not real good with saying this, but ..." He glanced over at Gordon. "I'll never forget."

Gordon waved him off. "You would've done the same if it were Sasha or Mika. Besides, it's because of you we're all alive and that mess got exposed in the first place."

"Mmm." Westfield nodded.

They sat in silence for a while longer. A shadow approached.

"Sorry I'm late. Anything yet?" Zhou Murong said, dressed in sunglasses and a floral print Hawaiian shirt, board shorts and flip flops. Far cry from his typical immaculate style.

"You showed," Westfield said.

"Nothing yet," Gordon said.

"Let's wait a moment," Murong crossed his arms.

The three waited, silent, watching the distant blaze sink into the ocean. A slight disturbance of the water at the edge of the pier around the wooden pilings caused them all to lean forward.

"Sasha?" Gordon whispered.

The waves lapped against the pilings with a light hypnotic slapping. Gordon felt afraid to move, the air stuck in his lungs, anticipation hovering in his chest.

"Sasha," Gordon's voice broke. "I miss you so much. Please speak to me." His voice hung on a razor's edge of emotion. He listened but received no reply.

The beach was empty now, the sun descending beyond the reach of the distant horizon in glows of orange and purple, a chorus of tree frogs rising in the air with a peaceful trill. Unable to help himself, the burly Hawaiian hunched forward and cried, his shoulders shaking with little tremors.

A sad sound emanated from beneath the pier, an echo of her father's tears. "Papa, please don't cry."

Gordon's eyes flashed wide, searching the dark water around the pier. "Sasha?"

"I'm here," Sasha replied quietly.

"Oh, Sasha," Gordon said falling to his knees and then to all fours in an attempt to get as close to the water below as possible. "Sasha, you … are you okay? Did they hurt you?" He mumbled, struggling to see through eyes wet and hot.

"I'm okay, Papa," Sasha said, her voice that of a wounded child.

"Oh, let me see you. Please," Gordon said.

"You don't want to see me," she whispered.

Gordon wiped his face and straightened, a fatherly self-control creasing his features. "Sasha Kaimana Kino," he said his voice taking on a stern baritone. "You are a precious gift, a daughter of the sea. And you are prefect in whatever form the great ocean destined to make you. Let me see you."

After a long moment, light ripples of water pushed at the edge of the pier. Sasha swam into view, eyes turned down in shame.

Gordon gasped, his hands raised to his mouth. "Sasha. My Sasha … look at you."

Sasha's lips quivered, tears dripping from her eyes.

"You are the most beautiful thing I have ever seen." Gordon choked with emotion.

"You can't mean that," she said.

"I mean it. With all my heart. Come home to us."

Sasha lowered her head. "I can't. There's still too much I need to do. Too many questions."

Gordon swallowed back the desire to probe further. He smiled. "I brought you something." He grabbed the brown bag and leaned forward, setting it on the edge of the wooden boards.

With a flash of movement, a webbed hand snatched the bag from the pier.

"Oh, Papa." She made a small moaning sound as she tore through the wrapper and took her first bite. Gordon waited, unable to help the amused look on his face.

A moan of ecstasy hummed from Sasha's lips.

"I thought you deserved a veggie burger lettuce wrap with extra mustard and pickles from Hula Burger," Gordon said.

"Thank you. The importance of cooked food can't be overstated."

"When I got the message, I knew it was you," Gordon said. "Of course, I had to notify these two." Gordon cleared his throat. "Sasha, do you remember my friend Derrick Westfield?"

Sasha appraised Westfield, chewing thoughtfully. She set the garbage back on the pier. "Yes. I heard what you did. Thanks for trying to help me and my friends and for saving this big lug for me. I sort of need him." Her voice had softened.

"My pleasure, Sasha," Westfield said. "I think it's we who are in your debt. What Jager did was terrifying, to say the least."

"You sure you can't come home, dear?" Gordon asked.

"I can't. Not yet. There's too much at stake."

"The Erebos?" Murong said, placing a hand on Gordon's shoulder.

"Yes," Sasha said.

"It's bad, Sasha," Murong said. "We're looking at catastrophic biological and ecological effects if we can't get it off the sea floor."

"I know. Get it out of the ocean and somewhere safe, if you can," Sasha said.

"Easier said than done," Murong said. "The Department of Defense is all over the grid coordinates where *The Harbinger* went down. They want their experiment back."

"The DOD doesn't need it any more than Jager did," Sasha said.

"No one needs to have control of something like that," Westfield added.

"You're right, but right now, Sentry under Murong's guidance is the safest option." Sasha turned her attention back to her mysterious benefactor. "What's with the board shorts and sunglasses?"

Murong chuckled. "My organization attacked a United States Navy Battle Group and were branded as terrorists. I have to keep a low profile for a while." He plied his hands together. "It's so good to see you, Sasha. We didn't think you made it."

"The ocean wouldn't let me die."

"That sounds so mystical. What happened, really?" Murong asked.

"The orcas. They stayed with me, pushed me to the surface, supported me until I revived. They know I belong to them."

Gordon's eyebrows raised and he smiled.

"It's been weeks since," Murong said. "Where have you been?"

Sasha shook her head. "I needed some time to process everything. I've got too many regrets. I know what we did had to happen. I can't shake the feeling though, that Alvarez and his Strykers and some of the other sailors aboard those ships only did what they were commanded to do, what they felt was their duty. And I killed them for it."

"I'm not sure that's fair to you," Murong said.

"Well, it's how I feel," she said, a tremor in her voice. "I'd appreciate it if you would find out what you can about the wounded and deceased. If they had families, or if their families need anything. It's Jager's mess and they got held accountable for it."

Murong looked at her long before giving a reverent bow. "If you wish, Sasha. I will have my people look into it."

"Thank you." She bit her lip. "So, how are Max and Bodhi? Lemeaux? Tell me they're all right," she said.

"René is still alive, but he's had a hard time of it. For him, only time will tell." Murong paused. "Max and Bodhi are doing great. Their speech is returning with therapy, they're coming to grips emotionally with what happened to them, how their lives are fundamentally different now."

"I miss them," Sasha said.

"They've asked about you. They still believe you're alive."

"Don't confirm it for now, I need some more time. They'd feel compelled to come find me."

"I understand." Murong nodded.

"In the meantime, I've got something else to look into."

"Jager?" Murong said.

"I need to know he's dead, Zhou." Sasha's face turned grim. "I can't rest until I know."

"When will we see you again, my dear?" Gordon stood, his hands clasped at his chest. "Your sister, your mother and I, we need you."

"We will see each other again, Papa. But first I have to figure some things out about myself, about what I'm supposed to do with this … gift. I love you—which is why I have to go. Give Mom and Mika my love."

Gordon nodded. "You are loved, daughter. We will be here when you are ready."

"Aloha," Sasha said, drifting from sight as the deep bluish-purple of a cool island night descended.

"Aloha, Sasha," Westfield said.

"Aloha, my dear girl." Gordon waved.

"Sasha, wait," Murong said. He scanned the dark surface of the water, searching, seeing only the gentle lapping of the waves against the slick wooden pilings. "Sasha, what if something happens?" He called out, trying to keep his voice low. "Where will you be if the world needs you?"

"Where I'm needed most. Standing in defense of what's right," Sasha said. The spectral sound of her voice faded, alluring and mysterious, like a siren's song carried forth on the darkening waves of the pacific. "So shall we go."

Artist's Gallery by Michael David Ward

Erebos

Erebos Crash

Sasha Surf Competition

Sasha in Harmony with the Ocean

Sasha, Bodhi, Max and Gordon

Sasha exposed to the Erebos

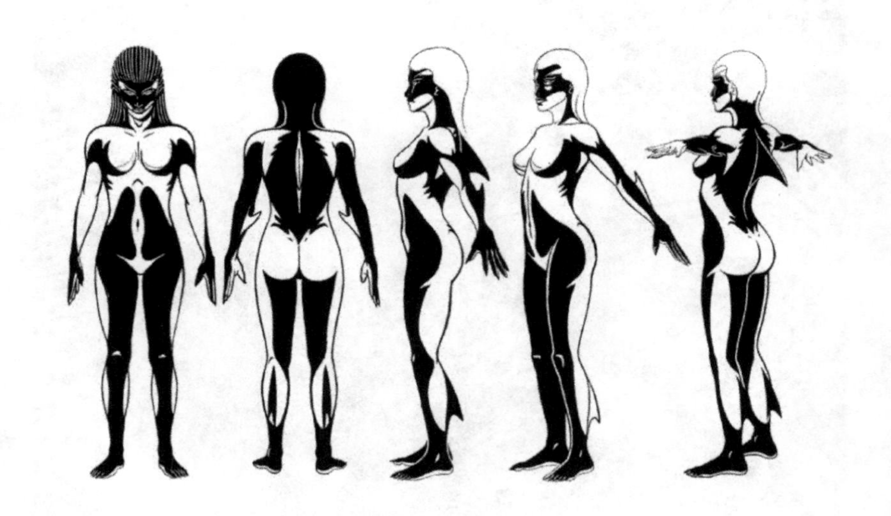

Early Concepts

Sasha Post Mutation

Sasha Resurfacing

Sasha Terrorizes the Vladimov

Jager aboard the Harbinger

Stryker Concept Art

Sasha Concept Art

Sasha Closeup

STU JONES

Breach Closeup

Stu Jones

A veteran law enforcement officer, Stu has worked in patrol, narcotics, criminal investigations, as an instructor of firearms and police defensive tactics and as a team leader of a multi-jurisdictional SWAT team. He is trained and qualified as a law enforcement SWAT sniper, as well as in hostage rescue and high-risk entry tactics. Recently, Stu served for three years with a U.S. Marshal's Regional Fugitive Task Force - hunting the worst of the worst.

He is the author of multiple sci-fi/action/thriller novels, including the multi-award-winning *It Takes Death To Reach A Star* duology and *Condition Black*, written with co-author Gareth Worthington (*Children of the Fifth Sun*).

Known for his character-driven stories and blistering action sequences, Stu strives to create thought-provoking reading experiences that challenge the status quo. When he's not chasing bad guys or writing epic stories, he can be found planning his next adventure to some remote or exotic place.

Stu is represented by Italia Gandolfo of Gandolfo-Helin-Fountain literary.

For more information check out stujonesfiction.com and follow on social @stujonesfiction